THE
WHITE
FEATHER
MURDERS

THE WHITE FEATHER MURDERS

a reggie da costa mystery

laraine stephens

For my darling Bob

Praise for The White Feather Murders

"A superb historical mystery with an engaging central sleuth in crime reporter, Reggie da Costa. Dark secrets, a poison pen, murder, and that tantalizing clue of the white feathers – what's not to love? Highly recommended."—Matthew Booth, author of the *Everett Carr Mysteries*

"In 1927 Melbourne, a scandalous newspaper column exposes five public figures, but when three end up dead clutching white feathers, crime reporter Reggie da Costa is drawn into a chilling mystery. As he investigates the link between the victims, Reggie must uncover the truth before the killer strikes again. A gripping, atmospheric, historical mystery, loaded with scandal and deception and spiced with a touch of romance. I highly recommend this fifth book in *The Reggie da Costa Mysteries*!"—Lori Duffy Foster, author of the *Lisa Jamison Mysteries*

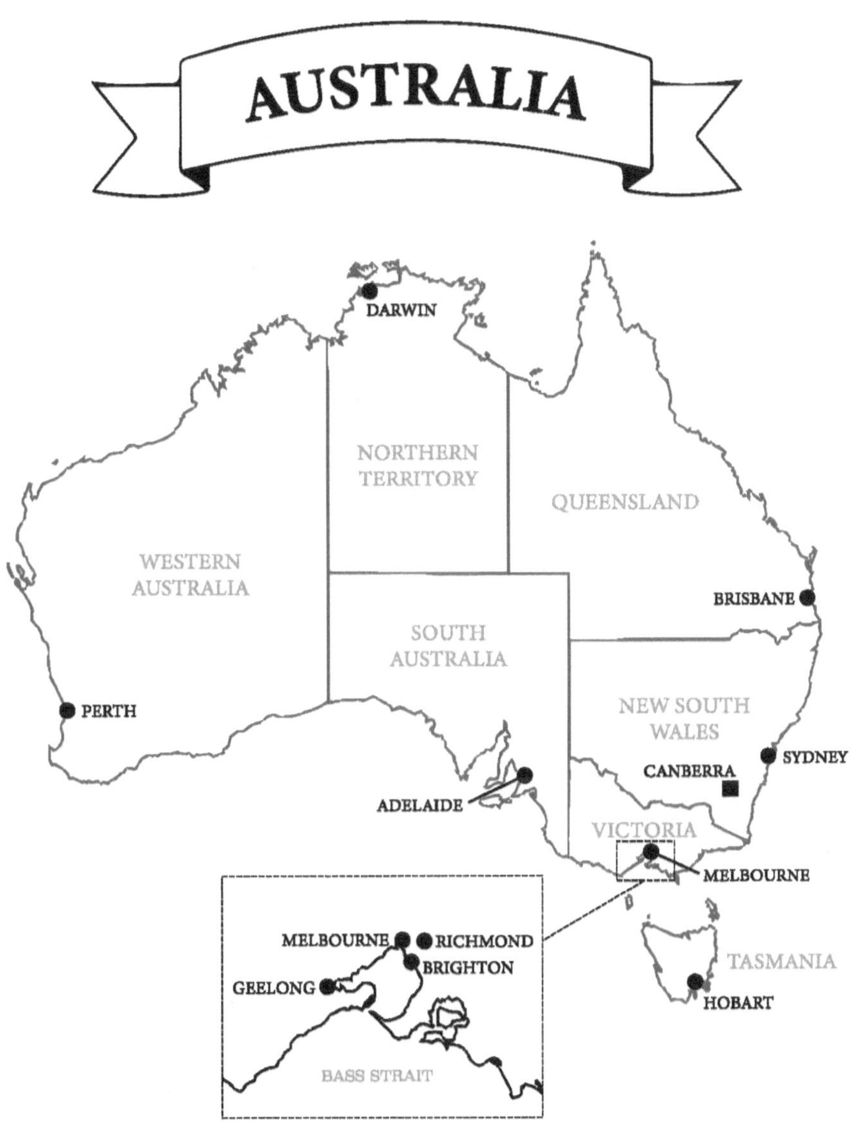

AUSTRALIA
DARWIN
NORTHERN TERRITORY
QUEENSLAND
WESTERN AUSTRALIA
SOUTH AUSTRALIA
BRISBANE
PERTH
NEW SOUTH WALES
CANBERRA
SYDNEY
ADELAIDE
VICTORIA
MELBOURNE
MELBOURNE
RICHMOND
BRIGHTON
GEELONG
TASMANIA
HOBART
BASS STRAIT

Prologue

He came back from the Western Front a shadow of a man. He was all but destroyed. While others returned with ruined lungs, scarred faces, missing legs, and arms, he was damaged beyond repair: his mind all messed up, like a pot of stew that has boiled down on the hob, just a few lumps left, no broth to hold it together.

They put him away. They eradicated any chance of recovery. Medicated to the eyeballs, his memory gone, just existing.

They let him out three months ago without telling me.

He stood in front of a train.

Chapter One

This was the time she most enjoyed when the audience had gone, and she was sitting alone in the small dressing room off the auditorium. She unpinned her hat and brushed her hair, staring at her face in the mirror. The light from the bare globe brought the lines on her face into high relief, the visible signs of a fight well fought, no holds barred, no inch given. That was what her life had been like, taking up the mantle of one cause until another presented itself.

The meeting had been a great success, the seats full of supporters, while a few loudmouth adversaries lined up along the back, trying to disrupt the flow of her speech. Unlike other speakers, she found abuse and vilification stimulating, pushing her on to destroy their arguments and dismantle their logic. And, when the sea of faces was turned her way, waiting for her next piercing exchange with an opponent, or another convincing and pithy argument, she knew that she had her supporters in the palm of her hand crying out for more, ready to join her in the battle against those who lacked the moral courage to stand up and be counted.

Prohibition was the only way, she had asserted not thirty minutes before, to stamp out the drunken behaviour of men who ruined families, bashed their wives, and neglected their responsibilities as fine, upstanding members of society.

'Look to America as an example,' she had said. 'Poverty and crime have disappeared because the government has been strong enough to crack down on the sale of alcohol. People's lives have been saved. Wretchedness and disease have been wiped out almost entirely, replaced by sobriety, happiness, and good health!'

Her claims had been rewarded with cheers and applause, drowning out the catcalls and boos emanating from the back of the hall. Tomorrow, the newspapers would report once again on her success as a firebrand in the Woman's Christian Temperance Union.

As she was about to finish her speech, a bottle sailed through the air, smashing at her feet. She looked up and noticed an angry man shaking his fist at her and yelling obscenities, before he was dragged from the hall.

'This is the price I pay in my quest to eliminate demon drink from society!' she cried to the audience. 'The government must act to restrict the licensing and advertising of intoxicating liquor. Without reform, violence will continue. And there are those who are benefitting from the sale of alcohol at the expense of downtrodden wives and families. Stand up and be counted!'

Her final words were greeted with cheers. She nodded to the audience and left the stage.

And now, seated in the dressing room alone, she opened a drawer and reached in, her fingers finding the reassuring neck of a bottle. She uncorked it and let the silvery liquid refresh her dry throat, relax her. Everyone deserves a reward for a job well done, she told herself. She breathed a sigh of relief and took one last swig, then put the bottle in her handbag.

Home. To bed.

As those thoughts came into her mind, the lights went out. She sat stunned, then felt a surge of anger. The caretaker had once again forgotten that she was still there. They had an agreement that she would turn off the lights and lock up when she left. Damn man.

She lit a candle and, as she reached for her bag, she heard the door open behind her. In the mirror, she could see the dim outline of a man wearing a hat and coat.

'Who is it? Step into the light.'

Silence. She felt a degree of uneasiness, then reasserted herself, mustering that bloody-mindedness that never seemed to desert her.

'Get out or I'll scream.'

'Who will hear you?' he whispered. 'No one, tonight.'

The hairs on the back of her neck rose as she heard his words. She reached for the hairbrush and stood up, brandishing it as if it were a weapon. 'Out!'

He chuckled. 'I don't think so.'

Within seconds, he had reached her and pinned her arms behind her back, tying them with a thin piece of cord which bit into her flesh. She looked up at him defiantly.

'What do you want?'

'Revenge.'

She screamed.

He clamped a leather-clad hand across her mouth and thrust her back into the chair. 'Not so brave now,' he growled as she slumped down, trembling violently. 'Scream again and it will be the end for you.'

There was the clink, clink of glass as he removed two bottles from his bag and set them down on the dressing table.

'Here's your favourite. Gin. A little nip to start with.'

He uncorked one of the bottles, watching her closely. She shook her head, her eyes wild with fear.

'Head back.'

He forced her mouth open, pushing the neck of the bottle between her teeth. The liquid slid down her throat. She gagged and spluttered, but his grip on her was tight.

'You've always enjoyed the limelight, Mrs Burns. But you've never given one thought to the consequences of your words and actions, or the damage that you do. I'm going to make sure that your death makes headlines in all the newspapers for all the wrong reasons. No one will forget you.'

* * *

They found her in the alley outside the meeting hall early the next morning.

'She's dead,' the doctor said as he examined her. 'Asphyxiation, brought on by excessive consumption of alcohol. Gin, by the smell of it.'

'Isn't that—?' asked a bystander, tut-tutting as he recognised the dead woman.

'Yes, it is,' replied another.

'What's that in her hand?'

'It's a white feather.'

Chapter Two

The Argus newsroom was abuzz with the bell and whirr of typewriter carriages retracting as the reporters hammered out their stories to beat the deadlines. Phones rang and voices were raised above the clatter as the office boy was run ragged, dashing from one desk to another, carrying stories to the news editors upstairs or the compositors on the floor below. In the bowels of the building, the printing presses were thundering, spewing out the newspapers which would soon be bundled together and loaded into trucks, to be dumped on footpaths, or displayed on newsstands, or sold by newsboys, spruiking and squawking, 'Get your *Argus* here!'

With the door of his office closed to the chaos, Reggie da Costa, *The Argus's* senior crime reporter, studied his assistant, Will 'Dusty' Rhodes, who was sitting opposite him. As usual, Dusty was wearing his trademark patched and crumpled jacket. Despite Reggie's frequent assertion that appearance was as important as dedication to the craft of crime reporting, it was clear that this message had not taken root in the two years during which Dusty had worked for him. There had been a brief period when he had smartened himself up, but that had been short-lived, never to appear again.

In contrast, Reggie was exhibiting his usual sartorial elegance, wearing cream-cuffed trousers teamed with a navy double-breasted jacket and red tie. His new, cream fedora hung from a hook on the hat stand behind him.

Reggie put his feet up on the edge of his desk, admiring his highly polished, cream leather shoes, and said, 'What have you got for me this week?'

Dusty flipped through the pages in his notebook. 'You asked for something different to the usual crime stories.'

'That's right. Something that will spark our readers' attention. Forget robberies, murder, and assaults for once. Something bizarre, perhaps.'

'And I've found just the thing, boss.'

Reggie sat forward, eyes alert, ears pricked. 'Go on.'

'Some of the strange theories about criminality from the past.'

'Such as?'

'The idea that criminals could be identified by their physical characteristics. Small heads, and lumps and bumps on the skull.'

'Dusty, please, we had enough of that in the Death Mask Murders case. No more phrenology, please.'

'Give me a chance, boss. This would be different. I've read about an Italian criminologist, Count Lombroso, who measured the powers of taste and smell in convicted criminals, their cranial capacity, and the way they walked. He even studied their tattoos.'

'Really?'

'But the most bizarre indication of criminal behaviour, according to him, was the eye colour of killers who committed crimes of passion.' Dusty paused for effect. 'Ice cold, blue, staring eyes.'

Reggie chuckled. 'Who, for example?'

'Dr Crippen, the American eye and ear specialist who murdered his wife and buried her in the cellar of his London house. George Joseph Smith, who drowned three of his wives in the bathtub. Frederick Deeming, who butchered and buried his wife and four children under the hearth of a fireplace in England, then murdered his second wife in Melbourne. They speculated that he might be Jack the Ripper. These killers shared one characteristic: They all had hypnotic, blue eyes.'

'Is that it?'

'I saved the best for last,' replied Dusty. 'The "Blue-Eyed Six" murdered Joseph Raber in Pennsylvania for his life insurance policies. Six killers, all with piercing, blue eyes.'

Reggie leaned forward, studying Dusty intently. 'You understand, don't you, that this "blue-eyed killer" theory is ridiculous?'

'Of course, but it is interesting. So, what do you think?'

'I agree that it has potential, but the bigger question is whether criminals are born evil. Or is it because of their upbringing? What you're suggesting is that there's a link between criminal tendencies and physical appearance, which is a stretch of the imagination if you ask me. The problem is that this subject is a bit too philosophical. You don't want to confuse our readers. They don't like to concentrate for too long, remember? They like to see things in terms of black and white, not shades of grey. Or blue, for that matter.' He pointed at Dusty's notebook. 'For the moment, I'd focus on everyday crime in Melbourne if I were you. Perhaps something more relevant to the crimes we're reporting on.'

Dusty nodded his head, his disappointment evident. 'You know best, boss. I'll put it aside for a while. But I'll be looking out for killers with staring, blue eyes.' He brightened visibly as a thought struck him. 'On a different note, there's been a development in the Squizzy Taylor saga.'

Reggie raised an eyebrow. 'Indeed? What's Melbourne's foremost gangster been up to this time?'

'Apart from fixing juries, selling illegal booze, and running gambling dens, he's about to be reunited with his sworn enemy, Snowy Cutmore.'

'But Snowy lives in Sydney.'

'Very true, but his wife has been seen in Melbourne.'

Reggie stroked his thin Ronald Colman moustache. 'Which means that Snowy will show his ugly face in our fair city soon.' He lit a cigarette and blew a smoke ring, watching it curl up into the air. 'Snowy Cutmore? I met him when he was part of the Fitzroy Gang back in 1923. Vicious. Hated Squizzy with a passion. It never surprised me when he joined the razor gangs up in Sydney. They say he took to using a razor on his enemies like a duck to water. Carved them up.'

Dusty nodded his head. 'He joined Norman Bruhn's gang up there.'

'Until Bruhn was gunned down in a Darlinghurst alley last June,' added Reggie.

Dusty lowered his voice. 'The word is out that Snowy was behind Bruhn's murder.'

Reggie tapped the ash off his cigarette. 'If that's the case, then it's highly likely that we'll see him down here soon. The Sydney mob will be after him.'

'Wasn't Squizzy also an ally of Bruhn?'

'He was in the past. There'll be fireworks when Squizzy hears Cutmore's in town. He'll want revenge. There's no escape for Snowy, either up in Sydney or down in Melbourne.'

'I'll keep my ear to the ground,' said Dusty. 'By the way, I saw Squizzy recently. You'd have loved his outfit, Reggie. Three-piece suit in russet brown check, with a cream, silk shirt and diamond tiepin. You couldn't miss him.'

'He models himself on the American bootleggers, although his taste is too flashy for my liking. Which reminds me, my wedding's not far off.'

Dusty grinned. 'I can see the headline now: "Reggie Romances Ruby. Wooed and Wedded,"' he declared, running his hands through his untidy thatch of fair hair. 'Just think, I'll be your brother-in-law by the end of the year.'

Reggie chuckled. 'You have a gift for alliteration. Seriously though, we'll need to put our family relationship aside while we're in the office. It wouldn't do.'

Dusty's face became unusually serious. 'Of course, boss. I would never take advantage of that.'

'Out of the office, it's fine. We can be friends. But here, I wouldn't want anyone to think that there's nepotism at work. If you apply yourself, you'll be rewarded, but not because you're family.' He lowered his feet to the floor and studied Dusty intently. 'Now to the important stuff. My wedding. Have you been to a tailor yet?'

Dusty pulled a face. 'Can't I pick a suit out from a catalogue?'

The look on his boss's face made the answer clear.

'Whom do you recommend, Reggie?'

'Wallace, Buck, and Goodes of Queens Walk.'

'They'll be expensive.'

'You have to understand, future brother-in-law, that when it comes to good grooming, and particularly when it involves me marrying Ruby, money is no object.'

Dusty's expression was one of resignation. 'I'll get onto it, Reggie. Perhaps Squizzy might lend me one of his suits?'

Reggie's raised eyebrows were answer enough to that suggestion. 'And Dusty. Another thing. I'll give you the address of my barber.'

Chapter Three

For over eight years, the stately home of Glenrothes in Brighton had been the meeting place for a group of older women, hosted by the formidable Mrs Mildred Bardsley Smith. Prior to that, when the now deceased Mrs Florence Darrow had brought the ladies together, their function had been to support the boys at the Western Front, by knitting socks, balaclavas, and scarves, or by preparing small food parcels to bring a smile to those who faced a diet of bully beef, tea, and biscuits. But the Great War was over, and their purpose had turned to charitable works, assisting those in financial difficulty or who were facing personal tragedy. Two new members, Clementine Crowe and Bertha Dankworth, had recently joined the group, based on their standing in society and their philanthropic endeavours.

Mavis da Costa, Reggie's mother, had been a member of the group since its inception. Despite being deserted by her irresponsible cad of a husband, Mario, who had also relieved her of her inheritance, Mavis had kept her place amongst the well-to-do ladies of the Brighton coterie due to Mildred's insistence that she be supported in her time of trial. Living comfortably in Richmond in a modest two-bedroom house, she still made the weekly train trip down to Middle Brighton Station and walked the half mile or more to the Bardsley Smiths' palatial home in Grosvenor Street.

The drawing room of the Victorian mansion was a study in elegance, with lush, olive-green, velvet, swagged curtains around its bay windows, exotic Turkish rugs over its highly polished floorboards, decorative cornices intricately painted in pinks and greens, and an impressive ornate ceiling rose, from which hung a Murano glass chandelier.

The ladies sat on Victorian armchairs carved from rosewood, with cushions upholstered in flesh pink velvet, sipping their tea from Royal Albert cups, while balancing their side plates on their knees. Everyone was on their best behaviour.

With the afternoon tea cleared away, Mildred drew the attention of the ladies to matters at hand, specifically their fund-raising efforts for charitable causes.

'I was thinking of holding a cake stall to raise money for the proposed Methodist Babies' Home in South Yarra. I'm sure the shopkeepers in Church Street wouldn't object. Perhaps we could start off the fundraising by donating five shillings each. What do you think?'

Edith McGillicutty nodded in agreement. 'Wonderful.' She took out her purse and placed two florins and a shilling in the centre of the table. Bertha followed suit.

'A new orphanage will take a lot of pressure off the Methodist Children's Home in Cheltenham,' Gladys Onions commented as she handed over her donation.

Mildred smiled. 'Over six hundred children will have been cared for by the time the new institution opens. It's a tribute to the administrators that most of them have been placed with families.'

'It does worry me that unmarried mothers have to pay the Home to take their children,' said Clementine as she placed her coins on the table. 'Is it right that these women are made to pay for the upkeep of their babies until they're adopted?'

Edith pursed her lips. 'Disgusting. Unmarried women having children.'

'Now, Edith,' remonstrated Mildred. 'We are good Christian women who must forgive those who transgress.'

Edith pulled a face. 'If that's what you think, Mildred.'

'I do.' She added another five shillings to the small pile of coins, then turned to Mavis. 'Are you in favour of the cake stall?'

Mavis was studying the contents of her purse. She looked up, startled. 'Pardon, Mildred?'

Edith leaned forward, the lens of her glasses glowing in the light from the chandelier. 'The cake stall. Concentrate, Mavis.'

'What's wrong, my dear?' asked Mildred kindly. 'You look distracted.'

Mavis played with the frilly collar of her fussy, pink blouse. 'Sorry, I don't seem to have five shillings on me.'

'Put it in next time,' Mildred replied, patting her hand. 'We can wait. Now, what news, ladies? Has anyone attended any interesting lectures or charitable events lately?'

'I attended a lovely concert put on by the children of the local Baptist kindergarten,' offered Clementine. 'It was delightful.'

'I was at a meeting of the Woman's Christian Temperance Union last week,' said Mavis.

Gladys looked shocked. 'But they're in favour of Prohibition! Does Reggie know?'

Mavis shook her froth of white curls. 'Of course not. He'd be horrified.'

Edith scowled. 'Alcohol should be banned.'

'My Reggie doesn't think so. He says that Americans have died from drinking methyl alcohol—I think that's the name—because of Prohibition. Illegal stuff, made in a still.'

'There's been more deaths from drunkenness and violence brought on by alcohol, if you ask me,' argued Clementine.

'Hear, hear,' added Bertha.

Mavis continued, oblivious to the dissent. 'Reggie says that they sell illegal liquor everywhere in America. They even carry it in hearses. Reggie says that mourners at funerals get drunk. He says it's out of control.'

Mildred touched her arm. 'If you don't agree with Prohibition, my dear, why did you go?'

'I wanted to hear Mrs Burns. She was the guest speaker. She was very convincing. And she had all the answers. The thing is—'

'What, dear?' asked Mildred.

'She was found dead outside the meeting hall the next morning. It's said that she choked on her vomit from drinking too much.' In hushed tones she added, 'Reggie told me that. Those were the exact words he used. He says that I'm not allowed to tell anyone until the coroner confirms it.'

The women sat back in their chairs, stunned and shocked.

Edith's dark eyebrows knitted together. 'That's terrible. It's hard to believe. Although I did read that someone in the movement had…a problem.'

Mavis looked at her intently. 'Where did you read that? Not in *The Argus*?'

Edith went red. '*The Truth*.'

Gladys couldn't help herself. 'You read *The Truth*? That gossip rag. Really, Edith?' A smile spread across her face.

Even Mildred and Mavis raised their eyebrows in astonishment. Rigid, austere, and uncompromising Edith McGillicutty read *The Truth*. After all these years, it was still possible to be surprised by those you thought you knew.

Chapter Four

The interior of the little terrace house, in a back street of Brunswick, reeked of gas when the neighbour went to investigate the source of the smell. He had climbed the fence and wrenched open the back door, only to be forced back gagging and gasping as a wall of fumes threatened to suffocate him. He took his handkerchief from his pocket, covered his nose and mouth, and went back in. When he stepped into the kitchen, he saw the figure of his neighbour propped up in her rocking chair. It beggared belief that she could survive the heavy, stifling onslaught of gas, but suddenly she coughed, and he threw himself towards her, holding his breath as he carried her from the house and around to the front.

Outside on the street, a gaggle of neighbours and voyeurs had arrived, staring down at the woman lying on the footpath. He yelled at one of them to ring the ambulance and police, while he shook her gently, trying to keep her conscious. Unexpectedly, she coughed violently and opened her eyes. They were red and weeping, the pupils dilated.

'Where am I?' she mouthed.

'You're alive, Beryl,' her neighbour replied. 'Help will be here soon.'

As if on cue, an ambulance rounded the corner, ringing its bell to clear a path through the crowd gathered on the road. Two attendants removed a stretcher from the back of the van and lifted the woman onto it, then checked her condition. The police arrived next, followed by the fire brigade, who went into action, breaking down the front door with axes. Gas masks on, they disappeared into the house. Soon they reappeared, reporting that there were no other occupants, then went back in.

Reggie coasted his new Belgian beauty, a 1927 red Minerva AC Open Tourer with a silver bonnet, into the curb behind the ambulance. He stepped down onto the footpath, flicked a spot of dust from his sleeve, and joined the group of anxious residents and curious onlookers who were watching the action.

He sidled up to one bystander and took out his notebook. 'Reggie da Costa from *The Argus*. What's happened here?'

'That bloke over there saved her. The one who's speaking to the copper. Gas. The woman inside was overcome. She looked dead, but they reckon she's survived. Don't know how, given the look of her.'

Reggie walked over to the man in question. 'You found her?'

'I did.' The man turned to him. 'Terrible business. Got a cigarette?'

Reggie nodded towards the house. 'Perhaps not the best idea given the situation.'

The man nodded vacantly. 'I was coming home from my shift. Smelled the gas. Jumped the fence and got inside just in time. Beryl was sitting there. I thought that she was dead at first.' He looked away, wiped his nose, and sighed. 'She's a strange one, alright.'

Reggie's ears pricked up. 'Strange? What do you mean?'

'She likes to be alone. You talk to her, and she'll ignore you. No family. No friends. I think she has problems, if you know what I mean.'

'Problems?'

'You only have to see her to know.'

Reggie shook his head. 'Know what?'

The man mouthed, 'Drugs.'

The crime reporter touched his nose and nodded sagely. 'Ahh.' He wandered over to where the ambulance men had placed the woman on the stretcher and peered over the shoulder of one of the onlookers. Beryl was not in the best of health. Apart from her red and inflamed eyes and hacking cough, she was a sad and sorry sight, a woman whose face was lined and wrinkled, despite appearing to be in her early forties. The skin on her neck was mottled in colour, her hair greasy and matted, her teeth yellowed, and her arms and legs wasted.

'Drugs, indeed,' thought Reggie, turning away at the sound of a motorcar pulling into the curb.

The unmistakable figure of Detective Inspector Clary Blain emerged from the patrol car. With his flushed face, a sign of his abiding love for Scotch whisky, his bulbous nose covered in spidery red veins, and with his trousers hitched up over his ever-burgeoning belly, Clary Blain was no picture of virile manhood, but his unappealing exterior masked a sharp mind and a determination to lock offenders away. And he was always open to sharing information with *The Argus*'s senior crime reporter in exchange for a glass of the finest whisky.

Reggie caught his eye, and they nodded at each other. Blain walked past him and spoke to the constable, a notebook in his hand.

The number of people outside the house had grown as word spread of an unfortunate accident. Mothers, carrying babies, and shift workers woken from their sleep had accumulated outside on the road, enjoying the novelty of a near death in their neighbourhood. It was almost a festive mood as those present speculated on what was known about the woman, which was very little.

Reggie strolled up the front path to stand next to the detective.

'She survived that?' asked Reggie, looking in through the open door.

Blain heaved a sigh. 'Almost to the point of no return, according to the medical attendant.'

'I'm surprised to see you here, Clary. Not your usual Criminal Investigation Branch case.'

'I was in the neighbourhood.'

The captain of the fire brigade came out of the house. 'All done here, sir. The gas has mostly dispersed. Little danger of combustion now. But the smell is awful, and I'm not talking about the gas. You can go in.'

Clary entered the house, the constable accompanying him. Meanwhile, Reggie interviewed a couple of other neighbours but was unable to find out anything significant about the woman.

Ten minutes later, Clary emerged and beckoned to Reggie to join him.

'Who is she?' asked the crime reporter.

'Miss Beryl Webb. She was employed as a nurse at The Melbourne Hospital, according to the bloke next door. She retired two months ago.'

'Retired? She doesn't look old enough to retire. What happened here?'

'Hard to tell. The tap on the stove was on. The neighbour found her sitting in a chair in the kitchen, looking as dead as a doornail. She'd had her dinner. Must have put the kettle on but forgot to light the gas. The door to the kitchen was shut, too, speeding up the process. In another few minutes, it would have been fatal. Do you want to take a look around?'

'Thanks, Clary.'

Detective Inspector Blain and Reggie covered their faces with their handkerchiefs and went into the house, the smell of gas still discernible. It was a small place, with a sitting room at the front and a bedroom off the hallway, which led down to a kitchen across the back. It was fair to say that the walls had not seen a lick of paint in years, and the carpet runner in the hall was worn back to the tufting in parts.

Miss Webb had been sitting in a rocking chair in the kitchen, a blanket over her knees, unconscious, according to Clary.

Reggie pointed at the table next to her chair. 'See that?' A used hypodermic needle lay on a dirty saucer.

The detective raised an eyebrow. 'Hmm,' was all he said.

Reggie took in the scene. The remains of dinner lay on a plate on the draining board, while dirty and chipped crockery from previous meals was piled up in the sink. The rubbish bin was overflowing with empty cans and bottles, as well as food scraps gone rancid. Reggie turned up his nose at the smell.

While Clary inspected the kitchen more thoroughly, Reggie took a moment to check the other rooms. The sitting room looked neglected, with dust on the floorboards and the fireplace unused. In the bedroom, he gagged as the smell of sweat and urine hit him. He covered his face with a handkerchief again and crossed to the dresser on which sat an empty wash basin. Next to it was a photograph in a frame, showing a woman and a man in their Sunday best. Probably her parents, given the style of clothing, Reggie thought.

Back in the kitchen, Clary Blain was taking notes while the police photographer captured the scene on film.

Reggie pulled a face. 'Disgusting place. For a nurse, you'd think she'd be more concerned with personal hygiene. You should see the bedroom. A pigsty. What do you reckon, Clary? An accident?'

'Can't see any sign of foul play.'

Reggie pointed again at the hypodermic needle. 'Seems the lady had a problem. You think she turned on the gas and forgot about it?'

'It looks that way. The windows were shut. So was the door to the front of the house. It wouldn't take long for her to lose consciousness, particularly if she was under the influence of drugs. She wouldn't have known a thing.'

'I've seen enough,' he added.

Outside, they watched as Beryl Webb was placed in the back of the ambulance.

Reggie noticed a flash of white. 'What's that?' he asked, moving forward to look.

A white feather fluttered to the ground.

'She was holding it in her hand,' remarked one of the attendants.

'That's odd,' said Reggie, picking it up. He examined it, twirling it in his fingers. 'You want it, Clary?'

The detective shook his head. 'All yours, mate.'

Reggie slipped the feather into his pocket and walked back to the Minerva. With one last glance at the van conveying the woman to the hospital, Reggie started the engine and headed down the road, back to his office.

Chapter Five

Ruby Rhodes shook her bob of wavy, red hair and relaxed into the deep cushions of her armchair, her green eyes moving towards the photograph of herself and her fiancé, Reggie da Costa. She smiled at the sight of the ruby and diamond engagement ring on her finger, then took a sip of sherry, her thoughts moving to the past.

It had been over two years since she had first laid eyes on Reggie and enlisted his help in solving the mysterious death of her estranged, identical twin sister. She had found it hard to understand how Katherine had been able to acquire a house and a motorcar on the wages of a museum assistant. Ruby quickly concluded that her twin's death was no accident, but the result of foul play, and she was determined to discover the killer.

At the same time, she had fallen in love with *The Argus*'s premier crime reporter. His choice of occupation was, to her, both stimulating and diverting. Tales of murder and robbery, and the nefarious activities of the main players in Melbourne's criminal underworld, such as Squizzy Taylor and Horace Striker, gave her an insight into another world apart from the staid and conventional existence of being secretary to the managing director of Smith and Sons Furniture. And soon, Reggie would be her husband, their wedding to be celebrated at The Stockade, the private club of none other than Horace Striker.

Ruby finished her sherry. Time to stop daydreaming, she thought. Her dinner guests would be arriving soon. She went out into the kitchen, where the leg of lamb was roasting in the oven. She put on her apron, peeled the potatoes, and cut up the carrots and beans. Next, she took a quick peek at the rhubarb pie that she had baked that morning.

'Smells delicious,' she concluded.

She opened the oven and added the potatoes to the roasting pan, then put the vegetables in a saucepan, ready to be put on the hob when the guests arrived. Reggie and his mother, as well as her brother, would be arriving shortly. It had been a while since she had seen Mavis, and she was looking forward to it. Her relationship with her future mother-in-law had been fraught at first, but these days, they chatted like old friends. However, there was one element of discord between them, and that was Mavis's view that Ruby should stop work when she was married. Despite Ruby's assertion that she needed something more to occupy her mind than staying at home, scrubbing floors, and ironing clothes, Reggie's mother was unmoved.

'It's the custom, my dear,' said Mavis. 'The husband is the breadwinner in the family.'

* * *

The meal finished and with Reggie and Dusty enjoying the last of the wine, Ruby cleared away the dinner plates and took them out into the kitchen. As she began to wash up the dishes, she was joined by Mavis, who took up a tea towel.

'Let me help you, dear. That was a lovely meal. The rhubarb pie was delicious.'

'Thanks, Mrs da Costa.'

'Please, call me Mavis. You'll be my daughter-in-law soon. You'll be family. And, when you stop working, we'll be able to meet up regularly.'

Ruby smiled. 'That's very nice of you, Mavis. But I'm not sure that I want to give up my job. It means a lot to me, and we could do with the money.'

'You'll be a married woman. Surely you can see that it's the proper thing to do?'

'Maybe it was once, but it's the 1920s and things have changed for women.'

Mavis pouted. 'What does Reggie think?'

'I don't know. We haven't discussed it yet,' Ruby admitted.

'Well, I think you need to. A wife should be at home, having the dinner ready for her husband when he comes home from a long day at work.'

'Hmm, I don't think so,' replied Ruby. 'I've been independent for a long time. It makes you see things differently. But I'll be happy to catch up with you regularly, whether I work or not. It will be so nice to have someone to confide in. I haven't had anyone like that since my mother died.'

Mavis touched Ruby's arm. 'Can I ask your advice, my dear? I know that I have Reggie to talk to, but sometimes there are things that I find difficult to share with him.' She paused, then blurted out, 'I'm thinking of taking the pledge and I don't know how to tell him.'

Ruby put the dishcloth down. 'You want to give up drinking? If that's your choice, I'm sure he will respect your wishes. No one should feel that they have to drink if they don't want to.' She took up the dishcloth again and began rinsing the dishes. 'By the way, wasn't that shocking about Mrs Burns, the president of the temperance movement in Melbourne? To make speeches condemning excessive drinking, and being found dead like that?'

Mavis nodded her head. 'That was a surprise. I've heard her speak, and she seemed so sincere. So convincing. And yet she drank like a fish, they say.'

Ruby turned back to her. 'You've heard her speak?'

'It was on the day she died.'

'Is that right? Did anything happen at the meeting?'

'There were people heckling her at the back of the hall. A man who was sitting near me threw a bottle and started shouting.'

'Goodness, me. What did he say?'

'Some of it is too rude to repeat. But he said that she'd ruined his life. His wife had left him. He was very angry. She pointed at him, telling him that he was the problem, not her. He got out of his seat and ran up the aisle towards her. It was all quite frightening.'

'What happened then?'

'Two big, burly men grabbed him and dragged him from the hall. He was out of control.' She looked at Ruby intently. 'Do you think that he might have had something to do with her death?'

'Probably not. Reggie says that she died from alcoholic poisoning, but he still might be interested to hear about it.' Ruby put the last of the plates and bowls in the cupboard.

'It was foreseen, you know.'

'Foreseen?' Ruby stared at her. 'Like in the stars? You're not having Tarot readings again?'

Mavis shook her head vehemently. 'No, it was in the newspaper, *The Truth*. My friend Edith saw it. She says that they didn't name Mrs Burns, but you could tell it was her they were talking about. A woman who drank too much and was in the temperance movement.'

'Have you told Reggie about this?'

'He'd think it was foolish.'

'No, he wouldn't. I think he'd find it intriguing. And Dusty would too. He used to work for *The Truth,* and I know that he still reads it. We're finished in here, so let's go and tell Reggie what Edith said.'

'I'm not sure—'

Ruby took both her hands. 'Come on, Mavis. Tell them what you've told me.'

'If you think so.'

Mavis followed Ruby up the hallway.

The two men were in the sitting room, smoking cigars and drinking port.

Ruby stood in the doorway, Mavis behind her. 'Reggie. Dusty. Listen to this. I think that you'll find it interesting.'

* * *

After taking Mavis home, the two crime reporters drove to Dusty's rented house in Port Melbourne, where he kept his collection of *Truth* newspapers. Although he was employed at *The Argus,* Dusty still enjoyed reading all the gossip and scandal that could be found within the pages of *The Truth.*

'Do you remember the article that Mother's talking about?' asked Reggie as the docks came into view. 'The one that was supposed to be about Mrs Burns?'

'I don't,' Dusty replied, 'but it's the sort of thing you'd read in the Poison Pen's column. That's where you find the most salacious gossip. It's brief, though, but there's enough detail to identify whom he's talking about. He doesn't name names, so it's hard to sue.'

'Who is this Poison Pen?'

Dusty shook his head. 'No one knows. He's a man of mystery, but I have to say that his information is usually correct. Where he gets it from is a mystery too, because his victims come from a vast array of occupations: lawyers, politicians, businessmen, theatre folk, high society, and social reformers. He targets those who are supposedly above reproach but are hiding dirty, little secrets. No one is safe.'

Reggie parked the Minerva outside Dusty's house and looked around at the warehouses and factories that occupied most of the port area. 'Talking about safe, is it safe to park here?'

Dusty smiled. 'My Australian Six has never been tampered with in two years.'

'Yes, but this is a Minerva. Belgian. The automobile chosen by royalty, nobility, and captains of industry all over the world. Six cylinders, 75 horsepower, capable of 100 miles per hour. Classy and stylish, much like me.'

'Point taken, Reggie,' said Dusty, stifling a laugh. 'There's a safe spot in the lane behind my place. While you shift the car, I'll ferret out my back copies of *The Truth*. I'll leave the back door open for you.'

* * *

Shortly after, Dusty was reading a Poison Pen article published a month earlier:

It is the POISON PEN's mission in life to lay bare the hypocrisy of those whom we foolishly admire for their principles and integrity. Social reformers, the clergy, the caring professions, politicians, and decorated members of

the armed forces are not immune from our scrutiny. The Poison Pen strips away the outer layers of these Pillars of Society to reveal their rancid core.

In this series, we unmask our first hypocrite for public shaming.

INTEMPERATE TEMPERANCE RABBLE-ROUSER TITILLATED BY TIPPLE

Banish the booze, she cried! One of the Woman's Christian Temperance Union's most vociferous defenders has called for the abolition of alcohol, in the manner of the Prohibitionist movement in America. Bleating from her pulpit in miscellaneous meeting halls around Melbourne, the Fiery One has ranted and raved about the dangers of booze, but, in reality, she is the ultimate hypocrite. One week ago, this Madam of Moderation was witnessed exiting a bootleg liquor shop. She was intoxicated to the eyeballs, her breath reeking of Demon Drink. The temperance advocate is decidedly intemperate.

Her secret has been uncorked!

[*The Truth*, September 23, 1927]

'What do you think, Reggie? Does that sound like Mrs Burns?'

'You can't ignore the play on words, Dusty. "The *Fiery* One." Mrs *Burns*? It looks like further investigation is required.'

'But the death was accidental, wasn't it?'

'It appears that way, but my reporter's nose has picked up the scent of something more insidious. It may come to nothing, but it's worth sniffing out.'

Chapter Six

On Monday morning, Reggie stood in front of Temperance Hall in Napier Street, South Melbourne, looking up at the impressive two-storey façade. It had been a more modest building in its early days, when it was a simple hall built by the Emerald Hill Total Abstinence Society. Additions meant that it could accommodate a few hundred people in its lecture hall, and could cater for social clubs, religious groups, and political societies, although being alcohol-free was its one defining prerequisite for use. There was still a sign stuck to the front door, advertising Mrs Burns' forthcoming address to the Woman's Christian Temperance Union on Friday, the 30th of September. It was a call to action; a call to ban alcohol and follow the path of the American Prohibitionist movement.

Reggie shook his head. From everything that he had read, the abolition of alcohol had only encouraged a black market in booze, and deaths had resulted from the consumption of illicit liquor. Whereas types like Mrs Burns claimed that poverty, alcohol-related disease, family violence, and crime were being eradicated in America, Reggie knew better. Grog shops were thriving, hiding behind the respectable façades of laundries, legal offices, and Turkish baths. Bootleggers and criminal gangs controlled the supply of beer and liquor; small stills were purchased for backyard brewing; liquor was smuggled in over the border from Mexico and Canada.

Prohibition imposed a blanket ban on drinking, to which Reggie objected strongly. Why should he, Reggie da Costa, submit to the wishes of a religious minority? Surely he should have a say in what he drank. Hadn't the six o'clock closing of hotels, which had been introduced because of the Temperance movement, only encouraged the 'six o'clock swill,' with drinkers over-imbibing before they went home? The Woman's Christian Temperance Union had not foreseen that drunken men would be lying in gutters outside hotels or going home full of grog.

It had been sobering, if that were the right word, to learn that his own mother was considering becoming teetotal. But what was more surprising was that she was in possession of information regarding the death of one of the Woman's Christian Temperance Union's most accomplished speakers, a firebrand who could whip up strong emotions in her audience and sway their opinions.

Reggie took the stairs up to the entrance and was pleased when the front door proved to be unlocked. He stepped inside. To his left was a small ticket office, while to his right was a storeroom, the door open, showing an assortment of brooms and mops, as well as cleaning products in large tubs. There was the sound of whistling coming from inside the hall.

Reggie pushed open the main door and took in the scene. Chairs had been stacked along the sides of the auditorium, leaving the main area bare. At the front was a stage with steps leading up to it on each side. Dust motes floated in the air, the result of the sweeping being done by the cleaner, who leaned on his broom and stared at the visitor.

'Can I help you?' he asked. He was in his early forties, wearing an old khaki shirt beneath his overalls and a flat cap over his black hair.

Reggie stepped forward. 'I'm Reggie da Costa from *The Argus*. I was hoping to speak to the caretaker.'

'That's me. Caretaker, cleaner, ticket seller. What's this about?'

'I'm investigating the death of Mrs Burns. Have you worked here long?'

'A couple of months.'

'Were you here on the night of her speech?'

'I was, and I've already spoken to the coppers. What's to investigate? She drank herself to death.'

'Could you answer a few questions, so that we can eliminate any doubts about her last hours?'

'I suppose so.'

Reggie took out his notepad and pen. 'When did you last see her?'

'Like I told the police, I didn't see her after she left the stage. The arrangement was that I'd be back in the morning to clean up. She liked to have a few moments to herself after the meetings.'

'You saw nothing out of the ordinary before you left?'

'The usual protesters who wanted an argument with her. But backstage is out of bounds. I make sure that everyone has gone and I lock the main door, and leave. She turns off the lights and exits by the stage door leading into the alley.'

'Could someone have hidden himself away?'

The man shrugged. 'Could have. But why would they? Her death wasn't unexpected, at least, not to me. She was a drunk. That's why she died. One night, I saw her drinking straight from a bottle after one of her meetings. She didn't see me; otherwise, I would have got the sack.'

'You've cleaned up the dressing room since her death?'

'On the Saturday morning after the meeting. I went out into the alley to empty the rubbish; that's when I found her. I thought at the time it was strange that she hadn't locked the door. She was always pernickety about things like that.'

'When you were in the dressing room, how many bottles did you find there?'

The man took off his hat and scratched his head. 'Funny. There were none.'

'Not one?'

He shook his head, perplexed. 'She has this big bag which she carries around everywhere. That was missing, too. I suppose someone could have taken it from the alley; the only thing is that this area is usually deserted early in the morning.'

'Did you notice anything unusual about the body, something you wouldn't expect to see?'

Again, the man shook his head. 'Nothing. Except—'

'Except what?'

'There was a white feather between her fingers. I noticed it when I checked her pulse. I thought it was strange. We don't get any birds in the building, and I know it wasn't in the dressing room before Mrs Burns' speech. She was very particular about cleanliness.'

'A white feather?'

'That's right. Is it important?'

Reggie sighed. 'I wish I knew.'

Chapter Seven

Later that same Monday, Clary Blain was sitting at his desk in the offices of the Criminal Investigation Branch. Recently, he had been promoted to the position of detective inspector. Despite the satisfaction that he felt in attaining his new rank, he was uncharacteristically subdued. It seemed to have taken an eternity for his skills to be recognised and rewarded, yet, in contrast, newcomer Homer Glass had been appointed as a detective sergeant at the tender age of twenty-nine, rising swiftly through the ranks in record time after arriving from Sydney only a year before. It seemed, to Clary, that the Victorian Police Force was being seduced by the appearance of flashy policing methods, rather than the hard slog that characterised his own career.

Amongst the criminal classes of New South Wales, Detective Sergeant Homer Glass had been known as 'The Undertaker,' because of his funereal appearance and the unfortunate habit he had of drawing his gun and shooting suspects, then asking questions later. His record of arrests, his command of police rules and regulations, and his 'take no prisoners' approach to policing were spoken about in hushed whispers of admiration by senior officers, so that when he moved to Melbourne, his arrival was welcomed. But from what Clary had observed over the last few months, Detective Sergeant Glass was not transparent in his police methods. In other words, he was corrupt. And he seemed to have taken a keen dislike to Clary Blain.

Clary tidied the files on his desk and pushed his chair back.

'Where are you off to?' asked Glass.

'None of your business,' he replied. 'And you'll accord me the respect I deserve by addressing me as Detective Inspector Blain.'

'It will be the pub.'

Clary took his bowler hat from the hat stand and stalked out the door.

By the time he reached The Duke of Wellington Hotel, on the corner of Flinders and Russell Streets, Clary had calmed down slightly, his high colour more a rosy pink than a firehouse red. Damn Glass, he thought, as he ordered a Scotch. Damn Glass, he thought, as he raised the whisky to his lips.

* * *

It was close to four o'clock when Reggie finally arrived at the hotel. He noted that Clary's complexion was more florid than usual, suggesting that the celebrations for his promotion a month earlier had lasted well into the present week. Blain was leaning against the bar. He was dressed as usual in a crumpled shirt and stained tie, his large belly protruding over the belt of his trousers.

'You've ordered already? What's wrong?' exclaimed Reggie as he noted the unusual sight of a full glass of whisky pressed between the detective's hands.

'It's that bastard Glass. Thinks he's a cut above the rest.'

'The Undertaker?'

'That's the one.'

Reggie tapped him on the shoulder and pointed to an empty table in the corner, away from the prying eyes and the flapping ears of the regulars who were sitting on stools at the bar.

'Have a seat. I'll get you a drink.'

By the time he returned, Reggie was disturbed to see that Clary was slumped in his chair, looking more downtrodden. Even the sight of another glass of whisky did little to enliven him.

'Thanks, mate.' Blain scratched his nose, his bloodshot eyes appraising his companion. 'Look around you, Reggie. What do you see?'

The crime reporter cast his gaze around the labourers, factory workers, railway men, and tradesmen who made up the clientele of the shabby, but popular 'Duke.'

'Badly cut trousers, uncomfortable hobnail boots, and grubby overalls. Not a decent, well-cut suit in sight.' He sniffed. 'Excessive perspiration.'

Clary banged down his hand, making Reggie jump. 'The working man, mate. Blokes who do it hard. An honest day's work for an honest wage. Not like the Glasses of this world. Your mob applaud him. You make out that he's better than the rest of us coppers. And now, he's the Chief Commissioner's darling.'

Reggie looked unconvinced. 'His approach is different, I'll give you that, but you're no slouch when it comes to solving crime either.'

'He's so patronising,' continued Clary, draining his glass. 'That habit he has of sniffing when he disagrees with you. That smirk on his face when you try to talk to him about a particular case. I'd love to wipe it off his face. And that copy of *The Victorian Police Manual,* which he keeps in his pocket. He's a stickler for rules and regulations when it suits him. I know for a fact that when he was in Sydney, he crossed the line on what a copper's supposed to do.'

'You must admit that his arrest record in Melbourne is impressive. He puts offenders behind bars.'

'*He* gets the pat on the back. *He* gets the headlines,' snarled Blain. 'What about the boys on the beat who pound the pavement and work hard? What about me? I spend days poring over a crime scene, checking evidence, and interviewing witnesses. I get results, too, but I don't get the attention. It's not fair.'

'Settle down, Clary. I can see why you feel the way you do. It's hard when someone else is taking all the credit. But what about Glass's appearance? It's appalling. Shocking haircut, that trademark black suit and tie, white shirt, and black shoes. No wonder they call him The Undertaker, even without considering that he's too ready to shoot first and ask questions later.' Reggie patted Clary on the shoulder. 'I'll get us another drink.'

He pushed through the crowd milling around the bar and called out to the bartender, 'Beer and whisky,' then handed over a ten-shilling note.

Drinks and change in hand, he came back to the table and placed the Scotch in front of Clary. 'Here's to your promotion, by the way.' He raised his glass and drank.

Blain held the amber liquid up to the light. 'Nectar of the gods,' he commented, downing it in one gulp. He waved the glass at the bartender. 'Another, mate.'

Reggie raised an eyebrow, then took a sip of beer. 'What's The Undertaker working on at the moment?'

'Officially, it's counterfeiting, but unofficially, I'm not sure. He's a secretive bugger. But you can be sure that he'll get the credit, not anyone else.'

They waited while the bartender refilled the detective's Scotch. When he had gone, Reggie said, 'What's this all about? What's upsetting you?'

Clary leaned forward and whispered, 'I reckon he's on the take.'

Reggie lit a cigarette. 'Be careful throwing aspersions around about your fellow officers, Clary. You know that he's popular with the Chief Commissioner. And the newspapers love him. It will look like sour grapes if you speak out publicly.'

Clary fixed his eyes on the whisky in his glass. 'You're right. I should try and forget about him. But I know he's after my job.'

'You got your promotion,' insisted Reggie. 'You shouldn't be worried.'

'I know. But he watches you. Looks for weaknesses. He spreads lies to make you look bad.'

'Has he done that to you?'

'Not yet, but he will.'

'Counterfeiting is on the rise. Coins, one- and five-pound notes, fakes everywhere. Reining it in will keep Glass busy,' Reggie assured him.

'He had a win on that, too. Busted a recent operation, and the court case went in his favour. He made sure that the boss heard about it.'

'Which case was that?' asked Reggie.

'Skelton, Gillian, and Ostberg. £12,500 worth of counterfeits printed on one side. Crudely done. They said that they were intending to use the other side for advertising purposes. Luckily, the judge saw through it and sentenced Skelton and Gillian to four years in prison with hard labour, while Ostberg was acquitted.'

Reggie nodded. 'That's two behind bars.' He inhaled and blew a smoke ring. 'What about that Temperance woman, Mrs Burns? The medical examiner's report must be ready. Accidental death or something more?'

'Alcoholic poisoning. Choked on it.' He lifted his glass, stared at the whisky, blinked twice, and put it down.

'You're sure that there's nothing more sinister?'

'No.' Clary looked up. 'What have you heard?'

'Nothing, nothing at all, in relation to that. How about that gang of thieves that you caught recently? Anything I can use in *The Argus*?'

'They were young,' replied the detective. 'Sons of the idle rich. Robbed a few houses and took off in a stolen car. They were caught throwing the loot into Albert Park Lake. Didn't know what else to do with it.' He sniggered. 'By the way, did you hear about our good friend, Squizzy Taylor?'

Reggie butted out his cigarette. 'Someone stole his car, then burned it. He's the laughing stock of Fitzroy, although I doubt if any of his fellow hooligans would dare laugh in his face. There's nothing like a criminal who complains when he's the victim. The boot on the other foot.

'I did hear, though, that Snowy Cutmore's missus is in Melbourne,' he added. 'That could mean trouble. If Snowy comes for a visit, he might find himself facing the barrel of a gun. And the finger on the trigger will be Squizzy's.'

'Cutmore's a wanted man up in Sydney, too. Bruhn's mates think he was behind his killing. Snowy's got nowhere to go. Melbourne and Sydney are dangerous places for him these days.'

Reggie gestured with his hands, picturing the headline. '"Squizzy Cuts Down Cutmore." What a great front-page story.'

'If I had my way, they'd both be dead,' mused Blain. 'Squizzy's like a little fly, buzzing around, causing trouble. It's time someone swatted him.'

The crime reporter chuckled. 'Two birds with one stone. I reckon your Undertaker would like to be involved in that one.'

Clary sneered. 'He'd never get caught in the middle of a gun fight. Might get himself shot.' He checked his watch and frowned, then gulped down the rest of his whisky. 'I've got to get back to the station. The Undertaker will be keeping a record of when I come and go. Bastard,' he muttered through clenched teeth.

Reggie watched as Clary pushed himself up from the table, weaving his way past the bar and out the door. He reached into his pocket, took out the white feather and twirled it between his fingers, his look thoughtful.

Chapter Eight

A white feather? Coincidence or something more? That was the question that Reggie pondered as he stood at the window of his rented flat above the grocer's shop in Swan Street, Richmond, looking down at the passers-by on the footpath below. He tightened the belt on his crimson smoking jacket, took a sip of his customary post-dinner Scotch, and turned away. It was time to review the circumstances surrounding the attempts on the lives of two apparently unconnected women. He opened his notebook and reread his case notes.

According to the caretaker at Temperance Hall, there were no empty bottles of booze in the dressing room the morning that Mrs Burns' body had been found, and yet she died of alcoholic poisoning. Had she put the bottles in her bag? Had the missing bag been stolen by an opportunistic thief before her body was discovered? Or was foul play involved? And what of the white feather that the caretaker had noticed in the dead woman's hand?

After interviewing the caretaker, Reggie had contacted the Woman's Christian Temperance Union for information on Mrs Burns, but they had been uncooperative. The fact that their premier spokeswoman had died in such scandalous circumstances was disrupting their campaign and interfering with their message. No one at the Union was prepared to speak about the woman or her private life.

Fortunately for Reggie, an archivist at *The Argus* had managed to find a profile of the lady, which had been written when she was promoted to one of the executive positions in the movement. After reading it, Reggie wondered if there were more to Mrs Burns than what was in the newspaper. Fortunately, although the reporter who filed the report had retired, he was prepared to speak off the record when Reggie telephoned him.

'My wife will make my life a misery if I speak negatively about Mrs Burns,' the former reporter admitted.

'Off the record, then. What can you tell me?' Reggie asked.

'I interviewed her a year ago. I must tell you that she was a very unpleasant person, no matter what my wife thinks. Opinionated, arrogant, not prepared to accept that there might be valid arguments against Prohibition. Obviously, I couldn't print any of that. I settled for details of her life growing up and how she came to embrace the movement. It was illuminating, to say the least.'

'In what way?'

'She was born in Kangaroo Flat, near Bendigo, the only daughter of farmers. Her father died when she was young, and she and her mother moved into town. The mother worked long hours while the daughter was cared for by a widow next door. From what I could gather, this lady was involved in community affairs, taking on one cause after another. Mrs Burns was influenced by her more than by her mother. It seems that before she finished school in Grade Eight, she had become very opinionated. Always made her point of view known. Unlike the widow next door, who took on charitable cases and spoke up for the poor and unfortunate, Mrs Burns had bigger fish to fry. She was asked to leave school because she dared to argue with the headmaster over the way the school was run. Not bad for a fourteen-year-old! Everything was either black or white, good or evil, no shades of grey.

'She married late, aged forty. No children. Her husband ran the post office in Kangaroo Flat. He enlisted in 1917 and died in France. She ran the store on her own but sold it shortly after, living on the proceeds and the money he had left her. I gathered that it was a relatively comfortable life. She was a member of the local branch of the Independent Order of Rechabites, which was opposed to the drinking of alcohol. Apart from that, she was involved in all sorts of causes, such as women's suffrage and the deportation of enemy aliens during the Great War. As I said, Mrs Burns was nothing if not opinionated.'

'She sounds like she would make enemies.'

'That's true, but surprisingly, you had to admire her. She was plucky and determined, stubborn. She had a way with words and could sway a mob. She was unafraid and you had to respect her, even if you didn't agree with her.'

Thinking back to that conversation, Reggie was unsure how to proceed with his investigation into Mrs Burns' death. *The Truth* column complicated matters, identifying her indirectly and asserting that she was a drunk. Her death and the nature of it, following so soon after the publication of the Poison Pen column, bothered Reggie.

He turned to his notes on the Beryl Webb case. She, too, had been found clutching a white feather. The existence of the feather begged the question: Was there a link between the two women?

His first attempts to gather information on Miss Webb were not particularly productive, but finally, he found a neighbour in whom she had confided. According to this woman, Beryl was forty-two, lived alone, and was antisocial. No relatives. No friends. Her last place of work had been The Melbourne Hospital. Her home had been left to her by an uncle, now deceased.

Reggie's impressions of the house confirmed that Miss Webb had little income, and what she had was spent on feeding her drug habit. Given the disgusting state of her living conditions and her poor health, it surprised Reggie that she had survived the gassing.

Reggie poured himself another Scotch and put the notebook down. It was a long shot, but he was curious to know whether Miss Webb had been the subject of one of the Poison Pen's columns. However, given that she was not a public figure like Mrs Burns but a reclusive former nurse, he doubted it. Despite his misgivings, he left a message with Dusty's landlady, asking him to bring in his collection of back copies of *The Truth* the next day, so that they could see if the Poison Pen had written about Mrs Burns *and* Miss Webb.

He drained his glass and turned his attention back to the hustle and bustle of the street below. What he wouldn't give for another story that would cement his reputation as Melbourne's premier crime reporter.

Chapter Nine

The next day, in the offices of *The Argus*, Reggie and Dusty pored over the pages of *The Truth*, searching for a Poison Pen column that might make some reference to Miss Webb.

'Here it is!' exclaimed Dusty. 'From nearly two weeks ago.'

Reggie stood next to him, reading over his shoulder:

CAUGHT IN THE DEADLY WEB OF THE DOPE SPIDER: ANGEL OF MERCY MEDICATES WITH MORPHINE

A secret inquiry at a major Melbourne hospital, into the actions of one of their nurses, has found that this 'Angel of Mercy' stole drugs from the hospital's medical supplies and her own patients to satisfy her insatiable craving for morphine. Her arms scarred from the bite of the needle, she injected herself even while on duty, her drug-addled state a danger to the patients under her care. When this despicable breach of trust was discovered, the "powers that be" forcibly retired the drug fiend rather than expose her to the public eye.

Now, she hides away, caught in the web of the Dope Spider, wallowing in the filth of a back room, the blinds drawn against the world outside. She should pay for the pain and torment she inflicted on her vulnerable patients.

[*The Truth*, October 7, 1927]

'What do you think, Reggie?'

'Sounds like Beryl. Former nurse. Kept to herself. I noticed a used hypodermic needle in the kitchen. And there's that play on words again. The *fiery* one was Mrs Burns. This one has spun a deadly *web*. Miss Webb. If we're going to confirm that this is the woman he's writing about, we need more than speculation. We need proof. I was wondering if we could find out anything more about her. Webb worked at The Melbourne Hospital up to two months ago. She supposedly retired.'

'I know a nurse there. I could ask her if Beryl was dismissed.'

'Excellent.' Reggie tapped the headline. 'If what the Poison Pen says is true, he's intent on exposing hypocrites and ruining reputations. What's his problem with Beryl Webb and Ida Burns in particular? Why choose them?'

'You think that what happened to them might be something more than an accident?' asked Dusty.

'Let's look at the facts. The first column appeared on the 23rd of September. Mrs Burns was found dead about a week later. The second Poison Pen article was published on the 7th of October. Miss Webb nearly died from gas inhalation four days after that.'

'It could be coincidence,' Dusty offered.

'Two cases: one death, one near fatality,' said Reggie. 'If you look at the case of Nurse Webb, there's also a chance that she might have attempted suicide. Perhaps she was humiliated when she was sacked, saw the column in the newspaper, and was afraid of being identified. Unlikely, I think, but possible. You should have seen how she was living, Dusty. It was nauseating. Filthy and wretched, she was. Perhaps she couldn't take it anymore. But when you consider that she was a drug addict, it's more likely that she turned on the gas and forgot to light it.'

Dusty nodded. 'Attempted suicide. An accident. Both are possible. But what about the feather? Where did that come from?'

Reggie shrugged his shoulders.

'And there's Mrs Burns and the missing bag and the feather. How do you explain that one, Reggie?' added Dusty.

'Nothing mysterious there, either, if you consider a simple explanation. The stage door is open, and a feather blows into the building. Mrs Burns picks it up, staggers outside, holding her bag full of bottles, and dies. A shift worker goes past, looks down the alley, sees the bag, and steals it. On the face of it, there's nothing to suggest that her death was intentional either.'

'But she did make enemies. And the caretaker said there were protests.'

'That's true,' agreed Reggie. 'If there is a link with the Poison Pen articles, did these women know him? Did they know each other? If these were something more than accidents, the only other conclusion is that there's some crazed killer out there with no apparent motive and a passion for feathers. It's a shame that we can't talk to this Poison Pen and ask him where he gets his information from.'

'The fact is that the Poison Pen has been writing this column for about five or six years and, as far as I know, no one has died up until now.'

Reggie nodded in agreement. 'If we could only find out who he is. We'll keep an eye out for developments, but I think there's no hard evidence linking these incidents together.' He folded up the newspapers and put them to one side. 'More importantly, what's happening about your suit for the wedding? You're not wearing that.' He eyed Dusty's crumpled jacket with the patches on the elbows. 'Have you contacted Wallace, Buck, and Goodes yet? Remember, it's evening wear. Very swish. Very stylish. Your sister's getting married and you need to look the part.'

Dusty's face fell. 'Next week, Reggie. I'll deal with it next week.'

The office boy knocked on the door and entered. 'Mr da Costa, Mr Flange would like to see you in his office.'

Reggie rolled his eyes. 'Tell him I'll be along shortly.'

The lad went red. 'I'm sorry, sir, but Mr Flange specifically wants to see you now.'

Reggie grunted. 'Tell him I'm in a meeting. I'll be there as soon as I can.' He turned to Dusty. 'By the way, when's the next Poison Pen column due out?'

'This Friday.'

'We won't have to wait long to find out if we're on to something sinister.' He stood up. 'Our esteemed sub-editor is waiting. It's a pity the Poison Pen doesn't target Curtis Flange. He'd be doing the newspaper world a favour if he did!'

Chapter Ten

It was a beautiful day in Spring. The park was at its best, with delicate, yellow roses in bloom, the last of the pink and white magnolia petals clinging to the branches, and the lawns freshly mowed. Near the lake, children were playing while their mother watched on, enjoying the warmth of the sun on her back. She chatted contentedly to another woman, who was rocking a pram containing a sleeping baby. Ducks bobbed up and down on the waters of the lake, while a male and female clambered up onto the edge and waddled away, followed by a conga line of ducklings. Almost everywhere one looked, the scene was one of serenity and contentment.

Mavis da Costa was sitting beside the lake, her head down. A deep melancholy weighed on her, making her oblivious to the laughter of children, the gardens of glorious Spring flowers, and the perfection of the day. Nothing could take away the chill that had spread through her, after a visit to the bank had revealed the perilous state of her finances.

'What am I going to do?' she whispered. She gazed up at the trees, their boughs swaying gently in the breeze, but they offered her no answer.

Her efforts to keep up with the Bardsley Smiths were draining her finances, what with the need to dress well, purchase train tickets to Middle Brighton every Thursday to meet with the ladies of her circle, and contribute to the charitable events that they organised. Not to mention the occasional donations she was obliged to make to assist those who were vulnerable, which was part and parcel of being a member of the Brighton coterie. If she showed a reluctance to contribute, there was always Edith to point it out and shame her in front of her friends. It was a sad fact that her life would have little meaning if her straitened circumstances forced her to abandon the group.

It was a conundrum which she was contemplating when a young man sat on the bench next to her.

'What a lovely scene,' he commented. 'I love coming to the park, don't you?'

She turned her head and looked at him. He was around thirty, conservatively dressed, rather plain in looks, with straight dark hair.

'It is,' she replied. She smoothed her dress and drew her handbag closer.

He pulled a small bag out of his pocket and threw some breadcrumbs onto the grass, attracting the ducks that were sunning themselves nearby.

'Would you like to feed them?' He offered her the bag and she took it, glad of the distraction.

'I could do with some cheering up,' she said. 'Life is hard sometimes.'

The man nodded. 'I know what you mean. There's a lot wrong with the world, but I try to take a more optimistic view of life. Something will turn up, I tell myself.'

Mavis rallied. 'Yes, I'm sure you're right. Something will turn up.' She smiled at him, attempting to banish the sad thoughts that had afflicted her only minutes before. For some reason, she felt the need to confide in a stranger, rather than her beloved son.

Reggie had been so good to her over the years, she thought, and had saved her from embarrassing situations where her trust in certain people, men in particular, had been proven wrong. She didn't want to ask him for help again, after her humiliating stint in rehabilitation two years before, due to her dependence on morphine. Reggie had assured her that it wasn't her fault; that it was that dreadful travelling salesman, Dr Hiram T Wishbone, who had been instrumental in her becoming addicted to the drugs which he claimed would relieve her insomnia. But she couldn't erase the shame of knowing that her future daughter-in-law, Ruby, had witnessed her in the grip of morphine.

And now, to confess that she was in financial difficulties would imply that she wanted Reggie to supplement her income, and that she would not do.

Her son was engaged to be married, and he needed all his money to ensure that his and Ruby's future together was rosy. Besides, wouldn't he think badly of her if he knew that she was in trouble again?

Mavis cast a quick glance at the man sitting next to her. He didn't look like the other men who had led her astray. He couldn't be classed as fashionable or handsome, and his manner was not that of a ladies' man. He seemed like a nice, young, serious fellow, not frivolous or flippant. Not like Valentine Peebles with his oozing charm and dodgy ways, who almost defrauded her of her money two years before. Indeed, this sober chap looked like he could be trusted.

'You remind me of my aunt,' he commented. 'She has lovely taste in dresses too.'

'Thank you, young man.' Her new blue dress, the same colour as her eyes, had flounces of lace on the bodice, and was the epitome of the new Spring fashions that she had admired in the shops, but at a fraction of the cost. She shook her froth of white curls and smiled at him again.

'You don't look like you'd have much in the way of problems,' she remarked. 'You look like a sensible person.'

'It's money in the end.'

'I know how that feels.' Mavis felt the weight of the world settling on her shoulders again. 'It's hard when you're on your own, and your sole source of income is dwindling.'

'Surely a lady such as yourself would have a husband who looks after her?'

'I did, until—' This was not the time to unburden herself about her absent husband, Mario, who had spent all her inheritance and had taken off with the maid, leaving her and her then thirteen-year-old son penniless.

The young man sighed. 'Ah, you're a widow.'

Mavis didn't reply. She was not about to contradict him with the truth because, in a sense, her husband was dead to her.

He seemed unconcerned by her lack of response and continued. 'It must be difficult for you. As it is for me. You see, I run my own business. I produce brochures and advertising catalogues. Posters for theatrical companies and suchlike.'

'That sounds interesting. You must be artistic.'

'Would you like to see some of my work?'

'Yes, please.'

He opened his briefcase and took out a range of advertisements for clothing, department, and furniture stores, entertainment, and motorcars.

'I know these companies,' she exclaimed. 'Buick, Foy and Gibsons, The Leviathan, Leggett's Ballroom. You are a clever man. Such beautiful colours. Do you design them yourself?'

'I have two assistants. But we're having a problem finding premises for the business.'

'Why is that?'

'My landlord says that I must vacate the property in a week. I've explored the rental market for small factories. They're expensive. What I need is a large garage, preferably brick, with a back entrance to an alley or street, so that we can load our goods easily and transport them to our clients.'

'My house has a garage like that.'

He looked at her in surprise. 'It must be private. Lockable. Not far from here.'

Mavis's rosy cheeks glowed. 'Mine fits that description. I don't use it. And I would never bother you. It goes across the back of the block with the doors opening onto the lane.'

'It sounds perfect!' he cried. 'But are you prepared to rent it out?'

Mavis regarded him coyly. 'What are you prepared to pay?'

'£10 per week.'

'Really?' Mavis was ecstatic. 'I never even thought of renting it. The garage is almost empty. There are a few boxes in there, nothing more.'

'I could clear it out for you. Could you take me there?'

'I'd be delighted, young man.'

He smiled. 'I can't tell you how happy you've made me. You won't even know we're there. By the way, my name is Damien.'

She paused. 'Call me Mavis.'

'Let's seal the deal with a handshake, Mavis.' He shook her hand. '£10 a week cash with four weeks in advance.' He reached into his trouser pocket and extracted £50 from a roll of banknotes.

'Here you are.'

Mavis's eyes opened wide at the sight of the money. She gave him a huge smile. 'You've made me very happy,' she said, slipping the notes into her handbag.

'Not as much as you've made me,' replied Damien, pushing the wad of money back into his pocket. 'Now, let's see this garage of yours.'

Chapter Eleven

I t was a sad fact of life that Reggie's previous boss, Floyd Kramer, had been forced into early retirement due to illness, and his temporary replacement, Curtis Flange, had been made the permanent head of the crime desk at *The Argus*. Flange was editor of the social pages, rather than an expert on Melbourne's criminal underworld. In Reggie's view, he was more interested in what the Horace Strikers and Squizzy Taylors of Melbourne wore, rather than their involvement in illegal gambling, illicit booze, prostitution, and armed robbery. To put it bluntly, Curtis Flange was out of his depth, which was obvious to everyone except those who owned *The Argus*. Reggie had to wonder if the rumoured family connection were true, one that made the newspaper's chief editor turn a blind eye to Flange's ineptitude. It could be the only explanation for the decision to appoint the gossip columnist as head of the crime desk, over the experience and skills of the one and only Reggie da Costa.

Reggie sat opposite Flange, having been summoned earlier to his office for a meeting. As usual, his boss resembled a schoolboy, home from boarding school, with his straight, slicked hair parted down the middle, and uniform of white shirt, black braces, and red bow tie.

As he waited for Flange to speak, Reggie was amused to note that his boss appeared to have grown inches since his elevation to Crime, as they were no longer sitting eye to eye. It occurred to the reporter that Flange must have requisitioned a higher chair, one specifically chosen to reinforce his superiority over his underlings, in more ways than one. The only other explanation was that a few inches had been sawn off the legs of Reggie's chair. These musings helped pass the time while Flange fiddled with the files on his desk, far too busy to give the crime reporter his immediate attention.

Finally, he looked up. 'Ah, Reginald. You've finished your meeting. I would prefer it if you dropped everything when I want to see you. Time is money, and my time is especially precious.'

'What did you want to see me about, Curtis?'

'Mr Flange,' he said in his high, reedy voice. 'I am Mr Flange.'

'What did you want to see me about, *Mister* Flange?'

Flange looked down at him, his chubby, rosy-cheeked face glowing in the light from the overhead bulb. 'I am concerned about your recent reports on Sydney crime.'

Here we go again, Reggie thought. 'In what way?' he asked.

'This Razor Gang business you're writing about. I don't understand it, and I doubt if your readers do either. Are all Sydney's criminals clean-shaven? Does not one have a moustache or a beard?'

Reggie sighed. 'The term "Razor Gang" has nothing to do with facial hair, Mr Flange. It has everything to do with the weapons they use. The New South Wales government brought in the Pistol Licensing Act this year. It is designed to restrict the use of guns. There are severe penalties for carrying concealed firearms and handguns.'

'What does this have to do with razors?'

'These gangs are using razors as weapons instead of guns. That way, they escape prosecution. You can buy one in a barber's shop for a few pence. They're easy to hide, unlike firearms. And if a thug pulls a razor on you, you can bet that you'll be intimidated. Being slashed or mutilated is not something you want to experience.' Reggie drew his finger across his throat. 'Imagine that being a razor?'

Flange went pale and played with his bow tie.

'My series of articles,' continued Reggie, 'concerns how Sydney crime differs from the crime we get in Melbourne. The public here don't have the fears that Sydneysiders do. In Sydney, the crime bosses are more organised, more professional. Crime is lucrative and the New South Wales Police Force is ineffectual, if not corrupt, compared to the Victoria Police.'

'Indeed, Reginald. But what does the situation in Sydney have to do with us in Melbourne?'

'There's a good chance that two players, one from Melbourne and one from Sydney, are going to come to blows. Snowy Cutmore's likely to move to Melbourne. His missus is here, and he's sure to follow. He and Squizzy Taylor hate each other. Cutmore's been involved in a Sydney gang leader's murder up there, and they reckon he's heading for our fair city soon to escape retribution.'

'Thank you for enlightening me, Reginald, but I still find the subject confusing. However, I do have some suggestions for how you can improve your coverage of crime.'

Reggie gazed at his boss, lost for words. Finally, he said in a low, menacing tone, 'What do you have in mind?'

'Your reports lack *panache*. They are, dare I say it, bordering on dull. Try to liven them up; create interest in our readers. For example, are the rich and famous in Sydney society going out as much? Are they holidaying on the continent for fear of staying home and being robbed or slashed? Do they employ more bodyguards to protect their jewellery and their expensive motorcars? Has this Razor Gang business affected their attendance at opening nights and art gallery exhibitions? I think that you could enliven your reports a little more, Reginald, by giving an insight into how these crimes are affecting the moneyed classes. Don't you agree?'

Reggie didn't trust himself to speak. Flange sat back and put his hands behind his head. 'And, while you're at it, more about what Squizzy Taylor wears. His silk shirts, fawn gloves, and velvet-collared coats. His patent leather shoes. Where does he buy them? Does he have them specially made? What about the cars he drives? American models, aren't they? Does this "Snowy" fellow have expensive tastes too?'

Reggie moaned, as if he were in pain.

Flange reddened. 'That will be all, Reginald. You can go.' He waved a hand dismissively and turned his attention back to the pile of papers on his desk.

* * *

Back in his office, Reggie took out the flask that he kept in the top drawer and took a hefty swig.

Chapter Twelve

Friday morning had arrived and, with it, the latest edition of *The Truth*. Reggie watched on as Dusty thumbed through the pages until he reached the Poison Pen's latest column.

'Here it is,' he said, and proceeded to read it out loud:

THE BLATANT BLEAT OF A BILIOUS BIGAMIST

Which former captain in the Australian Imperial Force, recently elected as a Member of Parliament, has denounced divorce in the House, but burned his fingers in a matrimonial pie made in his own kitchen?

We allege that the Not So Honourable Member, in his maiden speech, called for divorce to be harder to obtain. However, it appears that this Witness for Wedlock, who has publicly stated that he is a widower, is secretly separated from his first wife. He lived up to his name by bullying and tormenting her. Having recently tied the knot yet again, it seems that the Dishonourable Member has a 'dead' wife, who is well and truly alive and living in Geelong.

[*The Truth*, October 21, 1927]

The two men stared at each other as the import of what the Poison Pen had written sank in.

'It's Captain Badger, newly minted member of the Victorian Legislative Assembly,' said Reggie, chuckling. 'Who else could it be? Badger: to bully and torment. If others work this one out as easily as we did, there will be hell to pay. Imagine the repercussions? He will be reviled throughout the State of Victoria. Imagine the reaction of the Premier? He'll be outraged. He personally requested that Badger join the Party and stand for election as the standard bearer of family values.'

'I agree, boss. It must be Badger. If what the Poison Pen says is true, his former wife is out there. Not dead and not divorced. Badger will be branded as a hypocrite and a bigamist. And his new wife was 1923's Debutante of the Year. Imagine what her family is thinking!'

Reggie stroked his moustache. 'Someone will find the first Mrs Badger in Geelong. I'll guarantee she won't stay dead long!'

'Where does he get his information?' asked Dusty, running his fingers through his hair. 'Someone knows Badger's dirty little secrets and has fed them to the Poison Pen. And how long will it take before this news becomes public?'

Reggie looked up. 'Not long, judging from the look on Monty's face.'

As he spoke, *The Argus*'s political reporter dashed into the newsroom, a huge smile on his ruddy face. Jeremy Montgomery, known as Monty to his colleagues, was puffing hard, having scaled the two flights of stairs to his office rather than waiting for the elevator.

'It's bedlam out there!' he cried, waving a piece of paper in his hand.

All those sitting at their desks raised their heads from their typing to look at Monty, usually one of the newspaper's most phlegmatic journalists. It was said behind closed doors that his facial appearance was only capable of one expression: expressionless. Thus, seeing him in an animated state shook the newsroom to its core.

'What's happened?' asked one reporter, getting up from his chair.

'Parliament is in chaos!' Monty cried, the words tumbling from his mouth. 'Accusations are being thrown around the chamber. Bigamy. Divorce. Live wives. Dead wives. Lies. Hypocrisy. And who do you think is the butt of the insinuations?'

'Who is it?'

'The Honourable Cuthbert G. Badger.'

Cries of 'No!' filled the room, while Reggie and Dusty smiled at each other and nodded.

Monty paused for breath. 'The Honourable Member has released a statement. Let me read it to you:

Shocking accusations have been levelled at me today, based on the scuttlebutt and innuendo published in *The Truth* newspaper. I wish to rebut these lies and slurs on my character and reputation by affirming my previous statement that I am a widower. My former wife, Agnes, died in the Spanish influenza outbreak of 1919.

My recent bride, Daphne, is deeply distressed by this malicious gossip. She is a sweet girl who should not be exposed to such disgusting and absurd rumours, the result of the scandalous and defamatory comments of the Poison Pen. He is a coward who hides behind a nom de plume rather than face those whose reputations he ruins.

I will not succumb to the chatter of the ignorant and ill-informed.

I will not resign.

Hon. Cuthbert G. Badger.

'That's incredible. Has anyone found the wife? The dead one?' asked Bluey Talbot.

'Not yet, but someone will find her.'

Curtis Flange came running into the newsroom. 'She's alive! Not dead! A woman claiming to be Badger's first wife has contacted *The Argus*. She wants to speak to a reporter to tell her side of the story.' His face was glowing, his slicked hair wet with perspiration. 'I need to get to Geelong. Fast.'

Reggie stepped forward. 'You're a gossip columnist, Curtis, not a political reporter. You don't write lead stories. Monty should go.'

Flange stopped dead. 'Reginald, I resent that insinuation. And it's *Mister* Flange to you.'

Reggie turned away, disgusted. He hated the thought of what Flange might write: a silly, superficial piece, not the insightful, serious analysis that this situation deserved, given the political ramifications of Badger's deceit. Because, of one thing Reggie was sure, the Poison Pen had hit the mark this time. If the former Mrs Badger was not alive and living in Geelong, he'd eat his hat. On second thoughts, his new grey fedora, which matched his grey, pin-striped, three-piece suit admirably, was too good to eat. Perhaps he'd swap it for a slice of pineapple upside-down cake.

* * *

Fortunately, the editor of *The Argus* was not prepared to entrust Curtis Flange with the task of writing one of the biggest political news stories of the year. It was clear to all but Flange that what the former Mrs Badger was wearing and how she decorated her house, should not be the primary concerns of the article. He insisted that Monty be assigned the role and that he should commence the 48-mile trip to Geelong as soon as possible. Given that Monty lacked both a motorcar and a driver's licence, Reggie volunteered to act as his driver, although his motivation was not necessarily pure. He was dying to know what the politician's wife would have to say.

* * *

Geelong, a city with a population of 35,000 people, was situated southwest of Melbourne on the banks of Port Phillip Bay. Originally a starting point for fossickers making their way to the Ballarat goldfields in the 1850s, Geelong had become a destination in its own right, with the establishment of woollen mills, a whisky distillery, fertiliser plants, and the opening of the Ford motorcar factory in the early 1920s. Its declaration as a city in 1910 had enabled Geelong to discard the tag 'Sleepy Hollow.'

The silver bonnet of the Minerva AC Open Tourer gleamed in the sunshine as Reggie and Monty took the Geelong Road, leaving the city behind, a journey of at least two hours ahead of them. Reggie had put the top down, so that they could enjoy the scenery and feel the gentle breeze of a beautiful day in Spring.

'They used to call this road "the old glue pot," but the work they did on it back in 1920 has made all the difference,' observed Reggie. 'No more sticking to the surface. I wouldn't want to subject the Minerva to that!'

Monty's facial expression had reverted to normal: expressionless. 'Never wanted an automobile,' he commented. 'Not sure what the attraction is.'

Reggie shook his head, rendered speechless. What could he say to that?

They drove past acres of flat grasslands, punctuated with gum trees and small, wooded areas. Halfway to their destination, the tower of the former stately home of the Chirnside family rose up to their left above the trees. Recently purchased by the Roman Catholic Church, the mansion was now the home of Corpus Christi College. Further on was the township of Werribee, situated amongst a vast tract of grazing land, along with market gardens, orchards, and poultry farms.

'Perhaps we could stop for lunch and a beer at the Bridge Hotel on the way back?' suggested Reggie, while his colleague gazed absentmindedly at the distinctive granite peaks of the You Yangs rising to their right.

Monty was non-committal. 'If that's what you want.'

With the likelihood that there would be no stimulating conversation for the rest of the journey, Reggie fixed his eyes on the road and pressed his foot down on the pedal, his beloved Minerva responding as it surged forward, its engine roaring. Soon, they would be at their destination, which couldn't come quickly enough. The thought of an exclusive interview with the Honourable Cuthbert Badger's former wife warmed the cockles of Reggie's heart. And he was certain that Monty would not deny him the opportunity to ask a few questions, even though the political reporter was the designated representative of *The Argus*.

Chapter Thirteen

Dusty took advantage of Reggie's absence to pursue an idea that he'd hatched concerning the subject matter for his next article. Nearly three weeks earlier, Reggie had recommended that his upcoming report should be relevant to the crimes on which they were reporting. The Poison Pen fitted that description, but Dusty had no intention of tracking down the columnist from *The Truth* until Reggie gave him the word. Instead, he wanted to research the background to poison pen letters in general: Who wrote them, and the reasons why they did, with reference to some of the famous cases from the past. And, if the link between the Poison Pen column and Burns, Webb, and Badger could be proved, his article would supply useful, background material.

To this end, he asked his colleague at *The Argus*, Bluey Talbot, if he could pick his brains on the subject. It was known throughout the newsroom that Bluey had an almost encyclopaedic knowledge on the subject of crime, able to quote chapter and verse when it came to famous criminals and their transgressions, drawing on his forty years of experience as a journalist. If anybody could supply Dusty with background information, it was Bluey. They agreed to meet after work at the Duke of Wellington Hotel.

Dusty had already found a table and ordered two beers when he saw Talbot enter the public bar and head his way, pushing past the drinkers who were lined four deep at the bar. Bluey was in his early sixties, still possessing a fine head of red hair, although his beard was dappled with grey. His career with *The Argus* had been interrupted by the advent of the Great War, resulting in him spending four years as a war correspondent stationed in London and on the battlefields of France and Belgium. On his return to Australia, Bluey took up his former position at the newspaper as a reporter.

'Now, laddie, what's this all about?'

Dusty pulled out a notebook and pen. 'I was hoping that you might be able to help me with a report that I'm working on. It's about poison pen letters. This business with *The Truth* column has sparked my interest in the subject. I'm curious about why people write them and what they hope to gain by doing it, as well as any cases you might know about.'

'You don't want much, do you, laddie?' he remarked, with a rueful grin. Bluey took a sip of his beer, sat quietly for a moment or two, then nodded slowly. 'The common characteristic of the author of a poison pen letter is that he wants to remain anonymous, most probably because he knows that what he is saying in his letter is either mischievous, abusive, libellous, or threatening. And often the language in these letters is crude or malicious, language that the writer wouldn't use in their normal, everyday interaction with others.'

'Why do they home in on particular people?' Dusty asked.

'Usually, because of resentment or jealousy. Specifically, we don't often know. The victim may have done nothing wrong to deserve such a spiteful response. But the fact is that the writer of a poison pen letter usually knows their victim and has developed an obsession with them.' Bluey watched as Dusty took notes. 'Am I going too fast for you?'

'Not at all. Please go on.'

Bluey took another drink and put his glass down. 'In some cases, the identity of the writer may never be known. He may stop for no apparent reason. Perhaps he's exhausted his hatred after a few, well-phrased letters. Perhaps he fears exposure. Perhaps he moves away. Or the object of his attention does. I say "he," but it's an interesting fact that the author of a poison pen letter is most likely a woman.'

'I didn't expect that.' Dusty picked up his beer and took a decent swig. 'What effect do these letters have on the recipients?'

'That's a good question, laddie. They're not easy to ignore. The recipient may become suspicious of his neighbours, perhaps even feel unsafe. The victim may become suicidal. Some go to the police, while others try to expose their accuser themselves. But there's no doubt that the desired effect is to destabilise the recipient.'

'Can you give me specific examples?'

'Early this century, there was the case of the "Serpent Typewriter." She sent letters to some of the most respectable members of New York society, making false accusations. One woman was branded as a prostitute. Another was bombarded with pamphlets about alcoholism, drug addiction, and insanity, suggesting that she had a multitude of problems.'

Dusty frowned. 'That's nasty. Did they find out who was behind it?'

'This is where it gets interesting. It was a neighbour, Mrs Pollard, a member of the Episcopal Church and Daughters of the American Revolution. The jury acquitted her because they found it hard to believe that such a respectable member of society could do such things, even though her typewriter was identified as the machine on which the letters were written.'

'She got away with it.'

'Indeed, no. The poison pen letters started up again, but this time they consisted of letters and words cut out of newspapers. The police set a trap for Mrs Pollard, and she eventually confessed. She was fined but not jailed. In the end, public humiliation was a much more effective punishment for a person such as her.'

He tapped his finger on the table. 'There's one other case you can find in the archives: poison pen letters signed by "Tiger Eye." It happened only five years ago in Tulle, France. It's fascinating. They caught her in the end due to creative detective work. Look it up, laddie.' He checked his watch. 'Better get home. The missus will be expecting me.' He finished his beer and stood up.

Dusty reached out and touched his arm. 'I don't want to keep you, but could you spare a couple more minutes?'

Talbot sat down. 'What is it, laddie?'

'You were a war correspondent. Did you ever cross paths with Captain Badger?'

'Badger?' He pulled a face. 'On the battlefield, no. But I did hear talk about him, and it wasn't complimentary. I'm not sure how reliable it is, but I'll share what I know. Just don't quote me.'

Dusty put away his notebook. 'Go ahead.'

'Badger was sent to Western France. He'd been promoted quickly through the ranks of the 37th Battalion, becoming a captain, but there were doubts about his capability. His first major battle was at Messines in Belgium. That's the one that defined him for the rest of the war.'

'What happened?' asked Dusty.

'It was after three o'clock in the morning of the 7th of June 1917. Nineteen powerful mines were detonated under German trenches, south of Ypres in Belgium. Flames shot up in the air; the earth belched clouds of smoke. It was like a scene from Hell, according to those who witnessed it. When dawn broke, thousands of German soldiers lay dead in the rubble. Those who were still alive crawled on their hands and knees away from the craters.'

'Where does Badger come into this?'

'The battle which came after was carefully coordinated: a push to gain possession of Messines. But it came at a price: Nearly 7000 of the 3rd Division were either killed or wounded. Later, I heard that one of the officers showed a shameless lack of courage in the face of enemy fire. He sent his men over the top while he cowered in the trenches. This officer also ensured that those who witnessed his cowardice would never testify against him. They were accused of mutiny or desertion. Innocent men had their reputations ruined. The top brass didn't want to deal with it.'

'Who was the officer?'

'Cuthbert Badger.'

Chapter Fourteen

After two hours on the road, Reggie and Monty reached their destination, the outskirts of Geelong, where the politician's wife resided. Mrs Badger's little yellow weatherboard house could just be seen above the thick hedge that surrounded it.

'Staying incognito, I'd say,' remarked Reggie as they parked behind a green, Summit motorcar.

They walked through the gateway cut into the hedge and stepped up onto the front verandah. Reggie checked his reflection in the front window. He was pleased to see that his green, check travelling suit still looked freshly pressed, despite the long journey. He licked his fingers and smoothed his moustache. As he did so, he was surprised and a little bit miffed to see the figure of a woman inside watching him through the glass.

Mrs Badger opened the door before they could knock. She looked tired, with dark rings under her eyes and an air of resignation on her face which belied her relative youth, for she could not have been more than late twenties in age. She was slender and tall, wearing a plain white blouse and grey check skirt. This was a person whose youth had dissipated, Reggie surmised, judging by the flecks of grey appearing in her long, brown hair, which she wore in a bun at the nape of her neck. He noticed that she was not wearing jewellery, not even a wedding ring.

'Mrs Badger, I presume?' Monty stepped forward. 'I'm Mr Montgomery, political reporter from *The Argus*, and this is my colleague, Mr da Costa. May we come in?'

'Can I see some identification, please?'

'Of course.' He handed over his press card, which Mrs Badger studied and returned to him.

'I have to be careful,' she remarked. 'You could be anyone.'

She opened the door wide, and they followed her into a small sitting room, which was relatively spartan in appearance. A faded, floral couch, a wooden chair, and a cheap sideboard were the main items of furniture, their age and condition suggesting that they were either second-hand or obtained from a charity. On the mantelpiece above the fireplace was a framed family photograph and a vase of flowers.

'Please, have a seat while I make some tea,' she said. 'You've had a long drive.'

Reggie and Monty exchanged looks as they heard a back door slam and the sound of raised voices. A few minutes later, Agnes Badger reappeared carrying a tea tray, accompanied by a thin, clean-shaven man who could only have been her brother, perhaps five years older. Life appeared to have been kinder to him, Reggie observed, for he looked fit and well, and was dressed in a fashionable jacket with matching trousers. They made for an odd couple, he thought.

'This is my brother, Herbert Hawke. He's staying with me now.'

'That must be your motorcar out the front,' observed Reggie, addressing her brother.

Herbert moved across to stand in front of the fireplace, making no attempt to greet his sister's guests or reply to Reggie's comment. The surly expression on his face made it clear that he did not approve of their visit.

As Mrs Badger poured the tea and offered them biscuits, Reggie had a chance to revise his opinion of her. It was true that she had prematurely aged, but she possessed a pair of particularly fine, green eyes, not unlike Ruby's, and a clear complexion, remnants of the very attractive woman she had once been.

She took the remaining chair, her hands cradling the cup and saucer. 'I asked you here because I feel like this web of lies and deception has to end,' she began. 'I've lived with this since the end of the war, and I want to be heard.'

'How did the Poison Pen know that you lived in Geelong?' asked Reggie.

'I don't know. I've never spoken to the Poison Pen or anyone at *The Truth*.'

'Why did you contact *The Argus* rather than *The Truth*?' asked Monty.

'I didn't want to tell my story to them, because they would pick and choose what to report and exaggerate the facts to sell newspapers. I'm depending on *The Argus* to report our conversation truthfully. Can I count on you to do that?' She looked from one reporter to the other, seeking reassurance.

'I can guarantee that,' agreed Monty. 'In the interests of accuracy, would you allow me to take notes?'

She nodded, ignoring the scowl on her brother's face. 'It should be told.'

'You know that your husband has issued a statement denying everything,' said Reggie. 'He claims that his second marriage is legitimate.'

She sighed. 'I know that. However, he can't hide from the truth this time. I'm very much alive, and I won't be silenced.'

'Think twice before you do this, Agnes.' Herbert's deep voice drew their looks. 'Badger will want his revenge. He has a lot to lose.'

She glanced at her brother. 'I have lost a lot already.' She turned back to Reggie and Monty. 'We come from Hamilton in the Western District. Our parents ran a sheep farm. I met Cuthbert at a country dance. He was a city boy, staying with friends who ran the general store in town. The long and short of it is that it was love at first sight, at least, it was for me. He was fifteen years older, and I was young and inexperienced. Over a short period, he romanced me, and, by the time he returned to Melbourne, we were engaged.'

'When was this?' asked Monty.

'Late 1915. War had been declared, and Cuthbert announced his intention to enlist at the start of 1916. We were married, and he left two months later.'

'What was he like when you were first married?' asked Reggie.

She pursed her lips. 'I should have seen the signs of what was to come. He was always sure of himself. He ordered me around. I was too naïve to see that he was a bully. I took my vows seriously: to love and obey. But there was that charm of his that always convinced me that I was wrong when I questioned him. Unfortunately, by the time he came home from the war, that charm had disappeared. In fact, he gave me the distinct impression that he didn't like me at all.'

'Where did he serve?'

'Western France. His first major battle as a captain was at Messines in Belgium. I only know what happened because when he got drunk, he'd talk about it.'

'I've read about that battle,' said Reggie. 'It was a bad one. They dug tunnels under the German trenches and packed them with explosives. 10,000 Germans died. It's said that the explosions were heard across the English Channel.'

Agnes Badger nodded. 'He had nightmares about it. Calling out, crying. But when he was awake and sober, he was perfectly in control.'

'You left him?' asked Monty.

'Eventually. He'd become more violent as time went on. He tried to control everything I did. I told him he should talk to someone about his drinking and his nightmares, but that only enraged him. Finally, I packed a bag and hid it away in case I needed to leave quickly. I was afraid of him.'

'He hit you?'

She nodded, tears forming in her eyes. 'There was no one to confide in. My parents were miles away, and he'd stopped me having any friends. I had to scrape together any small change I could find, so that I had some money in case I wanted to leave in a hurry.'

'I wish that you'd told me,' said Herbert. 'I'd have stopped him.'

'You had enough problems of your own, without me.'

Reggie was curious to know what she meant, but Herbert had turned away.

'Where did you live at that time?' asked Monty.

'In East Melbourne. It was a big place. Cuthbert liked to impress people. He's still doing that. Member of parliament. Married to the debutante of the year. Nothing's changed.' She looked at the two men glumly. 'When I had enough money, I made my escape. He would have been mortified if the truth came out, so he spread the word that I'd died from Spanish influenza. I don't think he could cope with his friends and family knowing that I'd left him.'

'Didn't anyone query it?' asked Reggie.

'Cuthbert had a way about him. Very authoritative. No one dared question him. He made out that he was heartbroken, and that talking about it was too painful. He was a good liar. He told them that the funeral was a private one.'

'How did you end up in Geelong?'

'That was the easy part. Mum and Dad bought this place for when they came to Geelong, rather than staying in a hotel. Cuthbert didn't know about it, but I did. I wrote to my parents and told them I was leaving him, then asked if I could live here. They knew that I'd be in trouble if he found me, so they kept quiet. I also used an assumed name to protect my identity.'

'Who else knew that you were here?' asked Monty.

'Herbert, of course,' she said, nodding at her brother. 'No one else until the Poison Pen wrote his column.'

'I'm intrigued. What's your motivation for granting this interview?' asked Reggie. 'You could stay here incognito or move interstate.'

Agnes looked Reggie squarely in the eye. He could see the strength of her character shining through. Despite all that she had endured, including the lies that her husband had told about her death, and the humiliation of seeing another woman take her place, she was defiant.

'I want my side of the story to be heard and for Cuthbert to suffer,' she said. 'Everyone will know he's a bigamist and a liar and a violent husband who beat his wife. They will know that what *The Truth* published was true.' She paused, then added, 'I wish he were dead.'

Reggie turned to her brother. 'What about you, Mr Hawke? How do you feel about your brother-in-law?'

He paused. 'Unlike my sister, I don't want to see him dead.'

'What do you do for a living, by the way?'

Herbert took out his fob watch and checked the time. 'I'm between jobs, Mr da Costa. I'm exploring opportunities for advancement at the moment.'

'One last question, Mrs Badger,' said Monty. 'Do you believe that your husband should retain his parliamentary seat?'

'He should resign, if he has an ounce of ethics in his body. But I doubt that he will. I can only hope that the Premier sacks him.'

Monty stood up. 'I think we've got enough for now. I'll write up the report and forward it to the legal department first. It will appear in next Tuesday's paper. You understand that your husband will be very angry when he reads it. His marriage and his career will go up in smoke. He could be charged with bigamy. He might come after you.'

Agnes shrugged her shoulders. 'Let him do his worst. I don't care anymore. I'm not afraid. And, if anything does happen to me, people will know who did it.'

Reggie got up from his chair. 'One last question from me, Mrs Badger. Are you sure that you didn't give this information about your husband to the Poison Pen?'

She shook her head. 'I did not. And I have no idea who did. Or why.'

Chapter Fifteen

Ruby joined the group of women at the entrance to Temperance Hall, waiting for the doors to open to admit the audience for a meeting of the Melbourne branch of the Woman's Christian Temperance Union. Her red hair had been subdued and hidden beneath a cloche hat, to make her less recognisable, and she had worn one of her more conservative work outfits to remain incognito.

The previous night, she had suggested to Reggie that if none of the leaders of the movement would speak to the press, then she could infiltrate the group and try to elicit information about the deceased Mrs Burns, and who might possibly have had the motivation to kill her, if indeed that was what had happened. He was, at first, opposed to the idea, until Ruby reminded him that she had gone undercover to find her sister's killer, and had been mixing with murderers, armed robbers, gamblers, and gangsters.

'I'll be talking to women who oppose the drinking of alcohol, Reggie. There's no threat there.'

'I'm not sure about that,' he replied, chuckling. 'However, it does seem a logical way to gain insider information.'

Ruby took a deep breath and walked inside Temperance Hall.

The lights in the auditorium were on, rows of seats had been placed in position facing the stage, and a large banner advocating for Prohibition was displayed on the wall behind the rostrum. The gathering, about one hundred in all and predominantly female, filed down the aisle and took their seats, chatting to one another as they waited for the meeting to begin. The sign out the front of the hall announced that there would be a guest speaker: the Rev Dr J.L. Brandt, recently arrived from America. There was an air of expectancy given the distinguished reputation of the invited guest.

A hush came over the assembled group as the new president of the local branch stepped up to the lectern. She had an imposing presence, clad as she was in a heavy brown coat with a fur collar, and a wide hat that put her face in shadow. She stood silently, her presence drawing the eye and bringing with it total silence.

'For those of you who are new to the movement, my name is Mrs Agatha Skinner. I have come to this position through the unexpected death of our president, Mrs Ida Burns. I am distressed and heartbroken at the loss of our leader, a woman who was unafraid to take on the might of the alcohol industry. She did great things to publicise our cause, and for that we should be truly grateful.'

A murmur ran through the audience. Mrs Skinner waited and then resumed speaking.

'Despite the attempts of the press to smear our movement, I ask that you ignore the rumours and innuendo that you may hear regarding the nature of her death. We must stay strong. We must be united. We can only achieve greatness by putting aside that which distracts us, or divides us, and keep our eyes fixed on the prize that lies before us: total abstinence for every individual, and the introduction of Prohibition for every nation in the world!' Her voice was authoritative and fierce.

She paused as loud cheering erupted amongst the audience. When silence was restored, she introduced the guest speaker.

'We are privileged to have the Rev Dr J.L. Brandt with us today, who will give us an insight into the beneficial effects that Prohibition has conferred on America.'

The reverend doctor stepped up to the rostrum to tumultuous applause. He placed his hands on the sides of the lectern and leaned forward, his eyes sweeping across the faces of those in the front rows. His presence was formidable. A strong face, with bristling black eyebrows and square jaw, was framed by thick black hair swept back from a prominent forehead. He raised his hands for silence.

'Ladies, and those brothers amongst us who have seen the error of your ways, I bring you messages of support from those who attended the international convention of the WCTU in the United States of America. Prohibition has brought great benefits to my country. People are saving more money to spend on the necessities of life. There is a significant improvement in peace and prosperity in the home. Fewer people drink now than before Prohibition. Is that hard to believe, ladies and gentlemen?'

He paused, as if daring anyone to disagree with him. No one did.

'I have three daughters who have accompanied me to your fair country. They have travelled extensively across the length and breadth of America. The length and breadth. Last night, they told me that they have seen more inebriated men in the city of Melbourne than they have in the whole of America!'

Cries of shock and horror resonated across the hall. Once they died down, the guest speaker continued, enunciating the improvements that Prohibition had brought to his home country. Less poverty. Less crime. Increased wealth. Improved public health. The restoration of domestic harmony.

Ruby sat quietly, occasionally applauding or mouthing a cheer to give some semblance to the impression that she shared the opinions of those present. Inwardly, she was feeling distinctly sceptical of the claims that were being made and was disconcerted by the show of almost religious zeal that the audience exhibited. She listened to the calls for a referendum on the prohibition of alcohol, the arguments put forward in favour, and the dire consequences if it were not banned. She smiled and clapped and nodded, feigning enthusiasm. By the time the meeting was over, she was on friendly terms with the woman sitting next to her.

'I should introduce myself,' said her neighbour. 'I'm Mrs Beveridge.'

'Miss Street.'

They shook hands.

'Have you taken the pledge, my dear?'

'Not officially, but I'm considering it,' Ruby replied, remembering the second glass of wine she had declined the night before, when she dined with

Reggie.

'In that case, perhaps you might consider signing up as a member of the Woman's Christian Temperance Union? I could introduce you to Mrs McTavish, our secretary, if you'd like?'

Ruby smiled broadly. 'I would love that. The cause is so important.' She paused, as if reflecting on a problem that bothered her. 'It's so important to have a president who upholds the principles of the temperance movement,' she commented. 'Is Mrs Skinner different to Mrs Burns?'

'Most definitely. Mrs Skinner intends to take the branch in a new direction. Despite her fighting words today, she believes in changing attitudes through hosting forums. That way, people can hear our views and understand the benefits of removing alcohol from their lives. She wants to work with the government to make change.'

'And Mrs Burns? What was she like?'

'She provoked and divided people. That's why we've had so much trouble with protesters. Unfortunately, the Rev Dr Brandt today was already booked to speak, and his views accord more with those of our former president.'

'There was friction between Mrs Skinner and Mrs Burns?'

The woman looked around to check that no one was listening. 'There was no love lost between the two of them,' she whispered. 'There was talk that she wanted to oust Mrs Burns. But our former president wouldn't budge, even when the rumours started.'

'About her drinking?'

The woman nodded. 'It's very disappointing.'

'Did anyone else dislike her?'

The woman looked uneasy. 'I think I've said enough.'

Ruby realised that she had pushed too far.

Mrs Beveridge preceded her down the aisle and entered a room off the stage. 'Mrs McTavish will be with you shortly. There's some literature here that you can peruse while you're waiting.'

A woman, wearing a battered hat, dashed into the room. She was out of breath and looking harassed. 'Alma, can you come? There's trouble out the front. Protesters again. And my husband, too. Why won't he leave us alone?'

'I don't know, Mrs McTavish.'

'I'm sorry, Miss Street,' said Mrs Beveridge, addressing Ruby. 'Can you wait until we get back?'

'Of course,' replied Ruby, looking demure.

On the desk in front of her was a desk calendar, pens, and paper, and a pile of pamphlets extolling the virtues of abstinence. But what caught her eye was a box, containing a file of index cards, with 'Membership' written in thick, black letters on the front of it.

As the women departed, Ruby leaned over and pulled the box towards her. She thumbed through the cards until she found 'McTavish' and 'Burns.' She quickly memorised the addresses and returned the box to its previous position.

Her task completed, she stood up, only to have the secretary walk back in. By this time, the woman's hat was hanging perilously off the side of her head, only just secured by a hatpin.

'Please don't go,' she said, puffing. 'I'm Mrs McTavish. I'm sorry to have kept you. The situation is in hand. The police have arrived.'

'Does this happen often?' asked Ruby.

'I'm afraid so. My husband, Jim, is a constant source of aggravation. Fortunately, he took off when he saw the coppers. However, there are others who like to write threatening letters and protest at our meetings.'

'What is he upset about?'

Mrs McTavish sighed. 'Me. I took the pledge and took the children. I told him to go. He was angry with Mrs Burns for convincing me to leave him, rather than blaming the person responsible.'

'And who was that?'

'Why, himself. He's a drunk.' The secretary shook her head and extracted a blank index card from the back of the members' file. 'Please fill out your contact details.'

Ruby wrote down a phantom name and address, signed it, then handed it back to Mrs McTavish, who glanced at it briefly and filed it back in the box.

'Now, Miss Street, I'll type up the pledge if you'll give me a moment.'

She sat down at the desk and pulled the typewriter towards her, put a new piece of paper in the roller, and started to type. Once finished, she handed it to Ruby.

'Read this carefully. If you agree, please sign it.'

'It's very straightforward,' commented Ruby as she looked it over. 'However, I'd like to give it some thought before I make that commitment. If you don't mind, I'll take it home with me.'

'Of course. I'll give you an envelope to put it in. Once you decide to take the pledge, return the document to me signed and dated.'

'Thank you.' Ruby placed it in her handbag.

'Now, Miss Street, perhaps we could have a little chat about the movement, and what you can offer us?' she suggested.

'It's getting late,' Ruby said, looking at her watch. 'Perhaps next time.'

Ruby had endured enough for the evening, she concluded, without being cross-examined as to her drinking habits or the possible contribution that she could make to the movement. If she needed further information, she could always make another visit to Temperance Hall, even if it required a fair degree of hypocrisy on her part. It bothered her that she was misleading good people who were upstanding citizens, but a woman had died, and so, in this case, some measure of deceit was required. And she had gleaned two pieces of important information which Reggie might find useful. By attending the meeting, she had found out that the new president had coveted Mrs Burns' job, and that Mrs McTavish's husband bore a grudge against the woman as well. Two people were antagonistic towards the former president, but whether that was a motivation for murder was a question that Reggie da Costa could pursue, rather than she. Her conscience appeased, she stood up and left the room.

Chapter Sixteen

It was bedlam in the newsroom of *The Argus*. Three telephone calls had been received within minutes of each other, causing great excitement when the identities of those involved became known. When he heard the names, Reggie felt like all his Christmases had come at once.

The first telephone call concerned the apparent suicide of Cuthbert Badger, member of parliament, wife-beater, and bigamist. His body had been found by one of his parliamentary colleagues, who had been invited to have drinks with him before they went out for dinner on Thursday evening. The front door was unlocked, and the visitor had entered, only to discover Badger lying on the floor of the drawing room, his service pistol discharged.

The second telephone call had come ten minutes later, at six o'clock that evening, informing Reggie that there had been a shooting in Barkly Street, Carlton. Almost simultaneously, Reggie's contact at St Vincent's Hospital rang him to report that Squizzy Taylor, Melbourne's infamous gangster, had been admitted, unconscious and on the brink of death.

If Reggie felt an obligation to follow up the first story, given that he had interviewed Cuthbert Badger's former wife, it was the shooting in Carlton that took precedence. Melbourne's public would want all the details—the who, the why, and the how—and he needed to be at the scene of the crime. The Honourable Cuthbert Badger would have to wait.

Reggie's beloved automobile was parked outside the offices of *The Argus*. He took out his handkerchief and gave a quick polish to the hood ornament— the Roman goddess, Minerva—whose helmet was catching the last rays of the sunshine. Distracted by the beauty of his new motorcar, Reggie momentarily forgot the biggest story of 1927. Coming to his senses, he swore under his breath and slid across the brown leather bench seat to the driver's side, then pressed his finger firmly on the starter button. The automobile in gear, Reggie smoothly executed a U-turn in front of a startled pedestrian, joining the traffic travelling along La Trobe Street.

'Come on,' cried Reggie, impatient with the snail's pace of the vehicles in front of him. 'Let's go!' He planted his foot on the accelerator.

The Minerva responded, showing its ascendancy over the mediocrity of its competitors in the automobile world. In Reggie's expert hands, the car wove its way between trucks, horse-drawn buggies, cyclists, and motorcars, defying the laws of the road in the pursuit of a story. Reggie was deaf to the blasts of horns and the screams of pedestrians, and blind to the evasive tactics of other drivers and the shaking fists of those who missed death by inches, as he guided the flash of silver and red towards Carlton, intent on beating the press pack to the shootout which had involved Melbourne's most notorious gang leader.

As he turned into Barkly Street, Reggie saw three police cars parked on the side of the road, as well as a smattering of curious onlookers on the footpath. There was no sign of reporters. He breathed a sigh of relief and pulled into the curb in front of Number 50, a sombre bluestone cottage, which was one of five comprising Barkly Terrace.

Detective Inspector Clary Blain and several members of the Criminal Investigation Branch were gathered on the footpath, along with two ambulance attendants and a few uniformed police. Reggie got out of his car and hurried over to them.

'You were quick,' commented Clary. 'Who's your contact at Carlton police station?'

Reggie smiled. 'As if I'd tell you.' He pointed at the house. 'What have we got here?'

'Number 50 is a boarding house operated by Snowy Cutmore's mother, Bridget. Her son is dead. His mother was caught in the crossfire, but she'll survive. They've taken her to hospital.'

'I hear that Squizzy's in hospital too.'

'He's dead. The doctor said he took a bullet to the liver.'

Reggie shook his head. 'Squizzy Taylor dead. The source of a thousand crime stories, soon to be consigned to a grave, six feet under. I almost feel sad. You know that Cutmore arrived from Sydney on Sunday? He was seen at the Richmond races, Monday.'

'I'm aware of that,' said Clary. 'Two of my blokes escorted him from the racetrack.'

'Because of his criminal record?' asked Reggie.

'That's right,' confirmed Blain.

The crime reporter leaned forward conspiratorially. 'I heard that Squizzy was at the track too. Apparently, he and Cutmore exchanged threats.'

Blain cocked his head. 'Is that right? They've been feuding for years. Squizzy would feel that he'd have to make good on his threats, knowing him. He wouldn't like to lose face in front of Melbourne's underworld.'

Reggie pointed at the house. 'What happened in there?'

'As you'd expect, we don't know much, except the obvious. The witnesses are too afraid to spill what they know. All of them were engaged elsewhere, unsurprisingly.' Clary sighed. 'Cutmore's mother was in the kitchen cooking dinner. His wife was out buying milk. One lodger was asleep; the other was cutting wood out the back.'

'No one knows anything?'

'They never do, in cases like this. But we do know that Snowy was in bed when Squizzy and a pal arrived, uninvited. They shot Cutmore five times, killing him. Snowy managed one shot, hitting Squizzy. Squizzy and his mate got out of there quick smart.'

'And Squizzy went straight to St Vincent's Hospital.'

Blain nodded. 'It will take some time to uncover the truth about whether anyone else was involved in this. We do have some names, but any information we get from these blokes will be minimal. If you hear anything from your snitches, let me know.'

'I'll do that,' Reggie said. 'By the way, what's the story on Cuthbert Badger?'

'Detective Sergeant Glass has been assigned to that one. He wasn't too happy about it, but he had no choice. I can't be in two places at once.

However, preliminary inquiries indicate Badger committed suicide.'

Reggie stroked his moustache. 'I reckon there's more to it than suicide.'

Blain pulled a face. 'I hope you're wrong. I've got enough on my plate without adding another serve of potatoes.'

'You have a healthy appetite, Clary,' commented Reggie as he appraised the detective's sizeable belly. 'How do you like your spuds? Mashed or boiled?'

Chapter Seventeen

PISTOLS AT SIX O'CLOCK
SQUIZZY'S DUEL TO THE DEATH
By REGGIE DA COSTA, Senior Crime Reporter

Joseph Theodore Leslie 'Squizzy' Taylor was buried on Saturday in the family grave at Brighton Cemetery. He was 39 years old.

A diminutive man, who favoured loud, flashy clothing and American automobiles, Taylor ruled Melbourne's crime scene for nine years, from 1918 to 1927. He frequented the sporting clubs, the 'two-up' schools, the snooker parlours, and gambling dens of Melbourne's criminal underworld. He was seen in the dives of 'The Narrows' in Fitzroy and on the racecourses. He was known, too, as a jury-fixer, a pickpocket, a standover man, a robber, and a blackmailer.

Now he is dead.

The feud, between Taylor and his killer, John 'Snowy' Cutmore, dates from 1919 when Cutmore was a member of a rival gang. Moving to Sydney, Cutmore worked as a standover man, gaining a reputation as a violent and dangerous criminal with a string of convictions to his name. He returned to Melbourne very recently and moved in with his mother at 50 Barkly Street, Carlton.

On Monday, the 24th of October, Taylor and Cutmore came face to face at a Richmond race meeting. There was a confrontation between the two. Threats were made.

The following Thursday, Taylor fuelled his anger with liquor and, in the company of two of his bodyguards, hired a car to drive to Carlton, where he found Cutmore in bed, ill with influenza. Taylor produced a gun and aimed it at the stricken man. At the same time, Cutmore pulled a revolver from under his pillow and fired upwards from the bed, hitting Taylor in the side. A fusillade of shots rang out. Police report that all four walls bore bullet marks and that the floor was littered with empty cartridge cases. Cutmore died instantly when a bullet penetrated his heart.

Cutmore's mother, drawn from the kitchen by the sound of loud voices and shooting, was wounded in the affray. She is in a satisfactory condition in hospital.

Taylor fled the house and was taken to St Vincent's Hospital, where he died shortly after. He is survived by his wife, Ida 'Babe' Pender, a former jazz dancer.

Third gun mystery?

The discovery of a third gun, 200 yards from the shootout, has raised questions about who was responsible for the deaths of Cutmore and Taylor. Was this a gangland execution or a duel to the death between two criminals?

One thing is certain: The reign of Squizzy Taylor has come to a violent and bloody end. The King is dead. But who will be Melbourne's next crime boss?

Anyone with information should contact *The Argus* or Detective Inspector Blain at the Criminal Investigation Branch.

[*The Argus*, October 31, 1927]

Chapter Eighteen

The death of Squizzy Taylor was initially greeted with silence by the members of Melbourne's criminal classes, but, once the shock wore off, jockeying for the position left vacant by the little gangster began, with Horace Striker the first to stake his claim. Whether it was Horace Striker's exultation over Squizzy Taylor's death or a genuine desire to throw an impromptu party, no one was quite sure, but two days after Joseph Theodore Leslie Taylor was consigned to a burial plot six feet under, the doors of The Stockade swung wide to welcome guests to a Hallowe'en party.

Apart from Ruby and Reggie, and the rich and influential who craved Striker's company, the guest list was a who's who of Melbourne's criminal underworld: Sydney 'Siddy' Kelly, Albert 'Tankbuster' McDonald, and Henry 'The Two-Up King' Stokes, amongst others.

Ruby's relationship with Horace Striker dated from the time of her sister's murder. Her identical twin had led a double life: 'Katherine' by day, a conservative and conventional museum assistant; 'Miss Kitty' by night, wild and headstrong, frequenting the illegal gambling dens and private clubs favoured by Melbourne's underworld. To uncover Katherine's killer, Ruby impersonated her sister and infiltrated those places visited by 'Miss Kitty,' including Horace Striker's club, The Stockade. The gangster, who had been uncle to Katherine's slain fiancé, had facilitated Ruby's charade and, surprisingly, had become an unlikely friend. They had remained so, even after Katherine's killer was exposed. It came as no surprise when Horace offered his club as the venue for Ruby's wedding reception.

The Stockade had been decorated extravagantly for Hallowe'en and was lit by jack-o'-lanterns, the candlelight throwing fantastical shadows onto the walls. Large murals of graveyard scenes decorated the room, depicting ghouls and skeletons cavorting amongst the headstones. Small, hollowed-out pumpkins had been placed on the tables to act as ashtrays. Fake rats peeked out from under chairs, while large, hairy spiders hung from invisible threads, occasionally brushing up against the faces of unobservant guests, evoking screams of shock and horrified delight. Black, papier-mâché bats in mid-flight were suspended from the ceiling, and, in the corners, coffins had been propped with their lids partially open, their 'corpses' emitting the occasional moan or cackle of laughter. The waiters, carrying platters of hors d'oeuvres in their white-gloved hands, were attired in skeleton suits, their faces plastered with stark, white makeup. A five-piece jazz band, wearing red devil costumes, was belting out the latest popular songs, fronted by a female singer dressed in a skintight, red sequinned evening gown, brandishing a microphone in the shape of a devil's pitchfork.

The guests had embraced the spirit of the celebration, dressed in an array of Hallowe'en costumes: from werewolves, witches, and warlocks to Draculas and corpses. One man was apparently headless, holding a stick with a head attached, but closer examination showed a pair of shining eyes peering out through two holes in his shirt.

Reggie and Ruby, too, had given much thought to their choice of costumes. Wearing a chalk stripe, double-breasted suit, black shirt, and white tie, in the best tradition of America's mobsters, Reggie had slathered his face with ghoulish, white makeup and circled his eyes with a thick, dark kohl pencil. He had blackened the tip of his nose with charcoal and drawn a black outline around his lips.

Ruby, meanwhile, had chosen a silky, black floor-length dress, her flame-red hair adorned with scarlet horns. A broomstick in one hand and a small pumpkin handbag completed her costume, although it was quite restrained compared to what some of the other guests had chosen.

Reggie indicated the trio of gang leaders who were gathered near the door. 'Our friends from Melbourne's underworld haven't got into the spirit of

Hallowe'en. They're more concerned with maintaining their dignity and status in the face of all this frivolity.'

Sydney Kelly, Albert McDonald, and Henry Stokes had paid mere lip service to the theme: a bloodstain on Kelly's shirt; a Dracula cape over Tankbuster's three-piece suit; a jagged scar drawn on Stokes's face.

'Do you think they're happy to see an end to Squizzy?' Ruby asked.

'Henry Stokes is. Look at the smile on his face. The word is that he'll be going it alone. Taylor cramped his style. Too erratic. But I reckon he'll use Squizzy's methods—jury-fixing and violence, in particular—to get what he wants.'

'They look friendly, judging by the way they're chatting.'

Reggie shook his head. 'Not a chance. They'd stab each other in the back if they weren't in public. That blood stain that you see on Kelly's shirt would be real. Melbourne crime is like a giant pie, Ruby. Everyone wants a slice of the action, and the bigger, the better. That's why they're here tonight. Squizzy's dead, and they're celebrating. If you look closely at the mural on the wall, you'll see Squizzy's name engraved on one of the headstones.'

'What about Horace? Does he want a slice of the pie?'

At the mention of Striker's name, a lull descended over the place. But it wasn't Ruby's question that had brought it about, more the arrival of the man himself. Conversation died, the waiters almost stood to attention, and heads turned in the direction of the host, who was accompanied by his two most trusted bodyguards. Burke and Hare walked one step behind him, their eyes darting from one face to the next, watching for a discernible shift in facial expression, such as a nod or a wink to some associate who might be reaching into his pocket for a weapon. Reggie didn't doubt that the desire was there, amongst the assembled leaders of Melbourne's criminal underworld, to extinguish the power of their most astute and intimidating host, but to do so in such a public place would only lead to wholesale carnage. Fortunately, there was nothing in the behaviour of the guests to indicate a threat.

'Why do they call them Burke and Hare?' asked Ruby as she watched the three men enter the room.

'They're named after two Scottish grave robbers. The real Burke and Hare killed sixteen innocent victims and sold their bodies to the Edinburgh Medical College for dissection. That's how they made their money.'

'Did they get caught?'

'Hare agreed to give evidence against Burke in return for immunity from prosecution. Burke was found guilty of murder and hanged.'

'And Hare?'

'Last seen going over the English border.'

Ruby shook her head. 'That's awful.' She looked uncertainly at Horace's bodyguard, Hare, whose bloodless face, cropped, red hair, and cool, green eyes now seemed to convey a hint of malice. 'I'm not sure that I'll feel the same way about Hare. I always thought he was such a nice man.'

'As I've said to you before: The criminal classes are only nice to you when you aren't a threat to them.'

Hare's boss, Horace, nodded at Ruby as he strolled past, a retinue of hangers-on in his wake. She could never understand how he could remain so aloof, so in control. But, as usual, this tall, well-dressed man had a mesmerising effect on those who encountered him, commanding attention.

'No Hallowe'en costume for Horace,' noted Reggie, admiring Striker's beautifully tailored evening suit.

'He once told me that he likes to stand out from the crowd. He's succeeded again.'

'Look at that!' exclaimed Reggie. 'I wish I had a camera.'

Horace had made his way over to his three rivals, greeting them as old friends. They shook hands, slapped each other on the back, smiled and chatted, hostility put aside for one night as they celebrated the demise of Squizzy Taylor. Burke and Hare settled in close by, watching every move intently.

Reggie turned his attention back to Ruby. 'Let's dance.'

As they put down their champagne glasses and headed towards the dance floor, Reggie stopped abruptly.

'Well, I never,' he said. 'It's The Undertaker.'

'Who?'

He pointed at a man who was leaning up against the wall, watching the proceedings. Ruby was struck by his unpretentious garb. No Hallowe'en costume for this one. He was wearing a black suit, white shirt, and black tie, his hands in his pockets, his eyes roving from one guest to the next.

'Who is he?'

'The latest addition to the Criminal Investigation Branch, Detective Sergeant Homer Glass. Rumoured to be a favourite of the Chief Commissioner. He's on his way up through the ranks, fast. But what he's doing here, I have no idea. Or how he got in.' Reggie chuckled. 'Let's go and have a chat to him. This should be interesting.'

Up close, The Undertaker had smooth, pale skin, thin lips, and a slight overbite. Not a hair could be seen on his freshly shaven cheeks. He was drinking a beer, appraising Reggie and Ruby over the top of the glass as they approached.

'Detective Sergeant Glass, nice to meet you.'

'You have the advantage of me,' he said coolly, ignoring Reggie's outstretched hand.

'Reggie da Costa, senior crime reporter with *The Argus*. And this is my fiancée, Miss Rhodes.'

Glass leaned back against the wall, glancing briefly at Ruby before his gaze settled on Reggie. 'I've heard about you, da Costa. You're pals with Blain.'

'Detective Inspector Blain to you.'

Glass sniffed. 'If that's what you want to call him, go ahead.' He looked around, not pleased that his presence had been noted, especially by a reporter. 'What are you doing here?'

'I could ask you the same thing.'

'Hurry up. I'm a busy man. What do you want?'

'I believe that you're investigating the Badger case. Have there been any developments?'

'If there were, would I be telling you?'

'I'll make this simple. Murder or suicide?'

The Undertaker stared at him and sniffed loudly. 'I'll make it simple for you, too. The Honourable Member shot himself with his own gun.'

Reggie was not to be deterred. 'Was there anything at all that was slightly questionable about the crime scene?'

The detective shook his head. 'Of course not.'

'Did you check the body? Was Badger holding anything?'

'Why would I look?' he said. 'He was dead.'

'Have you checked the coroner's report?'

Glass pushed himself off the wall. 'You reporters are all the same, looking for stories when there aren't any. Dredging up stupid theories and fooling the public, making them think that you know something that the police don't know.' He turned to Ruby and looked her up and down. 'You could do better for yourself, miss.'

Ruby returned his gaze. 'I'm quite content, thank you.'

The detective drained the rest of his beer and slammed the empty glass on a table. 'I'll be off.' He headed towards the entrance.

'You still haven't told me what you're doing here,' Reggie called after him. He grunted. 'Clary's right, you know. Glass is bent. Mixing with the criminal classes invites suspicion.'

'But he wasn't talking to anyone,' commented Ruby. 'He looked like he was waiting for someone.'

Reggie nodded. 'You're right. But he's gone, so let's have some fun.'

He took her hand and they headed for the dance floor. 'Tango?' he asked as the band struck up.

'Yes, please,' she replied, leaning her broomstick against the wall. 'Let's do some black magic on the dance floor.'

Chapter Nineteen

A truce had been declared in the aftermath of Squizzy Taylor's death. The gangland feuds, fights, and rivalries had gone quiet, while the territory lorded over by the diminutive gangster was divided up and the spoils distributed. Henry Stokes appeared to be the main beneficiary, given that he had been in cahoots with Squizzy, although 'Siddy' Kelly and 'Tankbuster' McDonald made it clear that they wanted their cut of the profits from illegal gambling.

Horace Striker, on the other hand, sat back in his Shamrock Street terrace, biding his time. He had considered making a play for Squizzy's share of the rackets but had concluded that his portion was sufficient for now. His interest in extending his influence into the halls of power occupied his thoughts. When he had first met Ruby, in the months after his nephew's murder, he had intended to finance the election of a candidate into the Victorian parliament, one who would do his bidding, but that had backfired badly when the plan had been exposed by none other than Ruby's crime reporter brother, Dusty Rhodes. Horace also belatedly realised that the selection process for a 'puppet' was very important; he needed someone whom he could control, someone predictable who would do what he was told. Such a candidate was not easy to find, because those who chose the political path were usually egotistical and mercenary. Consequently, Striker decided to let the matter cool and find yet another way to wield power.

Meanwhile, back in the offices of *The Argus*, Reggie was hoping that the gang wars would flare up again soon. Such rivalries were his bread and butter, although he had come around to the view, most likely due to the influence of his fiancée's ethical sensibilities, that it was perhaps better that violence did not return to the streets, given that innocent people could be caught in the crossfire. As a compromise, he hoped that gang warfare would erupt again, but behind closed doors, reducing the death count.

Apart from the occasional armed robbery, drug deal, or bootlegging operation gone wrong, the pages of *The Argus* were relatively crime-free, affording Reggie with the opportunity to pursue his investigations, yet again, into the deaths associated with the Poison Pen column in *The Truth* newspaper.

He opened the file and reflected over what he had learned.

The death of Mrs Burns, president of the Woman's Christian Temperance Union, appeared to be suspicious, rather than the result of alcoholic poisoning. Ruby had managed to elicit some useful information from her visit to the meeting hall, implicating two possible suspects: Mr McTavish, scorned husband, whose wife had been persuaded to leave him by Mrs Burns, and the new president, Mrs Skinner, who had disagreed with Mrs Burns about the direction of the Union and had coveted her job. But whether either of them had sufficient motivation to kill was another matter. When weighing up the likelihood that either McTavish or Skinner was behind the murder, the probability was that it was the former. Anger was a powerful motivator, and it was more likely that Mr McTavish had sought revenge on the woman who had destroyed his marriage. Alternatively, it was hard to imagine that Mrs Skinner would have done the dirty deed herself, but there was always the chance that she had employed someone to kill Mrs Burns.

And yet, there was a third possible motive for the murder of the former president of Melbourne's Temperance Union: to bring an end to the Prohibition movement and the return of extended hotel hours. Hoteliers and legal distillers had much to gain from removing one of the most vocal advocates for abstinence. But would they resort to violence to achieve their aims? Without a name, Reggie was inclined to put this third possibility aside for the moment.

Reggie turned to his notes on the Webb case. Dusty had delivered on his promise to interview his friend who worked at The Melbourne Hospital.

The nurse reported to him that Beryl Webb had been questioned, after three of her patients had been given the wrong medication with dire results. Her behaviour raised eyebrows, leading to rumours that she was an addict, who had indulged her drug habit while on duty, putting the patients in her care in danger.

A subsequent investigation by the hospital revealed that Webb had faked patient records to get her hands on more supplies to feed her addiction. It was possible that patients had not been administered with the medication they required to quell their pain. She had also accessed the drug-dispensing cabinet and removed vials of morphine. The hospital attempted to deal with the issue quietly by asking her to resign, but the family of one affected patient had kicked up a fuss and forced the hospital to fire her. When asked the name of the patient, Dusty's friend had given it, on condition that she remain anonymous. Her job would be on the line if he revealed his source. Reggie had recommended that Dusty should interview Mr and Mrs Longfellow, the patient's parents.

The rest of Beryl Webb's story was self-evident. Exposed as a drug addict, she had hidden herself away, fuelling her habit and withdrawing deep into herself until death almost came her way. Was it possible, Reggie asked himself, that someone connected to one of the patients at the hospital had decided to take their revenge on Beryl Webb because of her negligence? That was a scenario worth considering.

Coming soon after the Poison Pen's third exposé was the suicide, or possible murder, of the Honourable Cuthbert Badger. Information had been sought and received from Detective Inspector Clary Blain earlier that morning, after Reggie's chat with The Undertaker had yielded little or no information.

'Glass is either incompetent or lazy, Reggie,' Blain declared as they stood on the steps outside Russell Street police headquarters. 'He's not interested in the case. He's prepared to rubber stamp it as "suicide." The constable's notes suggest otherwise.'

'What are you going to do?'

'I think that further investigation is warranted, but I don't have the time or manpower to follow it up myself, what with Squizzy's death and the repercussions arising from that. I've told Glass to take another look, and I'm going to apply pressure to make sure he does.'

Clary took a deep breath. 'Just this once, I'll give you copies of everything that I have, because I trust that you will follow up any leads. However, I expect that you will fill me in on *everything* you discover before you write it up in *The Argus*.' He took a folder out of his bag and handed it to Reggie. 'We have a deal?'

Reggie nodded. 'It's a deal. By the way, I saw Glass at The Stockade last week.'

'The Stockade? What was he doing there?'

'Ruby thought that he was waiting for someone. I reckon we spoiled his plans and he left.'

Clary scratched his nose. 'Consorting with criminals. That's interesting. Thanks, mate.'

* * *

With the police file on his desk, Reggie had spent the next hour poring over it.

The detective in charge, Homer Glass, had found that the deceased had died from a self-inflicted wound; one shot through the heart; one bullet discharged. He had fallen backwards, hitting his head on the cast iron surround of the fireplace. A copy of *The Argus* was on the table, open to the article written by reporter Jeremy Montgomery after his interview with Agnes Badger, who had accused her husband of bigamy. The proximity of the newspaper article to the body was proof, in the detective's view, that the former soldier had committed suicide after he had read it. His reputation was in tatters, his second marriage deemed illegal, and his political career had come to an abrupt halt, now that his duplicity had been publicly aired.

In the file, there were photographs of Badger's body before it was removed from the house. He was lying on his back, arms outstretched, holding the service pistol which had fired the fatal shot. Also, there was a note in the report to the effect that the gun was registered to Captain Badger.

Reggie looked closely at the photograph of the body. The gun was clutched in Badger's left hand. That was odd, he thought. No right-handed person could shoot himself with his left hand unless he had steadied the gun using both hands. Was Badger left-handed? He made a note to follow that up.

Reggie flipped through the other photographs, comparing them. Fortunately, the police photographer had done a good job of showing the position of the body in relation to the furniture and fixtures of the room.

There was also a report provided by one of the constables who had attended the scene. He had been tasked with interviewing the neighbours on the day of Badger's death. He had noted that a woman was seen leaving the premises that morning. The neighbour had provided the policeman with a detailed description of the visitor: Tall, thin, in her late twenties, and with straight brown hair pulled back into a bun, wearing a grey overcoat and hat. 'Dowdy' was the word that the neighbour had used to describe her. Reggie nodded his head. The former Mrs Badger, resident of Geelong, fitted that description. A Summit motorcar, green in colour, had been parked outside Badger's house earlier that day. Reggie made another note to follow up the lady's movements, as well as her brother's.

The same neighbour had not heard any shots fired around the time of the woman's visit, but then he would not have heard anything, he told the constable, because he was deaf. How inconvenient, thought Reggie.

In the folder was also the medical examiner's report. Reggie laid the diagrams out on his desk and proceeded to read the notes that accompanied them.

According to the report, the trajectory of the bullet had been at approximately 45 degrees to the horizontal, entering the heart in an upwards direction. It appeared that the deceased had fallen backwards, hitting his head on the surround of the fireplace behind him. A large amount of blood had issued from the wound, indicating that death was not instantaneous. Residue around the wound suggested that the bullet was fired from close range. Fingerprints on the weapon showed that the barrel had been grasped in one hand, with the forefinger on the trigger.

In one section of the report was a list of possessions found on the body. Apart from the clothing and personal items that had been documented, there was one scrap of information that would have appeared incidental and insignificant to anybody but Reggie. The medical examiner stated that Captain Badger was clutching a white feather in his right hand.

Reggie sat back in astonishment. Here it was again.

He took a swig of whisky from the flask in his desk drawer, shook his head, and stared into space. How could Badger hold the barrel of his gun in one hand and pull the trigger, then be found with arms outstretched, clutching a feather in his right hand? He would have needed both hands to steady the gun. There had to be another person present who had staged the crime scene to look like suicide.

Three seemingly unconnected crime scenes. Three white feathers. It was no longer possible to regard the feather as incidental. There was a message there, and it came from the killer.

The question was: What did these three people have in common? Did they know each other? Or did each separately know the killer? And where did the Poison Pen and his column come into this? Of one thing Reggie was certain: He needed to break the story of the White Feather Murders before others made the connection between *The Truth* column and three seemingly isolated incidents.

Reggie looked up at the clock on the wall. He realised with a start that he had lost track of time. He was supposed to pick up his fiancée and his mother to take them to Flemington racecourse, where, in less than five hours, the horses would thunder around the racetrack vying for the prestigious Melbourne Cup.

Another thought struck him. The next Poison Pen letter was due to be published on Friday, only three days away. Who was next on the list, and were they going to die too?

Chapter Twenty

Two hours earlier, her umbrella shielding her from the rain, Ruby had stood outside the address listed on Mrs Burns' membership card. The president of the Woman's Christian Temperance Union had been renting a small weatherboard cottage not far from Temperance Hall. There was a board propped up against the fence indicating that the property was available for rent, and what pleased Ruby the most was that the landlord was about to nail the sign in place.

'Excuse me,' said Ruby meekly, clutching a capacious handbag to her chest and looking appropriately demure, 'is it possible to see through the property?'

The landlord straightened up and brushed the raindrops from his jacket. It was Melbourne Cup Day and he wanted to be away as soon as possible. Yet here, in front of him, was a clean and tidy woman, a potential tenant, and it seemed silly to ruin the chance of letting the place quickly because of a horse race.

'Of course,' he said, removing his hat, 'but I warn you that I haven't had a chance to clear out the house. The lady…left unexpectedly.'

'Aah,' said Ruby, nodding. 'A furnished house would suit me admirably, if that's possible. And it would be a week or so before I could move in.'

'You have references?'

'Indeed, I do. I'm down from the country. I've secured an excellent job as secretary to the owner of a furniture factory. If I'm interested, I'd be happy to supply you with those documents.'

The man opened the gate and beckoned for her to go in. 'I need to put up this sign. Would you mind looking through the place on your own?'

'Not at all.'

Ruby propped her umbrella on the porch and entered the house. It was a sparsely furnished home with a parlour at the front, two small bedrooms, and a kitchen at the back. Everything was neat and tidy.

The sound of hammering broke the silence. Ruby surveyed the front room, wondering where she should start. Her purpose in coming there was to find the threatening letters that Mrs McTavish had spoken about, which might shine a light on why someone would want Mrs Burns dead. She pulled out a couple of drawers on the sideboard. Tablecloths and napkins. No letters.

Moving quickly through into the main bedroom, she checked the tallboy, but found only underwear, nightwear, jumpers, and cardigans, neatly folded. The bottom of the wardrobe yielded nothing of interest apart from half a dozen bottles of gin. Ruby raised an eyebrow.

Mrs Burns had used the second bedroom as a dining room, with a table and four chairs, but no other furniture. Ruby sighed. The kitchen, too, seemed an unlikely place to store anything of a personal nature, so she returned to the main bedroom and cast her eyes around the room. It was inconceivable that a woman would have no private papers, letters, or official documents in her possession. She remembered that her own twin sister had hidden incriminating evidence in a cache beneath the floorboards. She got down on her hands and knees next to the bed and groaned as she felt her stockings snag on the rough edge of a board.

Ruby lifted the bedspread and peered underneath. A small metal trunk had been pushed beneath the bed. As she pulled it out, she realised that the hammering had stopped. Time was short, and she'd have to move fast before the landlord came inside. She undid the latch and pushed the lid back on its hinges. Inside were official-looking documents and some cash, which she ignored. But her eyes fixed on a wad of letters, still in their envelopes, held together with an elastic band. She slipped them into her handbag and closed the lid of the box, then pushed it back into place under the bed.

The floorboards creaked in the hallway. Ruby stood up quickly and smoothed down her skirt.

The landlord stood in the doorway. 'What do you think, miss?'

Ruby managed a sad smile. 'It's nice, but I need to be closer to the railway station. It would be a long walk in the morning.'

'I see. Well, if that's the case, I'll show you out.'

Outside, the rain had stopped. Ruby furled her umbrella and checked her watch. She had an hour to get home and dress for the Melbourne Cup. Unfortunately, there was no time to examine the letters; they would have to wait till later. Her hope was that they contained the threats referred to by Mrs McTavish, the Temperance Union's secretary. And, if they did, this would provide Reggie with some possible suspects in Mrs Burns' murder.

As she boarded the tram that would take her down to Flinders Street station, Ruby felt uneasy about what she had done. Not only had she deliberately misled the landlord, but she had done the same with the secretary of the Temperance Union.

She wrestled with her conscience as the tram lumbered down Sydney Road towards the city, the bag with Mrs Burns' correspondence on her lap. There was no doubt that by taking on her sister's identity two years earlier to find Katherine's killer, she had widened her horizons by experiencing the seamy side of life offered by Melbourne's criminal underworld. And, in so doing, she was not the same person that she had been before Katherine's murder. The old Ruby would never have considered bluffing her way into Mrs Burns' home or pretend that she wanted to join the Temperance Union. The old Ruby was respectable, conventional, and law-abiding. Which begged the question: Where was that person now?

As Ruby stepped down from the tram, she calmed her doubts by assuring herself that her actions might be instrumental in uncovering a killer, and a clever one at that. And, with that rationalisation, she had to be content.

Chapter Twenty-One

Clary Blain lifted the glass to his lips and drained the last of his whisky. It was Cup Day, and he was drinking alone in the Duke of Wellington Hotel. Not even the thought of his winnings from the fiver he had placed on Trivalve could lift his spirits. Feeling dejected, he stared at the dwindling level of Scotch in the bottle in front of him, contemplating if his career was headed in the same direction. It was an unfortunate truth that since the arrival of Detective Sergeant Homer Glass, Clary's reputation and career prospects with the Victoria Police had nosedived.

That morning, after the police who would be patrolling Flemington racecourse were briefed, there had been jubilation when Glass announced the arrest of three men on charges of counterfeiting. Even the chief commissioner came out of his office and slapped Glass on the back.

'Well done, detective sergeant,' Blamey said. 'You have a future here, my lad.'

A circle of admiring colleagues surrounded Glass as he related his triumph to all and sundry. Inquiries had been ongoing for six weeks, he told them, culminating in the raid on a Moffat Street, Brighton Beach house, during the early hours of that morning. A complete plant for making counterfeit banknotes had been seized, along with two thousand £1 notes which were packaged ready to distribute at the Melbourne Cup.

'How did you track them down?' asked one of the junior detectives.

'We had a description of one of the suspects,' announced Glass, his smirk making Blain's skin crawl. 'We saw him in the city two weeks ago and followed him closely that day, then shadowed him to Brighton Beach. He never suspected a thing! The blinds on the house were drawn, and the garden was neglected. The neighbours thought that the place was unoccupied. We kept surveillance going day and night, waiting for the opportunity to raid them. It was clear that they wanted to use Cup Day to pass the fakes, given that no one would notice anything unusual at Flemington racecourse with so much money changing hands. And we caught them red-handed. They'd divided up the fakes and had stuffed them in bags ready to leave for the racetrack.'

He turned to Blain. 'By the way, sir, if you need any advice on catching criminals, you know where to find me.'

Clary didn't give Glass the satisfaction of acknowledging his remark. He turned his back on the man and put on his hat, ready to leave the office for the day.

'Off to the pub, *sir?*' Glass called after him.

He was on the verge of reprimanding him when Chief Commissioner Blamey appeared in the doorway.

'Blain. A word.'

Clary took off his hat and followed his boss into his office, unnerved. It was evident from his tone that Blamey was displeased.

'Take a seat.'

The chief commissioner was a former military man, chief of staff of the Australian Corps to Lieutenant General Sir John Monash in the Great War. He had been appointed to deal with the grievances that had resulted in the Police Strike of 1923. The Victoria Police needed an able and fearsome leader, it was believed, one who was ready to speak his mind, which he did once Clary took a seat opposite him.

Blamey opened the folder on his desk and passed Blain a sheet of paper. 'How do you explain this?'

Clary glanced at the letter and frowned. 'I can't, sir.'

The chief commissioner took it off him and began to read:

Inspector Blain,

You should know that Squizzy Taylor is planning to visit Snowy Cutmore at his mother's house at 50 Barkly St Carlton tomorrow evening. Blood will be spilled.

A friend.

He put down the page and eyed the detective inspector. 'What do you have to say to that?'

'Nothing, sir. It's the first time that I've seen it.'

'It was found in your files on the Taylor murder, yet you did nothing about it.'

Clary shook his head. 'As I said, sir, I've never seen it before.'

Chief Commissioner Blamey was not convinced. 'You were promoted recently, but I believe that it was a mistake. Your record shows that you were demoted for drinking on duty some years ago, but since that time, you have acquitted yourself with distinction. Until now. It's a disappointment that you failed to act when you were warned that a shooting was going to take place. Admit it, detective inspector, you are in the wrong. The deaths of two men and the wounding of an elderly woman are the result.'

Clary looked down, contemplating what he should say. He sighed. 'I would never disregard a note like this. I am not derelict in my duty.' He looked Blamey in the eye. 'I need to ask how you gained knowledge of this letter.'

The chief commissioner leaned forward. 'An anonymous telephone call was received by one of our officers. The caller stated that he had sent you a letter on Wednesday, the 26th of October. You will see that the date and time of receipt have been written at the top. Taylor and Cutmore died the next day. You had plenty of time to round up Taylor and put him in custody while Cutmore was moved to a safe location. We do not need Sydney's gang warfare transferred to our fair city of Melbourne.'

'Who was the officer who took this call, sir?'

'That piece of information remains confidential. I have no desire to see you vent your resentment against a fellow officer.'

'Was it Glass, sir?'

Blamey ignored the question. 'How far have you got with Squizzy's murder, Blain?'

Clary took a deep breath. 'The police report has almost been finalised, sir. An automatic pistol—the third used in the deaths of Taylor and Cutmore—was located in the cistern of the lavatory at the house where the shooting took place. It was a Webley automatic pistol containing two cartridges. The two other guns are believed to have been used by Taylor and Cutmore. One was found in Squizzy's pocket at St Vincent's Hospital, and the other was picked up in a laneway near Cutmore's house. This third pistol suggests that another party may have been involved in the shooting.'

'And have you located this third party?'

'Not as yet, sir, but our enquiries are on-going.' He paused, then added, 'The coroner has returned an open verdict. There is insufficient evidence to determine who fired the fatal shots that caused the deaths of Leslie Taylor and John Cutmore.'

Blamey stood up. 'That will be all, Blain. You are on notice. I expect better from my men.'

As he walked back to his desk, Clary saw that The Undertaker was watching him, a sly smile on his face. He came up close to Glass and leaned down, so that they were nose to nose.

'I know it was you,' he whispered. 'I'm not going quietly. I'll be watching you very carefully from now on, so you'd better be careful.'

With that, Blain jammed his hat on his head and stalked out the door.

'You'll get what's coming to you, Glass, if I have any say in it,' he muttered as he walked away from police headquarters. 'You're corrupt. I know you are.'

He had wandered aimlessly at first around the streets, his mind rehashing his conversation with the boss. The Undertaker was firmly ensconced in Russell Street Headquarters, protected and admired by the upper echelons of the Victoria Police. No one would listen to his theories on Glass's dodgy behaviour, given that he had no evidence. As usual, he found his way to the only establishment where he could relax and not be judged: the Duke of Wellington Hotel. Here he could brood in silence, filling the void with alcohol.

The bartender came up to him, a full bottle in hand. 'A whisky, sir?'

Blain nodded. 'Fill her up.'

Chapter Twenty-Two

'Two murders, one attempted murder, three feathers,' said Reggie over dinner.

The Melbourne Cup had been run and the crowds had gone home, after 120,000 people had witnessed Trivalve's win at Flemington racecourse. And after Mavis had been deposited back at her home, Reggie and Ruby had a chance to chat about the deaths that Reggie had dubbed 'The White Feather Murders.'

'What does it mean?' Ruby asked. 'Why does the killer leave a white feather at the crime scene?'

Reggie finished his meal and pushed the plate aside. 'There's the obvious explanation. A white feather means cowardice. It was handed out to men to shame them into enlisting in the Great War.'

'I understand that,' replied Ruby, 'but how can you link a nurse, an ex-soldier turned politician, and a Temperance Union president together, if that's the answer? It makes no sense.'

'Were they cowards because they didn't admit the truth about themselves?' suggested Reggie. 'Webb was a drug-addled nurse who was a danger to the patients in her care. Burns drank, despite claiming to be teetotal. And what about Badger? He was opposed to divorce and an advocate for the sanctity of the family, but proved to be a bigamist.'

'But why does the murderer choose them?' challenged Ruby. 'There are hypocrites everywhere. What is the link? Doesn't a white feather symbolise peace too?'

'Given that two of these people were murdered, that doesn't seem likely.'

'Why don't you take a look at Mrs Burns' letters?' suggested Ruby. 'They're in the bag in the hallway. They might give you a clue.'

She picked up the dishes and carried them out to the kitchen, while Reggie poured them both another glass of wine. When she came back, she found him examining the first of the letters.

He looked up at her as she watched him. 'You're right. I need all the clues I can get. I must beat the rest of the press pack before they catch a whiff of this story. Hopefully, these letters suggest a potential murderer. It's time we found out who was threatening Mrs Burns.'

'Let me help you, Reggie.'

He handed her half the letters, and they started to read, the only sound being the occasional motorcar travelling down Tanner Street.

'Found anything?' asked Ruby.

'Not yet,' replied Reggie as he placed another innocuous message from one of the Temperance Union members on a pile. 'All these people. So prepared to ignore the wants and needs of those of us who like a drink.' He shook his head in dismay and took another sip of wine. 'It's all black and white to teetotallers: Drink is evil, abstinence is good.'

'All things in moderation, I say.'

Reggie looked up and grinned. 'That's the spirit.' He extracted another letter from its envelope. 'Well, what about this?' He frowned as he read it:

Dear Mrs Burns,

As a friend of the movement, I wish to bring this to your attention. I overheard our vice president talking to someone on the telephone. She called him Mr Striker. I've read about him in the newspaper. He's one of those gang leaders. I don't know why she was talking to him, but I fear for the future if Mrs Skinner becomes our leader. What's she doing mixing with criminals?

Yours sincerely,

A Concerned Member.

'How can that be, Reggie? Why would Horace be on friendly terms with someone from the Prohibition movement?'

'Because Prohibition would remove legal alcohol from the market and allow Striker to sell bootleg liquor at inflated prices, that's why. You can't wipe out the public's taste for alcohol through banning it. Prohibition in the United States has seen a rise in crime, despite what the Temperance advocates say. Striker would make a lot of money if he monopolised the illegal market.'

Ruby shook her head and sighed. 'It worries me if Horace is involved. I regard him as a friend, and he's going to host our wedding party. Do you think we should refuse his offer?'

'Nothing's proven,' replied Reggie. 'We don't know that Striker is implicated in Mrs Burns' murder. We don't know if he was in cahoots with Mrs Skinner. The letter doesn't make that clear.'

'You regard Mrs Skinner as a suspect?'

'Perhaps. How's this for a scenario? Mrs Burns confronts Mrs Skinner after she reads this letter. Skinner is angry. She's ambitious. She decides to have Burns killed.' Reggie paused, frowning. 'But I can't accept it. It sounds like the stuff of motion pictures, not like the inner workings of a temperance union.'

'I agree,' said Ruby, 'but money is a powerful motivator, if Horace offered to pay Mrs Skinner to cooperate with him.'

'Again, the letter doesn't say that.' Reggie laid it aside. 'Let's keep going. Let's see what else is here.'

'Listen to this one,' Ruby said.

Leave my wife alone, or you'll be sorry. You'll regret the day you interfered in my marriage.

'It's anonymous.' She put it aside and read a couple more. 'The language is stronger and more threatening in these ones. Whoever wrote them has a temper.' Ruby frowned as she studied the letters, comparing them. 'That's strange. All three are written on the same typewriter.'

'How can you tell?' asked Reggie, looking over her shoulder.

'It's like handwriting. Think about it. Each person writes differently: the way they form letters, the way they hold their pen, how hard they press the pen into the paper.'

'I understand that, but how does that relate to typewriters?'

'Typewriters have different makes and models, but there may also be differences in the spacing of the letters, or a key might be damaged or not aligned properly.'

'If you look at these letters,' she continued, 'you'll notice that the "t" is missing part of the horizontal line on the right. The "o" leans slightly to the left. And the bottom part of the "g" has a nick in the bottom curve.'

Reggie stared at her in amazement. 'How did you see all that? I mean, I've read about this, but never seen anyone analyse it before.'

Ruby looked at him coolly. 'It's my job. I use a typewriter every day. But, if you must know, one of the ladies in the typing pool explained it to me. She was helping the police a few years ago when they were gathering evidence against a criminal who was sending threatening letters in a protection racket. It intrigued me at the time so I decided to explore it. Fascinating, isn't it?'

'*You* still surprise me, my love. I find *you* fascinating.'

Ruby laughed. 'You'll be even more surprised when I tell you where the typewriter is kept.'

Reggie could hardly conceal his excitement. 'Where?'

'At the Woman's Christian Temperance Union meeting hall in South Melbourne.' She opened her handbag and searched through it, until she found the envelope bearing the pledge which had been given to her by Mrs McTavish. 'Compare this one with those letters.'

Reggie read aloud:

I promise to abstain from all intoxicating liquors as beverages and discountenance their use by others.

His eyes flicked from one page to the other. He shook his head in wonder. 'What a woman. You're right.'

'Of course, I am. And I'll bet the author is Mr McTavish, husband of the secretary. He would have known there was a typewriter in the office. He'd use that rather than have his handwriting recognised, particularly by his wife. It would be the work of a few minutes to type this when the hall was left open temporarily. By the way, I have Mrs McTavish's address too.'

'Great work, Ruby. I'll get Dusty to check Mr McTavish out.'

'Do you think he's the killer?'

'Hard to say, but a threatening letter is proof of motivation.'

Ruby returned to the letters, putting some aside until she held one up.

'What about this one, Reggie? The letters have been cut out of the newspaper and stuck on a sheet.'

I know your nasty little secret. You're not only a hypocrite, but you've ruined the life of someone special to me. Revenge will be sweet.

KK.

'That's worth keeping,' said Reggie. 'It certainly fits with the language used in the Poison Pen column, about her being a hypocrite and a drunk. What a shame that the writer didn't sign it with their full name.'

They spent another fifteen minutes reading the rest of the letters and checking them against the envelopes for clues as to their origin. Two more were threatening, but anonymous. The remaining ones were not significant, as they related to the agenda of the union and were signed.

Reggie and Ruby sat back and finished their wine. They looked at the little pile of letters warranting further investigation: three from McTavish, the aggrieved husband, the one from 'A Concerned Member,' and the one from the writer, 'KK,' promising revenge.

'It's a start, Ruby. McTavish is in the frame and we may have to take a closer look at Horace Striker, given his telephone call with Mrs Skinner.'

'Oh dear,' she replied. 'I do like Horace and I'd hate to think that he had anything to do with Mrs Burns' murder.'

'Despite your friendship with him, you must face facts: Horace may not kill anybody with his own two hands, but his gang does what they're told. If he wants someone dead, it will happen. He's a gangster, Ruby.'

'How would you broach that question with Horace?'

He shrugged his shoulders. Reggie remembered a time in the past when he had written a scathing article about Striker and suffered the repercussions: an unpleasant experience in a back alley with two of his bodyguards, leaving him with a bruised face and black eye, cut lip, and sore ribs.

'Perhaps we should forget about Horace,' he said, wincing at the memory. 'I think that it's unlikely that he would be behind these murders. The white feather doesn't fit with his *modus operandi.*'

Ruby brightened up immediately. 'I agree.'

Reggie took her hand. 'Yes, let's forget about him. It's been a big day, my love. The Melbourne Cup, a winning bet on Trivalve, and time spent with the two most wonderful women in my life. What more could I want? By the way, you looked lovely. Green suits you.'

Ruby smiled shyly, twisting her ruby and diamond engagement ring around her finger. 'Thank you, Reggie.'

He looked at the clock. 'I should go. It's work tomorrow.'

'Before you do, there's something I wanted to mention. Can I ask, Reggie, whether your mother has come into money? She had a couple of £5 bets at the races, which is unusual for her, and she was carrying an expensive handbag. I saw it in Georges department store in the city. It costs £20.'

'You must be mistaken. Mother doesn't have much spare cash. She's always been frugal because she had no choice. My rotten father bled her dry before he took off.'

Ruby wasn't convinced. 'Maybe the bag was a copy. Not the real thing. Still–'

Reggie stood up. 'I'll go.' He leaned forward and kissed her tenderly. 'I'm glad you and Mother get on well. It's important to me. Hopefully, we can keep her away from mercenary men like the Valentine Peebles of this world.'

Ruby laughed. 'From what you've told me, your mother is easily charmed.

She's a trusting soul, and that shouldn't be underrated, but she does get into trouble.' She sighed. 'Her conscience would be guilt-free, unlike mine lately. Pretending to be teetotal. Pretending to be someone I'm not.'

'Remember, it's all in a good cause. Finding a murderer. But you need to be careful, my love. Don't put yourself in harm's way on my account. Let me do the dirty work.'

Ruby nodded. 'I've compromised myself enough lately. My conscience is hurting me.'

'That's what I like about you. You're a good person.'

'Most of the time.' Ruby smiled sadly. 'Do I really help you?'

'Of course you do. And to be honest, I'm pleased that I can sit down and talk about my cases with you. You're a good sounding board for me.'

She smirked. '"Ruby Rhodes. Secretary and sounding board." I must see if there's a job advertisement for me in the Classifieds.'

Reggie chuckled and patted her arm affectionately.

The smile left her face. 'There's something else I need to say. It's about getting married.'

'You're not having second thoughts?'

'Definitely not.'

'You're not happy about me moving into your house? You'd rather live elsewhere?'

'Oh no, that's fine with me. It's the sensible thing to do.'

'Is it the large wardrobe I'm having made for the second bedroom?'

'Of course not.' She took a deep breath, her words coming out in a rush. 'I don't want to give up my job at Smith and Sons, yet. It's important to me. I don't want to sit at home. I don't want to have morning teas, or chat about the weather, or knit socks and jumpers to fill in my time. I'm good at what I do, and I'd like to continue until children come along.' She looked at him anxiously, waiting for a reaction.

Reggie took her hand. 'It's the twentieth century. Society is changing fast. For a long time, I wanted a wife who would stay at home, but then I met you. If it makes you happy, keep working.'

Ruby's face lit up. 'Thank you. I'm glad that you understand. And there are advantages to me working. Think how many more suits you'll be able to buy to fill that monstrous wardrobe you're having made. But please keep a tiny space in it for my clothes.'

Reggie chuckled. 'A tiny space? I think that we can manage that.'

Chapter Twenty-Three

TOXIC POISON PEN
<u>**MURDER MOST FOUL: WHITE FEATHER DEATHS**</u>
By REGGIE DA COSTA, Senior Crime Reporter

Who is *The Truth*'s Poison Pen columnist, and is he linked to two mysterious deaths and an attempt on the life of another? And why has a white feather been found at each crime scene?

One month ago, the first target of this anonymous member of Melbourne's press was the leader of the Melbourne branch of the Woman's Christian Temperance Union, Mrs Ida Burns. Despite campaigning for the prohibition of alcohol and haranguing those who drank to excess, it was alleged that the president had a drinking problem, confirmed when she was found dead from alcoholic poisoning in an alley next to the South Melbourne meeting hall. She was clutching a white feather.

A fortnight later, the Poison Pen denounced a nurse who neglected her patients while in the grip of an addiction to morphine. Shortly after, Miss Beryl Webb was found close to death in her home in Brunswick, the gas tap on the stove open, and a white feather in her hand. Two months earlier, she had been forcibly 'retired' from her job at The Melbourne Hospital, although this was done on the quiet. Sources have confirmed that she had stolen drugs from patients and from hospital supplies. She is recovering in a Salvation Army rehabilitation hostel.

The latest death is that of the Honourable Cuthbert Badger, formerly a captain in the AIF, who was a member of the Legislative Assembly. The Poison Pen column unleashed a blistering attack on him, accusing him of hypocrisy. Badger's speeches denounced divorce, yet he was a bigamist, his first wife still alive. Six days later, he was dead, with a white feather in his hand. According to Detective Sergeant Homer Glass, the officer in charge of the investigation, Captain Badger committed suicide. How was that possible when the right-handed Badger was found with a gun in his left hand?

Even though there is no evidence to suggest that the victims knew each other, they are irretrievably linked by their appearance in the current series of the Poison Pen columns, in which they are ridiculed for being unethical, hypocritical, and, at times, downright immoral.

Mystery surrounds the circumstances of the deaths of Mrs Ida Burns and the Honourable Cuthbert Badger, and the hospitalisation of Miss Beryl Webb, despite the explanation offered by the police, who have seemingly ignored the presence of a white feather at each crime scene.

Comment has been sought from Detective Sergeant Homer Glass. At the time of publication, no reply has been forthcoming.

[*The Argus*, November 2, 1927]

Chapter Twenty-Four

The investigation into the death of the Honourable Cuthbert Badger, Member of the Legislative Assembly, had taken a new turn with the publication of Reggie's latest report, one that Homer Glass did not appreciate. It was apparent that Detective Inspector Clary Blain had read the article in *The Argus* and, consequently, had gone over Glass's head. The Undertaker had been summoned to Blain's office.

'I see that you're persisting in your view that Badger committed suicide,' Clary barked, the veins in his nose bright red. 'Did you see da Costa's report in *The Argus*? He makes the coppers look foolish, and you're supposedly in charge of this investigation. I've read the medical examiner's and constable's reports, and they warrant action on your part.' He shook the case files at him. 'Why didn't you read these reports properly? I shouldn't have to do your work for you. I have enough to deal with tying up the final details surrounding Squizzy's murder.'

'I'm busy with the counterfeiting racket, *sir*,' Glass replied. 'I don't have time to follow up dead ends.'

Blain was not to be sidetracked. 'May I remind you that I'm still your superior officer, despite your best efforts to discredit me. Badger's neighbour saw a woman entering the politician's home on the morning of his death. It's as plain as the nose on your face that she's either a witness or a suspect. But you haven't made any effort to identify her. And, if you'd followed up the medical examiner's report, you'd have asked whether Badger was left- or right-handed, given the gun was in his left hand.' Blain leaned forward, the alcohol on his breath nearly causing Glass to gag. 'He was right-handed. A probationary constable would have questioned that, but not you. I wouldn't have you in my squad if I had my way.'

Glass sniffed, his indignation on display, but Clary was not finished with him.

'Find out who this woman was. Get a description of his former wife to start with, and, if she doesn't fit, look at the other women in his life. And investigate this white feather business. Or do I have to do that for you?' He threw down the files and glared at him. 'Now, get out and do some real police work!'

The Undertaker was seething as he stalked out of the office. Damn Blain. Questioning him like he was a police recruit, not a seasoned investigator. He had no choice but to follow orders, albeit unwillingly.

He gave two junior detectives the task of identifying the woman and was not pleased when one of them returned an hour and a half later with a photograph showing the mystery woman on the arm of the late Captain Badger.

'Here you are, sir. It's his former wife, taken on their wedding day. I found it amongst his personal possessions. I spoke to the neighbour, who confirmed that it was the woman he saw.'

With Badger's estranged wife, Agnes, identified as the visitor on the day of his death, the Geelong police were tasked with transporting Mrs Badger to Russell Street Police Headquarters. The interview was scheduled for Friday, coincidentally the same day on which the next Poison Pen column was due to hit the newsstands.

* * *

Detective Sergeant Glass was sitting in the interview room, waiting for Mrs Badger to be shown in. He was attired in his usual black suit, white shirt, and black tie, his pale complexion washed out even further by the glare from a naked overhead light. He opened the folder and straightened the pages so that they aligned exactly with the edge of the table.

The door opened and Agnes Badger walked in, accompanied by a policeman. Glass scrutinised her, eager to learn what he was dealing with. He noted that she looked thin and drawn, as she glanced briefly at him through tired eyes. Behind her, the constable took up his position next to the door.

'Mrs Badger, have a seat,' began Glass. 'I have a few questions for you regarding your relationship with your ex-husband.'

'My husband,' she corrected him. 'We are not divorced.'

He sniffed. 'Could you tell me the exact nature of your relationship with Captain Badger in the weeks prior to the publication of *The Truth* column?'

'There wasn't one. He didn't contact me, and I didn't contact him. In fact, he didn't know where I was living, and I don't think he cared. He was too busy with his new wife and his political career.'

Glass didn't like her attitude. He decided to change tack. 'Why did you give information about Captain Badger to *The Truth* newspaper?'

'As I've said to those nice reporters from *The Argus*, I didn't. I have no idea where the Poison Pen got it from. It certainly wasn't from me.'

'We only have your word for that.' He leaned forward, tapping his pen and trying to unsettle her. 'In brief, you abandoned your husband, left him to fend for himself, and sold your story to the newspaper to hurt his career. You were jealous of his success, success that he managed without your support.'

Agnes Badger never wavered. 'From your description of my husband, it's obvious that you never met Cuthbert,' she replied. 'He was a violent man. Leaving him was the only way I could have survived. Another few months and it would be *my* body in the mortuary, not my husband's. He was a brute.'

Glass sat back, formulating his next question. 'You were seen visiting your husband's house on the 27th of October. Why were you there?'

'I received a telegram from him the day after Mr Montgomery published his article about me in *The Argus*. I was dismayed to discover that Cuthbert had tracked me down. He told me that if I gave another interview to the newspapers, he would take legal proceedings against me. I decided to have it out with him. I'd tell him to his face that he had no power over me anymore. I had no assets so he couldn't sue me, and I refused to be silenced. And, if it meant going to jail, I'd make sure that the whole of Victoria knew him to be a wife-beater, hypocrite, and bigamist. He wasn't going to scare me anymore.'

'You have this telegram?'

'I threw it out.'

'You went to his house. Did he know that you were coming?'

'I didn't tell him. When I knocked on the door, there was no answer. It was ajar, so I pushed it open and went in. I found Cuthbert on the floor. He was dead.'

Glass leaned forward. 'You found him dead? Did you think he'd committed suicide?'

Agnes Badger smiled for the first time. 'Cuthbert Badger? Suicide? I don't think so. He regarded himself as a gift to society. In his view, we were lucky that he'd set foot on the earth.'

'You concluded that he'd been murdered?'

'That's right.'

'Who would have a motive to kill him apart from you?'

Agnes shook her head. 'How would I know? I never saw him after I left him and moved to Geelong eight years ago. Up until that day when I found him dead.'

'If you had to speculate?'

She shrugged her shoulders. 'He was a bigamist. Perhaps his sweet, new wife shot him. I know how good that would feel. Or her father? Perhaps he hired a hitman to finish off the son-in-law who'd lied to his daughter and brought humiliation on the family? And what about the enemies he made as a politician?'

Glass had had enough. A confession would put an end to speculation and get Blain off his back.

'Or what about a former wife with a grievance?' he countered. 'A woman who felt that she'd been cast aside and who wanted to pay him back? A woman who was missing out on the high life, being the wife of a member of the Legislative Assembly.' The Undertaker picked up his pen.' Perhaps you'd like to give me the details?'

Agnes sighed. 'Don't you understand? I didn't want anything from him. Neither his money nor his name. I was going to ask him to divorce me. I was ready to act as the guilty party. To admit that I'd deserted him. But I have no regrets about telling my story after *The Truth* exposed him. It was time that the public knew him for what he was. He deserved what he got: the humiliation, the mortification, being publicly shamed in parliament, and a bullet through the heart.'

'You fired that bullet. You shot Cuthbert Badger.'

'I did not.'

The Undertaker stood up and shook his finger at her. 'You murdered your husband, and I'll prove it.' He nodded to the constable. 'Escort Mrs Badger out.'

As she left the room, Glass sniffed. Taking her to court would require him to prepare a case against her, because she had shown that she could resist pressure. Interviewing witnesses, examining the evidence, and finding any clues that would send Agnes Badger to the scaffold would be time-consuming. It would have been so much easier to have rubber-stamped Badger's death as suicide, which would have allowed Glass to give his attention to the things that mattered: his rapid ascent through the ranks of the Victoria Police and the demotion of Detective Inspector Clary Blain. But he was stuck with a murder case and a suspect, as well as a superior officer who would be looking over his shoulder to check that he was doing things properly. *Properly.* It was a damned inconvenience. For the first time, he wished he were back in Sydney.

Chapter Twenty-Five

HYPOCRITICAL HIPPOCRATIC OATH

The miraculous medico now mediocre: his hand faltered, the scalpel slipped, the patient died, or worse, lived on. From slaughterman to surgeon in the blinking of an eye.

The Poison Pen has tracked the doctor back to his roots, as a butcher in a slaughterhouse. His abattoir experience equipped him to skin the hides of beasts, but not to experiment on human beings in hospitals and mental asylums, attempting procedures that not even qualified doctors would dare to do.

Now this mutilating medico sits amongst those of the dignified ranks of the Victorian Branch of the British Medical Association. He thinks that he's outfoxed the authorities, but he's soon to learn that the henhouse door is shut.

[*The Truth*, November 4, 1927]

Reggie and Dusty stared at *The Truth*.

'Who is it this time?'

'This one's beyond me,' admitted Reggie. 'I don't have a clue who it is, but it should be easy enough to find out. I'll telephone a friend of mine who's the secretary at the Medical Association.'

'What if these accusations are true?' said Dusty. 'Imagine the repercussions?' He ran his fingers through the tangle of his hair. 'Unqualified. Operating on patients in lunatic asylums. Perhaps performing brain surgery. Using them as guinea pigs in experimental operations. That's unspeakably awful.'

'This takes me back to the Death Mask Murders case,' said Reggie. 'Mental institutions could operate outside the law. Patients were locked behind walls and had no choice but to submit to the doctors and administrators who ran them.

'Dr Silas Bacon, a friend of mine, worked in one, and he told me what they were like. It took two doctors to have you committed, and eight to get you out. That was back late last century, and I doubt if much has changed.'

Dusty shook his head. 'An unqualified physician operating on patients without any proper checks made into his background. It beggars belief. I wonder whether the Poison Pen is performing a public service, warning us about these people.'

'Imagine what damage this doctor has done,' agreed Reggie, tapping the article in *The Truth*. 'And he's on the Medical Board.'

'Despite all that, he might be in danger,' suggested Dusty. 'When you find out his name, are you going to warn him about what's happened to the others named in the Poison Pen column? The fact that two have been murdered?'

Reggie stroked his moustache. 'Perhaps he should pay for what he's done.'

'I don't think that we can be judge and jury,' said Dusty, shaking his head. 'If the Poison Pen has signed his death warrant by writing about him, we should let him know about the other cases. Don't you think so, Reggie?'

'I'm not sure about that.'

'But what about our moral duty? We need to warn him.'

Reggie snorted. He sat back and rested his feet on the edge of his desk, admiring his green and white two-tone shoes. 'Careful, Dusty. Remember that morals and crime reporting are not necessarily compatible. Sometimes, we must step outside the accepted standards of behaviour to uncover a crime. By extension, if everyone did the right thing, there would be no crime and no stories for us to report on. Ergo, crime reporters would cease to exist. In the end, you don't want to put us out of a job, do you?'

'Hmm. Food for thought,' replied Dusty, scratching his head. 'By the way, I loved your last report. That headline was great.'

'You mean "Murder Most Foul: White Feather Deaths"?'

'That's right. However, there's room for improvement.'

'Indeed? What have you thought up this time?' asked Reggie, chuckling in anticipation as Dusty handed him his suggestion typed on a sheet of paper. 'Very clever,' he read. '"Murder Most Fowl: White Feather Deaths. Inspector Blain Hatches Plan to N-egg-ate Sergeant Glass's Poultry (Paltry) Investigation."' He looked up. 'Your best yet.'

His face grew serious. 'However, I caught up with Clary yesterday. He's in the depths of despair. He reckons that Glass is after his job. Apparently, Glass set him up by placing a false letter in his case notes warning that Squizzy was about to kill Snowy Cutmore. The implication was that Clary was negligent.'

'Glass would do that?'

'Clary thinks so.'

'Did Clary have any information on the White Feather Murders?'

'The Undertaker interviewed Agnes Badger. She admitted to being at Badger's house on the day of the murder but claims that he was dead when she arrived. Clary says that they can't press charges because there's no conclusive evidence tying her to the murder. No blood on her clothes, no fingerprints of hers on the gun, nothing except her pleasure at her husband's demise.'

'How did she get to East Melbourne from Geelong?'

'Train from Geelong; tram from the city.'

'If she'd had blood splatter on her, she would have been noticed,' Dusty commented.

'That's right. Badger was shot at close range.'

'I thought that Glass said it was suicide.'

'He did. But the medical examiner's and police reports suggest the opposite.'

'Badger had enemies,' said Dusty. 'I heard talk that his conduct on the battlefield left a lot to be desired. There'd been whispers, according to Bluey Talbot.'

'Such as?'

'Incompetence, bullying, and even cowardice. He silenced his critics by accusing them of desertion or mutiny.'

'That fits with what his wife told us. Cowardice. White feather material?'

'Sounds likely. Which reminds me, did you tell Blain about the white feather theory?'

Reggie nodded. 'I did. He reacted like I'd expected him to. He's prepared to accept that there might be something to it, but the Badger case is in Glass's hands, so there's not much that he can do. Clary's overwhelmed with work, and he's under pressure from the chief commissioner.'

'Did you mention the Poison Pen column to him?'

'He thinks it's a stretch of the imagination. He's not prepared to countenance that the Poison Pen and the white feather are connected. That doesn't surprise me.'

'What about Glass? Is he going to follow up the white feather theory?'

'In the end, he's not going to take any notice of the white feathers because they complicate matters. And I must admit that, without the white feather, there is nothing to link the victims. Different *modus operandi*—asphyxiation, alcoholic poisoning, a shooting—and three people from completely different backgrounds: a temperance advocate, a nurse, and a politician. Maybe we are wrong. Maybe it's coincidental. But I don't think so. And it makes for a great story. We've got the public interested. If we're going to confirm the link between the victims and prove that the white feather has significance, we do need to find out who this doctor is and have a chat with him before he ends up dead holding a white feather.

'Think about it. We know almost nothing about each of these victims. This is our chance to find out if this doctor knew Burns, Webb, or Badger. And does he know the Poison Pen?'

'That's worth pursuing,' agreed Dusty. 'What if I work the case from a different angle? What if I visit one of my former colleagues at *The Truth* and ask him if the Poison Pen is the source of the information or if someone is feeding it to him?'

'Good idea. They'll talk to you. While you do that, I'll try to identify the doctor. And one more thing: I want you to follow up a bloke called Jim McTavish. He's the husband of the secretary of the Temperance Union. See what you can find out about him. We think that he wrote threatening letters to Mrs Burns. Here's his address.'

Dusty jotted down the details and left the room.

Reggie picked up the telephone. 'Put me through to the Victorian Branch of the British Medical Association.' He took his feet off the desk and reached for a pen and paper. 'The secretary, please.'

Chapter Twenty-Six

It was at the Melbourne offices of *The Truth* that Dusty had cut his teeth on the fundamentals of newspaper reporting. In response to tip-offs, he and his colleagues would be off and racing, trying to keep ahead of the press pack for the latest news stories, scandal, and gossip, particularly those with a sensationalist edge which would simultaneously shock and delight the newspaper's readers. The eccentric and unpredictable *Truth* journalists, with whom he'd worked, had played fast and loose with the facts and were always on the lookout for a new 'crusade' or angle. Nearly every subject was fodder for a story, particularly if it impacted harshly on the 'man in the street,' because the newspaper's major audience was the working class. Defamation suits were levelled against the newspaper with monotonous regularity, but *The Truth*, with its large readership, ignored the outraged cries of those that it libelled and continued giving the masses what they wanted.

Dusty Rhodes had moved on to the newsroom of *The Argus* after a year, becoming Reggie's assistant at the crime desk. He had learned much in that time and had developed into a 'respectable' journalist, eschewing the wild ways of his former colleagues. What he hadn't left behind him was the love of a good headline, garnished with a heavy dose of alliteration. He still cherished the title of his final article for the newspaper. It focussed on an elderly, unfaithful husband named Elias Budd, who had been caught out in a hotel with his mistress. The headline read 'An Ancient's Amorous Antics Nipped in the Budd.' Setting foot in that establishment again would bring back fond memories of a time that would not be repeated, certainly not at

The Argus.

And as Dusty stood in the bedlam that was his former workplace, he smiled to himself. Telephones were ringing, reporters were smoking and drinking as they took calls, stabbing at typewriter keys, yelling for the office boy, arguing, and complaining. How he missed it! He strode across the newsroom, acknowledging the occasional face that he recognised, until he was standing in front of the desk of his former colleague, 'Crabby' Crabtree.

'Hello, mate,' said Dusty, raising his voice so that he could be heard over the hubbub. He cast an eye over the skinny, wrinkled man with the thinning hair plastered to his head, and was amused to see that Crabby was still wearing the same black, woollen jumper that he'd worn every day when Dusty had been an employee of *The Truth*.

'Well, well, Dusty Rhodes.' Crabby eyed him up and down. 'You haven't changed a bit. I thought that you'd be wearing three-piece suits and expensive shoes now that you've gone up in the world at *The Argus*.'

'Not a chance,' replied Dusty. 'I want to stay true to my working-class roots. Reggie's tried hard to change me, but I keep on resisting.'

'Good for you.' He looked at him thoughtfully. 'I expect this isn't a social call. Are you here with a purpose?'

'I am. Can we go somewhere quieter for a chat?' He looked around him. 'Any suggestions?'

'What about the pub?' replied Crabby.

'I'm sorry, mate, but I'm on a tight schedule. Is there a room somewhere?'

'The archives, that's where we'll go.'

They went downstairs and entered a storage room where back copies of *The Truth* were stacked into bookshelves, each month and year clearly marked. A wizened old man looked up from his reading as they entered.

'Help you, gents?'

'No thanks, Henry. Looking for a quiet spot.'

'You found the right place, Crabby. I'll nick out for a drink while you're here. You can have the place to yourself.' He looked Dusty up and down. 'You look familiar. Where did I see you last? On a wanted poster?'

Dusty laughed. 'Good to see you again, Henry.'

They settled in the corner of the room, facing each other.

'I'll get to the point, Crabby. I'd like to know who the Poison Pen is.'

'What's your interest?'

'No reason. I'm curious, that's all.'

'And I'm the Queen of Sheba.'

Dusty sighed. 'Alright, I'll tell you. It's to do with two deaths in the news lately. Mrs Burns from the Temperance Union is one, and The Honourable Cuthbert Badger is the other. The Poison Pen described Burns as a hypocrite, a drunk. Badger was pilloried as a bigamist. Both true, it appears. And both were dead shortly after *The Truth* published the Poison Pen's column.'

'I admit that surprised me,' said Crabby. 'What about the third one? The Angel of Mercy. She survived, didn't she?' Crabby cocked his head to one side. 'You're drawing a link between the column and these deaths?'

'You haven't changed, mate.' Dusty smiled. 'Still a shrewd one. It's true. But finding the link depends on finding out who this Poison Pen is.'

'I heard that Badger's former wife was taken in for questioning.'

'The evidence against her is circumstantial. So, if it's not the wife, who is it? That's why I'm here.'

Crabby screwed up his face, his expression almost comical. 'You think it's the Poison Pen? Not a chance, Dusty. He's been here for a few years, and this is the first time that anyone's attempted to link him with a murder. He writes gossip. He spreads rumours. Some of what he writes is damn ridiculous, unbelievable, usually libellous. But suggesting that he's a killer?'

'I'm not saying that he is, but I'm curious as to where he gets his information from.'

Crabby shook his head. 'No idea. I've never met the fellow; only read his column. He doesn't have a desk. He sends his column in by courier once a fortnight. He could be a woman. He could be the Prime Minister. He could be the Archbishop of Canterbury. But he's not a killer. At least, I don't think so. I have heard a rumour that he's a former policeman, but I don't know for sure.'

'Who would know?'

'It's a closely guarded secret. What he writes is inflammatory. It's a condition of his employment that he remains anonymous; otherwise, he might be shot by a disgruntled husband or a member of the public. The boss knows, I reckon, but you'll never persuade him to reveal a name.'

He leaned forward. 'Come on, Dusty. I understand why Badger might upset someone enough to murder him. That's what politicians do. But what's the story on Burns and this Webb woman? What did they do to make someone want to kill them?'

'Burns was a firebrand. She made enemies. Legitimate hoteliers and distillers would be shut down if Prohibition were introduced. Husbands were unhappy when their wives banned the booze.'

'Fair enough too,' agreed Crabby.

'And Webb was responsible for the deaths of some of her patients. She faked records and took the morphine that was prescribed for them, so they suffered in the end. Imagine how their families felt when they found out?'

'She left the stove on. Isn't that a possible explanation?'

'It's possible, but you must ask the question why the Poison Pen picked these particular people as subjects for his column.'

'What about the latest one: the phony doctor? Have you identified him, yet?'

'Reggie's working on it.'

Crabby scratched his head. 'If it were me, I'd be looking for a link between this doctor and the nurse. Find out if they worked together.'

'That's a good idea. I'll do that. But I come back to my original question, Crabby. Who is the Poison Pen, and how do I track him down?'

The reporter sat back in his chair, surveying the back copies of *The Truth* stacked on the shelves. 'If only these walls could talk.' He rubbed his cheeks and said, 'Again, if it were me, I'd try a good old-fashioned bribe. Every second Thursday at two o'clock, a courier delivers the Poison Pen's column in a sealed envelope to the front desk. I reckon that £1 might persuade him to tell you where he collects it from.' He paused. 'You didn't hear that from me.'

Dusty nodded his head and did a quick calculation. 'That will be the 17th of November. Ten days to go.' A slow smile spread across his face. 'I can see the headline now: "Will the Newshound Nab the Nib of the Pernicious Poison Pen?"'

Crabby chuckled. 'You never really left us, did you?'

Dusty shook his head and sighed. 'Old habits are hard to break.'

Chapter Twenty-Seven

Reggie sat in the waiting room adjoining the surgery of Dr Herman Fox. It was imperative that he interviewed the Poison Pen's latest subject before the public and the press pack found out who he was and forced the doctor to retreat from view. He had managed to get an appointment for Tuesday morning and had given a false name to the receptionist.

'The doctor will see you, Mr Richmond.' As she spoke, the doctor appeared in the doorway and invited him to enter.

The room was unexceptional for a doctor's surgery, furnished as it was with a desk, two chairs, a couch, and a drugs cabinet. On the walls were an eye chart and an illustrated diagram of the muscular system. Unsurprisingly, there was no indication that Dr Fox was previously a butcher in an abattoir. Everything was tidy and hygienic, as was the man himself, with his short, neat haircut, scrubbed face, and sparkling white shirt beneath a doctor's white coat.

Fox took his seat on the other side of the desk and opened a new folder, on which he had written the name 'Reginald Richmond.' His pen in his hand and a blank sheet of paper in front of him, Fox was ready to start a new patient file.

'Now, Mr Richmond. Can you tell me what brings you here today?'

'I'm afraid, Dr Fox, that I'm here under false pretences. My name is Reggie da Costa, and I'm a reporter with *The Argus*.'

The man looked shocked. He put the pen down and shook his head. 'I don't understand.'

Reggie paused before he answered. 'I am investigating some murders.' He took an envelope out of his bag and removed some press clippings, then spread them on the doctor's desk, pointing at each one as he spoke their name. 'Mrs Ida Burns. Died from alcoholic poisoning. Miss Beryl Webb. Hospitalised with asphyxiation. The Honourable Cuthbert Badger. Shot dead.'

Fox looked perplexed. 'What does this have to do with me? And why did you give a false name?'

Reggie ignored him. 'Each of these people was featured in *The Truth*, in the Poison Pen column.'

'I'm not familiar with—'

'Each of these people was accused of being a hypocrite and deceiving the public. Burns was president of the Temperance Union in Melbourne, yet she drank heavily, Webb was a drug addict and a nurse, and Badger railed against divorce and was a defender of the sanctity of the family, but, in fact, he was a bigamist and a wife-beater.'

'I still don't see—'

'Each died about a week after their hypocrisy was revealed in *The Truth*. A fourth person has been publicly exposed. A person who worked in an abattoir as a slaughterman, then represented himself as a qualified doctor during the war. Afterwards, he found work in a hospital and a lunatic asylum. He has a comfortable practice and is on the board of a medical association.'

The blood drained from Fox's face. He stared at Reggie, unable to speak.

Reggie looked around him. 'Your surgery is quite bare, Dr Fox. No hooks hanging from the ceiling, no animal pens, no saws, no blood.'

Recovering his composure, Fox rose to his feet. 'I think you should go.'

'Sit down, sir. You need to see something.' Fox hesitated and sat down again. Reggie took Friday's Poison Pen column from the envelope and placed it in front of the doctor. 'It won't take long for your identity to become known. Your qualifications don't exist. Your service at the Mont Park Lunatic Asylum and your place on the board of the Victorian Branch of the British Medical Association will accord very nicely with *The Truth*'s description of their latest hypocrite.'

Fox was defiant in the face of Reggie's accusations. 'There are others who have filled those positions. Why do you think that it's me?'

'Your name fits with the description. Mrs Burns was the "Fiery One." Miss Webb was a "Dope Spider." Captain Badger bullied and tormented his wife. That is, he *badgered* her. And now you.' Reggie tapped the article and read from it. '"He thinks that he's outfoxed the authorities, but he's soon to learn that the henhouse door is shut." That's you, Dr *Fox*.'

'You're deluded.'

'I don't think so. And I'll prove that it's true.'

'What do you want?' Fox asked, his eyes darting from the newspaper clipping to Reggie's face.

'Nothing, except some information, which would explain the Poison Pen's choice of subjects. Tell me if you knew any of these people: Mrs Ida Burns; Miss Beryl Webb; Captain Cuthbert Badger.'

Reggie watched him carefully as he slowly said each name, and noted a slight flicker in Fox's eyes as the name of the nurse passed his lips.

'Miss Webb. You knew her. Where did you meet her? Did you work with her?'

Fox shook his head defiantly. 'I've never heard of her.'

'What about the Poison Pen? Do you know him?'

The doctor had had enough. 'Get out. I've never read *The Truth*. Gossip and scandal.'

'This is your last chance, Dr Fox. Where did you meet Miss Webb? She was a nurse. Did you work together in a hospital? Was she a friend, an acquaintance? It's imperative that I find the link before you die.'

Fox looked horrified. 'Die?'

'Tell me how you knew her.'

'I told you to get out. I'll ring the police if you don't leave.' He moved towards the door.

'I'll go,' said Reggie. 'However, in the interests of your safety, I'll give you forewarning of the danger that you are in. If I were you, I'd go on a holiday, perhaps to Tasmania or some small country town where no one knows you.

Leave now. Because there is someone out there who has a grudge against you and will track you down and kill you.'

The doctor faced him. 'This is ridiculous. That's not me they're writing about. And the idea that someone wants to kill me is ridiculous too.' He turned on Reggie. 'We had types like you at the asylum. They were committed because they'd lost touch with reality.'

'Here's my telephone number if you want to talk.' Reggie placed his card on the desk. 'You've done terrible things masquerading as a doctor. You should be punished, but death is perhaps a bit extreme. I'll say this one more time: go into hiding. Now.'

He took one last look at Dr Fox as he stood in the doorway. The man was trembling, his face white, as he stepped forward and slammed the door in Reggie's face.

Chapter Twenty-Eight

Melbourne had been gripped by an unseasonable heatwave three weeks out from the start of summer. It had been over ninety degrees for the past few days, the winds blowing from the north, with no sign that the weather was about to break.

Mavis da Costa was in the kitchen, preparing a birthday dinner for her beloved son, Reggie, and his fiancée and her brother. The back door and the windows were open, but gave no relief from the late afternoon heat. Mavis wiped the perspiration from her forehead and pulled at her dress, which was sticking to her back. She had gone to a great deal of trouble, choosing an excellent cut of meat for the main course and baking an elaborate angel food cake for dessert, with frosted icing and sweet fruit sauce drizzled over the top. But the weather was making her fractious, and, although she was looking forward to seeing her guests, she was preoccupied with troubling thoughts which had intruded on her excitement as she prepared to celebrate her only child's 40th birthday.

The previous day had seen her at Mildred Bardsley Smith's home for the weekly meeting with her Brighton friends. It had begun as usual with afternoon tea served in the opulent drawing room of Glenrothes, followed by a discussion about which charitable causes they would support prior to Christmas. Proposals included a concert of popular Christmas songs and a performance of Charles Dickens' *A Christmas Carol*, with the actors drawn from the local schools. The venue was to be Brighton Town Hall. Mildred offered to make overtures to the headmaster and headmistress of the local grammar schools, while Edith volunteered to speak to the choir master at

St Andrew's to see whether the choir might be persuaded to participate.

'I know him well,' she declared. 'He won't refuse.'

'Not if he knows what's good for him,' whispered Gladys.

'There's only seven weeks to Christmas, so we need to get these events approved,' said Mildred. 'Costumes need to be sewn, and the local traders asked to make a contribution.'

There was a lot of nodding of heads and murmurs amongst the group. A short discussion followed, and the formal part of the meeting drew to a close.

'Now, ladies, what news?'

'What's Reggie investigating, Mavis?' asked Gladys expectantly. 'Any murders? Robberies?'

'Really?' tut-tutted Edith. Despite the look of disapproval on her face, her eyes were firmly fixed in Mavis's direction.

'You know the Poison Pen's column in *The Truth*?' asked Mavis. 'About a person who claimed to represent the temperance movement, but was actually a drinker? You were right, Edith. It was Mrs Burns. And there's *more*.'

'More?' asked Bertha. 'I've missed out on this. What's happened?'

Mildred smiled at the new member of the group. 'I should explain. Mavis's son is Reggie da Costa. He's a crime reporter with *The Argus*.'

'*Senior* crime reporter,' Mavis said. 'My Reggie says that Mrs Burns *and* Captain Badger were found dead after the Poison Pen accused them of hypocrisy.'

'How did Captain Badger die?' asked Clementine.

'Shot dead.'

Edith scowled. 'We've read about that, Mavis. It's old news.'

'What about the "Angel of Mercy"?' asked Gladys, ignoring Edith.

'Miss Webb. She was a nurse.' Mavis lowered her voice. 'Gassed, but she survived.'

The ladies exchanged looks and leaned in, waiting for the next tasty titbit of gossip.

'She was a drug addict.'

There was an intake of breath as the ladies took in the dreadful truth about Miss Webb's brush with death.

'I had no idea,' said Edith. 'Is there a connection between this Poison Pen person and these attacks?'

'Reggie doesn't know, but he'll find out.'

As she spoke, the maid came in. 'Excuse me, ma'am,' she said, addressing Mildred Bardsley Smith. 'Reverend Herring is at the door. He asked if he could speak to you briefly.'

'Of course.' She turned to Mavis. 'Could you collect five shillings from each of the ladies for the Methodist Children's Home Christmas Appeal while I'm with the reverend?'

'Certainly, Mildred,' Mavis replied.

The remaining ladies dutifully opened their purses and pressed coins into Mavis's hand. All eyes were upon her as she removed £1 from her handbag and added it to the pile. There was an intake of breath, and eyebrows were raised.

Edith spoke first. 'My goodness. You've had a change of fortune. Where did you get that from?'

'Have you come into money?' asked Gladys, her eyes wide.

Mavis met their stares. 'I have a man who pays me each week.'

Bertha was shocked. 'A man?'

'What do you mean? A man pays you. For what?' asked Clementine.

'My garage.'

'Really? Your *garage*?'

'Yes, he rents my garage.'

Edith's dark, button eyes glinted through her glasses. 'What does he want your garage for? Are you sure that it's the garage he wants?'

'Edith, what are you saying?' Mavis protested. 'You can't be suggesting anything…indecent?'

Clementine sniggered and winked at Bertha.

Mildred Bardsley Smith swept into the room, immediately sensing the change of mood. 'What's going on here?'

There was silence until Edith spoke up. 'Mavis was telling us about the man who gives her money every week, for services rendered.'

Mildred cast her eye over the blushing Mavis. 'There must be an explanation for this.' She waited, but Mavis was silent, overcome with embarrassment. When nothing more was offered, Mildred cleared her throat and declared, 'I think that we should move on to other matters.'

But the damage was done, and the meeting had broken up shortly after, the salacious gossip not spoken of again, but certainly central in the minds of four of Mavis's companions. She had left first, unable to stomach the thought that she was being viewed as acting in an improper and immoral manner, the subject of wild speculation.

* * *

And now, a day later, as Mavis stood in the kitchen with her son, his fiancée, and Ruby's brother about to arrive, she felt the weight of the world on her shoulders again. She was expected to put on a happy face and pretend that everything was rosy, when her reputation was at stake. Without the camaraderie of Mildred's little group, life would become meaningless. Friendship and social status were the benefits of acceptance, and it was with growing apprehension that she realised all was in jeopardy unless she could defend herself against rumour and innuendo.

Mavis rallied as she heard someone knocking at the front door. She took off her apron, checked her hair in the mirror in the hallway, switched on the fan in the dining room, and opened the door to her guests.

* * *

The dinner plates had been cleared away, and the candles on the cake burned brightly as 'Happy Birthday' was sung with gusto. Even Reggie joined in, a broad smile on his face.

'An angel food cake. How delicious,' said Ruby.

Mavis cut the cake into portions and distributed them around the table. 'And before you eat, I have a little something for my dear son.' She handed over a box wrapped in bright, blue paper tied with a navy ribbon.

'I'm a lucky man,' declared Reggie. 'My lovely wife-to-be and future brother-in-law have already presented me with a Waterman's Combination Writing Set. A fountain pen and matching pencil, all the way from London. Now, what do we have here?'

Reggie looked curiously at the present, tore off the wrapping, and opened the box. Inside was a nine-carat gold Rolex watch with a leather band. He stared at it, astonished. Treating it like it was a fragile work of art, he lifted it gently from its velvet holder and slowly rotated it, marvelling at the workmanship. Everyone was silent, in awe that Mavis had gifted her son such an extravagant present.

'Mother—' For once, Reggie was lost for words. 'It's beautiful. But how could you afford this? You didn't buy it off a thief, did you?'

'Don't be ridiculous. Of course not.' Mavis's eyes filled with happy tears. 'My dear son deserves the best. You'll be able to wear it on your wedding day.'

Reggie put it on his wrist and showed it to Ruby and Dusty. 'You shouldn't have, Mother. You can't afford this.'

'I appreciate your concern, dear boy, but my financial woes are over. I've been meaning to tell you. I rented out the garage at the back of the house to a nice, young man. He is very generous.'

Reggie frowned. 'What young man? Who is he? Why didn't you talk to me first before you took that step?'

Mavis pouted. 'It's my house, and I have the right to do what I please.'

Sensing a growing air of tension, Ruby stepped in. 'I'm sure that your mother is perfectly capable of looking after her own interests.'

Reggie raised an eyebrow. 'Are you certain of that?' He was about to say more when he registered the look on his fiancée's face. 'Of course, Mother, if he leaves you alone. And he's quiet. What does he want the garage for?'

'Damien is a printer. He's a polite, well-mannered man. He produces lovely pamphlets and posters. Every week, he puts the rent in an envelope and leaves it in the letterbox, so I hardly know he's there. Does that satisfy you?' she asked archly.

'I wish that you'd spoken to me first, but he sounds acceptable from what you've said.' He looked down at his new timepiece. 'I do love the watch. It's very generous of you.'

Satisfied, Mavis turned to Dusty. 'Now, Mr Rhodes, you've been quiet tonight. How is *The Argus* treating you?'

'Very well, thank you,' he replied. 'Reggie has taught me well.'

Mavis's cheeks glowed. 'How lovely. And can I ask what you're working on?'

'I'm writing an article on poison pen letters. It will appear in next week's newspaper.'

'How interesting. Is this to do with the murder case that Reggie's been talking about?'

'Indirectly. It's background material, essentially. I'm more concerned with how these letters affect their recipients.'

'In what way?' she asked.

Dusty leaned forward, keen to share what he had learned recently. 'Rumours and gossip can have a terrible effect on the lives of innocent people who have done nothing wrong.'

'That's so true,' agreed Mavis, looking flustered. 'Innocent. They've done nothing wrong.'

'Simple situations are twisted to sound nasty and scandalous, when the truth is pure and innocent.'

'So unfair,' she agreed, fanning herself with a napkin.

'I've read cases where respectable people are accused of immoral behaviour. They have no way to defend themselves. Some even contemplate suicide.'

'I can understand that. It's unbearable,' she said, with a sob in her voice.

'And you don't know the identity of the accuser, so you can't confront them,' he added.

'But, even if you do, it's impossible. I tried to explain, but they wouldn't listen!' Mavis cried. She fiddled with her dessert fork, pushing the piece of cake around the plate, then flung down the fork, while tears rolled down her cheeks.

Dusty stared at her in shock. 'Mrs da Costa, what's wrong? Is it something I said? Is it the weather? Is the heat affecting you?'

Mavis glanced from one face to another and fled from the room, leaving her guests bewildered. Reggie was about to go after her when Ruby laid a hand on his arm. 'I'll go.'

She found Mavis sitting in the kitchen, her head in her hands, sobbing. Ruby put her arm around her.

'What is it, Mavis? Something Dusty said upset you. Do you want to tell me about it?'

She raised sad eyes to Ruby, tears coursing down her pale cheeks. 'They're saying things about me, awful things.'

Ruby took a breath. 'Who's saying these awful things? Perhaps you could explain?'

Mavis nodded, her face a picture of despair. 'I was at Mildred Bardsley Smith's last week. I gave £1 towards the Christmas fund. They asked me where I got the money from, and I tried to explain about the garage. It came out all wrong, Ruby. They stared at me and pulled faces, and Edith suggested that I was getting the money…improperly.'

'Oh dear. Did you explain about the man, Damien?'

'I tried, but they kept on interrupting me. They implied things about Damien and me. It was awful.'

'Surely not Mrs Bardsley Smith? She's not like that.'

'Not Mildred. She wasn't in the room. And she knows me better than that. It's the others.' She paused. 'I don't know what to do. I'm afraid to go back there because they'll look at me, judge me.' She started to sob again.

Ruby sighed. 'People like to gossip. They don't understand the hurt and damage it does. It's like those poison pen letters that Dusty was talking about. Innocent people accused of doing bad things when they haven't. You know that it's often the result of jealousy?'

Mavis looked at her through her tears. 'Jealousy?'

'That's what Dusty says in his article. They're jealous of the person that they're writing about. They resent the fact that the person is prettier, has a nicer personality, or, maybe, has a smart son.'

Mavis opened her eyes wide. 'Jealous of me? Do you think so?'

Ruby nodded her head. 'Dusty says it's often the case. The thing is, Mavis, that if you stop going to Mrs Bardsley Smith's, it's sending a message that you're in the wrong. That you have something to be ashamed of. And you don't. I'd recommend that you have a chat with Mildred. Explain what happened and tell her the truth.'

'You think so?'

'I'm sure of it. She's a moral person, and she won't like what's been said about you.' She took out her handkerchief and handed it to Mavis. 'Wipe your eyes. We need to go back to Reggie and Dusty. They'll be concerned about you. And, if you don't mind, we should tell them about this. It's obviously causing you great distress, and the sooner we deal with it, the better. What do you think?'

Mavis sat for a moment. 'Thank you for listening to me, Ruby. You're very kind.' She squeezed her hand. 'Perhaps I should talk to Mildred. She's stood up for me in the past.' She blew her nose. 'Could you go first and tell your brother and Reggie for me? I find it embarrassing.'

Ruby smiled at her. 'If that's what you want, I'll do it.'

Chapter Twenty-Nine

Dusty was going for his daily walk near the docks at Port Melbourne. A hot, northerly wind whipped off Port Phillip Bay, while the seagulls wheeled overhead, screeching and dipping down into the white caps of the waves. Off in the distance, in the direction of Geelong, ominous black clouds were gathering, an indication of the coming storm which would give relief from the heat that had enveloped Melbourne for the past week.

Dusty had strolled past Station Pier up as far as Princes Pier. He watched as the R.M.S. *Otranto* slowly edged away from the wharf, pulled by two tugs. On board were passengers bound for London, who had spent the preceding twenty-four hours experiencing the delights of the city of Melbourne. On the wharf were friends and family, bidding them goodbye, and no doubt wishing that they, too, could embark on an adventure across the Indian Ocean, through the Suez Canal, and on to Great Britain. If the storm clouds moving across the bay were any indication, Dusty thought, the passage out through The Rip into Bass Strait would be adventure enough. It was renowned as being an unpredictable stretch of water, the graveyard of many ships, particularly when there was a combination of forceful winds and strong tides.

It had been a different picture, three days earlier, when Dusty took his usual walk. It was early, but Station Pier had been busy, with a ship being unloaded by wharf labourers, while hundreds of passengers waited with their luggage for transport to the city. A significant portion of them were new settlers on the assisted passage program, called the Empire Scheme, while some were to be employed as domestic servants or farm workers, the latter from southern Europe. Soon, they would be experiencing the trials and tribulations of adapting to a new culture, perhaps a new language, and would be seeking housing and employment. Leaving behind their homelands and families would be hard at first, but he wished them well.

As he strolled back along the thin stretch of beach between the two piers, watching the R.M.S. *Otranto* manoeuvre through the waves out into the shipping lane, he considered again the gulf between rich and poor: Those on *Otranto*, in their spacious cabins, would enjoy the delights of fine dining or games on deck, while those who craved a new life, free from wars and the travails of the class system back in Europe, had endured the cramped conditions and restrictions of being steerage passengers as they sailed to the New World. He knew where his sympathies lay. Living in his suburb of Port Melbourne, he saw unemployment and poverty close at hand and understood the effects of social inequality.

'Is it guilt,' Ruby had suggested, 'because you've had a good education and others haven't had that opportunity?'

He had reflected on that and agreed that it was perhaps the case. Seeing injustice firsthand each day had made him more determined to be a voice for the worker. Being a reporter made it possible to publicise such things, the articles on political corruption that he'd written two years ago being a case in point. His feelings were not always shared by his fellow reporters. Indeed, Reggie had accused him of overthinking things, worrying too much about ethics and morality, and perhaps he was right.

Dusty sat on one of the pylons of Station Pier and took the newspaper he was carrying out from under his arm. Indeed, he was proud to see that the editor-in-chief had given his opinion piece a prominent position in *The Argus*. He smiled to himself as he read it again:

A PLAGUE OF POISON PENS
By DUSTY RHODES, Crime Reporter

The battlefields of the Great War were awash with poison—

mustard gas and phosgene—which inflicted terrible suffering and even death on our soldiers. And now, we see the effects of yet another poison—in the form of words—which has crept into our homes and towns, causing misery and suspicion. It is the scourge of the Poison Pen letter.

What do we know about these sickening scribblers? The author of a poison pen letter is keen to remain anonymous, because what he asserts about his victim is often abusive, libellous, and sometimes threatening. He is essentially a coward, afraid to voice his opinion in public. Usually, he knows his victim and is motivated by jealousy and resentment. Why is sometimes not clear.

Let us take as an example the serene, fashionable, and once happy town of Coleford, in the county of Gloucestershire, England. In 1923, scurrilous letters, written in disguised handwriting or composed of words cut from the pages of newspapers, showed an intimate knowledge of the lives of those who resided there. Divorce proceedings, the destruction of the local bank's reputation, the ruination of relationships, and the misery of those innocent beings who were accused of all manner of misbehaving, brought about the intervention of Scotland Yard detectives, who hatched a plot to expose the writer of these poison pen letters. Half a dozen women were suspected, all residents of the town. Paper, envelopes, and even handwriting can be difficult to trace, but the detectives used an ingenious method to expose the culprit. Postage stamps, whose appearance had been altered by being treated with a particular chemical, were sold to one of the suspects. Shortly after, another batch of poison pen letters was sent with these stamps affixed, so it was a simple affair to identify the guilty party.

Not so fortunate was the situation of the small English village of Littlehampton, where poison pen letters disrupted

the serenity of life in 1921. For two years, letters flooded the seaside resort, with the result that a woman was convicted and sent to jail. On her release, the letters began again, and the same woman was locked up, although she protested her innocence. Imagine the dismay of the police and the authorities when poison pen letters were delivered to mailboxes, despite the alleged author being incarcerated? Distrust rocked the town, as a venomous stream of accusations, couched in vulgar and offensive language, destroyed marriages and families, wrecked relationships and reputations, and drove recipients to suicide.

But who was the Littlehampton Poison Pen? It remains a mystery, one which caused unimaginable damage to the lives of those who lived there.

[*The Argus*, November 14, 1927]

A raindrop landed on his arm, announcing the coming storm. Thick, black clouds were gathering, and the wind was rising. Dusty folded up his newspaper and gave the R.M.S. *Otranto* and its passengers one last look. Not for them the slums, warehouses, grinding poverty, and unemployment of Port Melbourne. But, judging by the state of the sky, they were in for a bumpy ride as they rode the waves back to their comfortable homes and estates in England.

He pulled his collar up and tucked the newspaper under his arm, then set off home, more certain than ever that he, Dusty Rhodes, would ensure that his writing reflected his sympathies with the 'working man' and with trying to make the world a better place.

Chapter Thirty

'Reggie, it's me, Clary. You need to get down here. There's been another white feather murder.'

Reggie gripped the telephone. 'Is it Dr Fox?'

'Who?' There was a pause. 'No, it's Everett Dwight. *Doctor* Everett Dwight. And he's holding a white feather. You were right, mate.'

Reggie shook his head. 'You're sure? I could have sworn—'

'No time for talk. Here's the address.'

Reggie jotted down the details, jammed his new Panama hat on his head, and took the stairs two at a time. His mind was racing, unable to comprehend that he might have been wrong.

'Dwight? Everett Dwight? The name doesn't fit,' he muttered to himself as he navigated the Minerva towards South Yarra.

Rockley Road was in a well-to-do area, about a mile away from Como House, the stately home of the Armytage family set in grounds overlooking the Yarra River. A small group of onlookers, mainly neighbours, were gathered outside Dr Dwight's two-storey Federation-style house, which occupied a substantial tract of land. It was fair to say that the doctor had done well for himself, if his early beginnings as a slaughterman were to be believed. In the front yard stood Detective Inspector Clary Blain, his hands in his pockets, interviewing a man wearing a bowler hat.

'There have been robberies around here, Mr Blain,' the neighbour was saying as Reggie approached, 'but never murder. Why kill him? It doesn't make sense.'

Reggie waited until the interview was over, then caught Clary's eye. The detective nodded his head, and Reggie stepped away from the growing crowd, still devoid of reporters, and joined him.

'Come inside, Reggie. See what you think.'

The crime reporter followed Blain inside. They entered a wide hallway, on one side of which was a staircase that curved upwards towards a landing lit by a skylight. Landscape paintings in ornate frames lined a hallway decorated in crimson, flocked wallpaper.

'It's like an art gallery,' remarked Clary. He pointed to a small ante room. 'The receptionist's office.' A woman was bent over in a chair, sobbing, occasionally raising her head to answer a question posed by a constable.

Along further was a bigger room, the door wide open, revealing a couch, desk, two chairs, and a filing cabinet. 'The consulting room.'

'Where's the body?'

'Upstairs.'

They climbed the staircase, with its intricately carved, wooden bannister and crimson carpet runner. It led to a landing giving access to the two wings of the house. Clary turned left and pushed open the first door.

A policeman was standing guard next to the body. 'Give us a few minutes, constable.'

On the floor lay the body of Dr Everett Dwight. He had been stabbed, evidenced by the thin trail of dried blood which had flowed from his chest to pool on the rug beneath him. The dark red of the blood stood out in stark contrast to the blue and white stripes of his pyjamas. Dwight was lying on his back, his face slack and pale, his thick, black eyebrows heavy over staring eyes.

'How long's he been dead?' asked Reggie.

'The doctor says it was early morning when he was attacked. We thought at first that it was a burglary gone wrong, but we found this.'

Blain bent down and pointed at Dwight's hand. A white feather was clutched between his fingers.

'Who found him?'

'His receptionist. She's downstairs being questioned. She had a key. Let herself in. No sign of Dr Dwight, which she said was odd, given that he was an early riser. She came up here, saw the door ajar, and found the body. She rang the police.'

'How did the killer get in?'

'No sign of forced entry. The window in the dining room downstairs was open. We found footprints in the garden. Male. We'll take a cast.'

Reggie's gaze took in the state of the room. The chest of drawers had been rifled, clothes pulled out and piled up on the floor. The wardrobe was open and the bedclothes thrown back.

'He heard the burglar and got up. It would be hard to sleep with this going on,' observed Reggie. 'Anything missing?'

'The receptionist said that the doctor kept drugs in the safe. It was bolted into the back wall of the wardrobe. As you can see, it's been cleared out. Also, she said that he wore an expensive watch, a Rolex. That's missing too. It looks like the killer was an opportunist, taking advantage of the situation.'

'You should notify pawnbrokers to watch out for the Rolex.'

'Standard police procedure, you know that.'

'Sorry, Clary.' Reggie shook his head and sighed. 'This looks more like a robbery gone wrong. There's no doubt in my mind about the killer's intention here. He wanted drugs and cash. Not revenge. Dwight disturbed him in the act. That's all there is to it.'

He turned to Clary. 'What do you know about the doctor? Did he work in an asylum? Was he qualified? Does he fit the Poison Pen's profile?'

Clary gave Reggie a long look. 'I normally trust your opinion, but in this case, I'm afraid you're wrong. I don't know the answers to your questions, but I do know one thing.' He pointed at the victim's right hand. 'It's a white feather, Reggie. Whether you like it or not, Dr Dwight is the latest victim of the White Feather Murderer.'

'It's Dr Fox who's the target.'

'Forget this Dr Fox. Forget the profile. Forget the Poison Pen. There's no proof of a link to him. And, if you won't let this theory go, consider that the Poison Pen might make mistakes. Maybe he got his facts wrong. Maybe there's no abattoir, no asylum, in Dwight's background.'

'I know for a fact that Dwight wasn't on the medical board. I have the list of names.'

'Honestly, Reggie. I get enough criticism at work without you questioning my judgment. Leave it alone and accept what's in front of you.'

Reggie frowned, exasperated. 'I can't explain it, but I know this isn't the intended victim. What if it's a simple case of a thief trying to cover his tracks by leaving a feather? Maybe he's trying to lead us astray? Do you know if Dwight had any enemies or financial problems?'

Clary shook his head. 'Not yet, but we'll check on that. Now, go back to work and write your report, mate. If you don't hurry, there will be ten reporters who'll beat you to it. I've given you a head start, so use it.'

He turned away as the medical examiner's men arrived, ready to transport the body to the morgue.

Reggie watched as they lifted the corpse onto a stretcher. Gut instinct told Reggie that this death wasn't one of the White Feather Murders. The killer had contrived to make it appear so. The Poison Pen had been accurate in his description of each of the previous victims, and Dwight didn't fit the profile. But Clary's comments could not be ignored. It was possible that the Poison Pen had got his facts wrong. Maybe there was no abattoir, no medical board. Maybe he had included them to make the story more sensational, a ploy to create controversy.

In the end, Reggie couldn't afford to miss out on breaking a news story, one that related to his ground-breaking report on the White Feather Murders. He could almost hear the whine in Curtis Flange's voice as he was asked: 'Why did *The Age* beat you to this story?'

Without an alternative course of action on offer, Reggie drove his automobile back to *The Argus* to compile a report for the next day's newspaper. His heart was heavy as he typed the headline, which he knew to be untrue:

POISON PEN PREDICTS DOCTOR'S DEMISE
ANOTHER DEATH AT THE HANDS OF THE
WHITE FEATHER MURDERER

* * *

Next morning, back at the crime desk, the telephone rang.

'Mr da Costa,' said the telephone operator. 'There's an angry man on the line who demands to speak to you. Will you take the call?'

'Put him through, Doris.' He heard the click. 'Reggie da Costa speaking.'

'I've finished reading this rubbish that you've written in the newspaper today. Dr Dwight isn't anything like you claim him to be. His background bears no relation to this Poison Pen description.'

'Who is this?'

'Dr Lynas Farrington. I've been an associate of Everett's for over twenty-five years. We went to school together. We trained as doctors together. We worked in the same clinic together, until recently. The suggestion that he worked in an abattoir is frankly ridiculous, as is the claim that he was unqualified. If Everett were alive, he'd sue you for libel.' His voice faltered. 'He was my friend. How could you make up such lies about him?'

Reggie took a deep breath. 'He was found with a white feather in his hand.'

Farrington exploded. 'So what? That doesn't excuse what you've written. You should be ashamed of yourself.' The line went dead.

Despite being shaken by the vehemence of Farrington's tone, Reggie felt vindicated if the truth be told. Dr Farrington had proved that Dwight wasn't the doctor referred to in the column. But how could he have explained to Farrington the quandary he'd been in? Follow his instincts and reject Dwight's death as being part of a series of murders, and perhaps be proved wrong, as well as giving *The Age* the opportunity to break the news of the latest 'White Feather' murder?

It was clear that there was only one explanation: The thief had copied the perpetrator of the other three cases by leaving a white feather at the crime scene. But try telling that to Blain or Curtis Flange? It would be an exercise in futility.

The fact was that Dr Dwight was not the subject of the latest Poison Pen column. It was Dr Fox. He was the only member of the medical board whose name fitted the play on words. His biography stated that he had studied medicine in Europe before the war, but the claim didn't specify which university, making it hard to check the authenticity of Fox's overseas qualifications, given that records had been destroyed during the war. Asking difficult questions would only make the medical community close ranks. And it was nigh on impossible to prove that Fox had ever worked in an abattoir. There would be no records, and such an enquiry would be treated as laughable at best, insulting or libellous at worst.

The thought struck him that if Dr Dwight were not the target of the White Feather Murderer, then Dr Fox was still in mortal danger. But, once he'd read Reggie's report in *The Argus*, why would he take notice of Reggie's warning?

Reggie sighed and ran his hand through his hair in exasperation. It crossed his mind that it felt dry. Time to replenish his supplies of Brilliantine. So much to contemplate, he thought. The Poison Pen, a killer on the loose, and the location of the nearest shop that sold hair oil.

Chapter Thirty-One

D r Herman Fox, a glass of wine in his hand, was relaxing after a long day at the surgery. It had been unpleasantly hot, with a warm, gusty, northerly wind affecting the moods of his patients, making them irritable and morose. He switched on the wireless and was pleased to hear the deep, soothing voice of Dr Polack discussing dental hygiene. Even more delightful was the prospect of listening to one of his favourite contraltos, Miss Gwendoline Butterrs, singing selections from the opera, *Carmen*, after Dr Polack's broadcast was over.

As the health program came to an end, Fox rose and shut the window, went out into the hallway, and checked that the front door was locked. Despite the reassuring article in *The Argus* that the person described in the Poison Pen column had been found dead, another victim of the White Feather Murderer no less, Fox could not quite dismiss Reggie da Costa's original advice that he was in danger. Unexpected noises—the sound of an automobile horn, a dog barking, the yelling of children out in the street— still made him jump. As the days had passed since he had spoken to the crime reporter, his fears for his own safety had lessened, but each night he re-read the Poison Pen column and wondered who had discovered his true identity. With the fortuitous death of Dr Dwight the previous day, Fox consoled himself with the thought that the Poison Pen had someone else in mind rather than him. His reputation and medical practice would remain unblemished.

Fortunately for Fox, the medical community had been unimpressed with the claims made in *The Truth*, whether they were about Dr Dwight or anybody else in the profession, because criticism from disgruntled patients was part and parcel of the job. Accusations against doctors only made them close ranks to protect their own. His colleagues would treat the claim that he was a butcher as laughable, particularly when his work on the battlefields of the Great War was taken into consideration. They would never believe it.

Sitting in his favourite armchair, the dulcet tones of Gwendoline Butterrs soothed him. Fox found himself reliving the past, prompted by the sight of his diaries shelved neatly behind the glass of his bookcase. They chronicled his journey from slaughterman to doctor. Reminiscing was not something that he often indulged in, but that night he felt obliged to acknowledge the role of fate in bringing him to his present position as a respected member of the medical profession.

As a young man living in a farming community in country Victoria, Herman Fox had found work in the local abattoir, at first sweeping and cleaning, but gradually being introduced to the management of animals before and during the slaughtering process. He was fascinated by the skills involved in removing their hides and internal organs, and in splitting carcasses using saws and knives. Unlike others who worked beside him, Fox enjoyed his work, becoming highly skilled at his 'craft,' as he termed it.

The war intervened, and he enlisted, eager to do his bit for the British Empire and 'defeat the Hun.' He chose to be a medical orderly, but kept silent on his previous employment as a slaughterman for fear of being derided or shunned. Ironically, once he was sent to the Front, his skills at anatomy were recognised and the medical teams, who patched up wounded soldiers and sent them back into battle, realised that they had amongst them one who could be trusted to assist with amputations and setting bones.

Fox could still remember that magical moment when one of the soldiers addressed him as 'doctor.' Within days, there was an acceptance amongst the military medical men that he was one of them. He was also fortunate because, in the casualty clearing stations and field hospitals set up to render aid to the wounded and dying, there was no time for the niceties of checking qualifications.

By 1917, Dr Fox was deployed to a hospital south of Ypres in Western

Belgium. The battle of Messines had begun, with an extensive list of casualties, both British and German. As he toiled through the long days, his reputation grew, and he was awarded a Military Medal for his work.

Shortly after, he was assigned to a London hospital, which primarily treated soldiers afflicted with shell shock. It was there that he was placed under the direction of the hospital's resident psychiatrist, a man who believed that electro-convulsive therapy could be used to cure war trauma. Fox's lack of empathy, regarding the animals he slaughtered at the abattoir, came in useful when mentally and physically damaged soldiers were subjected to therapies aligned to torture.

It was at this hospital that Dr Fox met Nurse Webb, for whom he felt an instant attraction. She, in turn, idolised him. In private, they pursued a relationship, but, in public, they were professional in their behaviour towards one another. Side by side, they tended their patients, confident that their use of new electric shock therapies was restoring the men to the point where they were ready to return to the battlefields.

During that year, Fox kept meticulous records of his experiments on patients at the London hospital. He felt a great degree of pride in his accomplishments and, with the end of the fighting, returned home and took up a position at Mont Park Asylum, made possible by a letter of recommendation from the psychiatrist at the London Hospital. By that stage, his relationship with Nurse Webb had ended.

The clock on the mantelpiece chimed ten, breaking his reverie. It was time for bed. Fox switched off the wireless and stood up. As he did, he heard an unfamiliar sound. His body tensed, and he leaned forward, anxious to identify the noise. He realised with a start that it was water running from the tap in the bathroom. He went out into the hallway. Light was shining in the gap beneath the bathroom door. He pushed it open and was aghast to see water pouring over the side of the bath and onto the linoleum. He leaned forward to turn off the tap and heard a low whistle from behind him.

Dr Fox turned towards the noise, but it was too late to protect himself. He felt and heard the thwack of metal against the back of his skull and fell forward, face down into the bath. As he gasped for air, his last memory was that of a heavy hand holding his head under the water.

Chapter Thirty-Two

The Undertaker stood over the bath, looking down on the fully clothed body that was submerged beneath the surface of the water. 'Electrocution, sir?' asked the constable, observing the wireless that had fallen into the bath, its cord still plugged into the wall.

'Definitely,' replied Detective Sergeant Homer Glass. 'The deceased was listening to the wireless while he bathed and inadvertently knocked it into the water.'

The constable looked at him aghast. 'But he's dressed, sir. Surely not?' He was about to say more when he was silenced by the look on his superior's face.

Glass sniffed, his displeasure obvious. 'Let's say that he had set up the wireless and switched it on. He was about to get undressed when he knocked it into the water. He reached in to retrieve it, received a deadly shock, and fell into the bath.'

The policeman was having trouble accepting the explanation, and unwisely persevered. 'He was running the bath when he was electrocuted. There's water all over the floor. So, who turned the tap off?'

Glass eyed him steadily. 'I suggest that you learn to accept what your superior says, Constable, if you want to get on in life. Questioning a detective sergeant is not advisable, unless you want to do night patrol. Am I making myself clear?'

'Yes, sir. Of course, sir. I'll leave you and check whether the photographer has arrived. If that's what you'd like me to do, sir?'

'Open the window first, to let in some fresh air.'

Glass waved him away, then turned back to the body. The eyes were half open, with dilated pupils. The body had gone through rigor mortis and was bloated, cold, and clammy. There were no signs of burns from electric shock, but that was of no concern to The Undertaker.

He glanced around the room, still damp from the water that had overflowed from the tub, and noticed something wedged up against the wall. It was a white feather. Glass frowned and put it in his pocket. As he did so, there was a knock on the door.

'Photographer, sir. Can I come in?'

'Yes, but don't take too long. This one's straightforward. Drowning by electrocution.'

He passed the ambulance men in the hallway and walked outside, taking in a few deep breaths as he surveyed the crowd of reporters, curious neighbours, and voyeurs who had gathered in the street outside. Word travelled fast when it came to an untimely death, he thought, particularly when the deceased was on the board of the Victorian branch of the British Medical Association.

Glass frowned. Amongst the throng was a nattily dressed forty-ish man wearing a well-cut, three-piece suit in brown wool with a cream shirt, and black and gold striped tie. Reggie da Costa. Senior crime reporter with *The Argus* newspaper. Blain's pal.

The Undertaker stepped forward as questions were thrown at him by the press pack.

'Is it Dr Fox, detective sergeant?'

'Is he dead? Murdered?'

'How did he die?'

'Is it true that he's been dead for a while? That his secretary found him?'

'I'll make a statement,' Glass declared. The group of reporters went silent, pens and notepads at the ready.

He waited, then spoke as if reading from a script. 'This morning, the body of Dr Herman Fox was found drowned in his bath by his secretary, Miss Myra Hockstetter. He had not attended his surgery this morning and was not answering his telephone. On finding her employer deceased, Miss

Hockstetter telephoned police headquarters. A police car was dispatched, and by 10:35 a.m., detectives were attending the scene.

'An intensive examination of the bathroom confirmed that the doctor had died as a result of electrocution and drowning.'

A voice broke the monologue. 'Electrocution *and* drowning. Which is it?'

Glass sniffed; his eyes fixed on the sartorially elegant form of Reggie da Costa. 'Both, Mr da Costa. But it will be up to the coroner to determine the cause of death, as you should know.'

He continued with his statement. 'The deceased was about to undress for his bath when he accidentally knocked the wireless into the water. Reaching in, Dr Fox was electrocuted and fell forward into the bath, where he drowned.'

'Was he lying face down or face up?'

The Undertaker summoned all his inner strength, so that he wouldn't snap at the reporter. 'Face up.'

Reggie stepped forward, so that he was close to the detective. 'If he fell into the water, he would be face down, Mr Glass.'

'Detective Sergeant Glass, to you.'

The reporter was undeterred. 'Fully clothed, about to retrieve the wireless, electrocuted, slips, and falls in. I'd suggest, Detective Sergeant, that the deceased would be face down in the water, *if* that's what happened. Have you considered foul play?'

'Naturally,' Glass snarled.

'Are you aware that Dr Fox was the subject of a Poison Pen column in *The Truth* nearly two weeks ago?'

'I'm surprised that you should say that, da Costa. Didn't you publish an article, only yesterday, stating that Dr Dwight was the person in question?' There was a murmur from the assembled reporters. 'Or don't you read your own newspaper?' Laughter broke out but was soon silenced as the detective attempted to put an end to Reggie's cross-examination. 'The Poison Pen didn't name anyone, as you well know, so the presence of a white feather on Dr Dwight's body was incontrovertible proof that he was the target of this killer.'

He turned to the circle of reporters, enjoying himself. 'In the police force, we tend to ignore salacious rumours and gossip when we're investigating crime. We look at the facts. We do not try to create panic amongst the public by spreading rumours of a killer on the loose, killing doctors by the dozen. Anything for a story, isn't that right, Mr da Costa?'

He paused, smirking. 'Are there any more questions? I'm a busy man.'

Reggie's voice broke through again. 'One more thing, detective sergeant. Was there a white feather at the crime scene?'

Glass's eyes flickered momentarily. 'A white feather? What rubbish is this? I've answered enough questions.'

Chapter Thirty-Three

Reggie drove off in the Minerva, his mind mulling over the latest death. He'd been right all along. Dr Fox had been the real target of the White Feather Murderer. How he wished that he had stayed true to his instincts, rather than identify Dr Dwight as the killer's latest victim in his report. Perhaps Fox might have survived.

There was still the question over whether this was the last victim, or if there were others on the list. He could only hope that Dusty would intercept the courier tomorrow when the Poison Pen's column was delivered to the editor of *The Truth*. It was imperative that the Poison Pen be tracked down and questioned as to his involvement in the White Feather Murders.

Detective Sergeant Glass had been adamant that Dr Fox's death was accidental, but his description of the scene suggested otherwise. A fully clothed man lying face up in the bath after being electrocuted, trying to retrieve a wireless? Implausible. What a shame that Clary had not been able to attend the scene, rather than The Undertaker. Blain would have allowed Reggie to access the house and use his advanced skills of observation to analyse what had occurred.

And there was Glass's reaction, which had not escaped Reggie's attention. That flicker of the eyes, when Reggie had asked about the white feather, was a giveaway, indicating that there had been a feather in the bathroom. Reggie had schooled himself on those brief, involuntary facial expressions, gestures, and eye movements that signalled people's true feelings, and he knew they couldn't be faked. Over the years, he had applied that knowledge when dealing with the criminal classes. Although they could be relied upon to lie, offenders could not conceal the truth on their faces.

Why pretend the feather did not exist? For reasons known only to The Undertaker, he had decided to conceal that fact. Reggie assumed that Glass was trying to avoid the necessity of interviewing suspects, searching for motives, creating links between the Poison Pen victims, and a myriad of other time-consuming tasks that a murder investigation involved. There was also the convenient death of Dr Dwight, who had been found with a feather in his hand. It wouldn't do to have two deaths attributed to the White Feather Murderer, when one would do. It was, as Clary said, a case of a detective who was lazy. And it appeared that it was up to Reggie to sniff out a killer, rather than the detective who had been assigned to the case.

As the Minerva gathered speed, Reggie regretted that Dr Fox had not confided in him. He should have taken his advice to get out of town until the danger blew over, but the murder of a fellow colleague in Dr Dwight had probably given him a false sense of security. There would be no way to ascertain if Dr Fox and Nurse Webb had known each other. If only the doctor kept a diary.

As that thought crossed his mind, Reggie braked violently and did a U-turn in front of half a dozen automobiles and cyclists, ignoring the screams and obscenities from those who had had a close brush with death. The secretary. She would know if Dr Fox had kept a diary. It was vital that he moved fast before she left the scene of the crime.

* * *

The house came into view within minutes, a constable posted outside. Reggie was relieved to see that Miss Hockstetter was sitting on the neighbour's porch, drinking a cup of tea. Most of the onlookers had moved on, now that the ambulance had driven away with the body of Dr Fox on board. The reporters had also departed, clutching notes taken from Detective Sergeant Glass's statement, which would form the basis of a report in the next day's newspapers. It didn't escape Reggie that he should be doing the same thing, but the prospect of linking Fox to Burns, Webb, or Badger was irresistible.

He approached the gate leading up to the neighbour's house and called out to the secretary, 'Miss Hockstetter, do you remember me?'

She looked up through bleary eyes and blinked twice. 'Mr Richmond, how are you?'

'Not too bad.' He pushed open the gate. 'I was passing by and I stopped to see what was going on here. I believe that Dr Fox has died in a horrible accident. Do you mind if I come in for a chat?'

The woman looked doubtful but nodded her head. She put her cup and saucer down on the bench and placed her hands in her lap.

'How can I help you, Mr Richmond?'

Reggie's mind was working fast. 'The fact is that I have this problem with my memory, Miss Hockstetter. Dr Fox was most helpful. He recommended that I make an appointment with one of his colleagues, an expert in the field, but I've forgotten the name. So silly of me, and I've lost the piece of paper that he gave me. Would he have written it down anywhere, do you think?'

Miss Hockstetter was nodding her head. 'Indeed, yes. Dr Fox was obsessive about record-keeping. He was amazing that way.' A tear rolled down her cheek.

Reggie stroked his moustache. 'He was a wonderful doctor. He even suggested that I keep a journal as an aid to memory. I was most impressed. I gained the impression that he had found that useful too.'

'You're quite right. Dr Fox was a great believer in diaries. He told me once that they helped him reflect on his life: his achievements and challenges, as well as documenting information that could be useful in his future endeavours.' She clasped her hands together and let out a sob.

'I'm sorry to cause you such pain, dear lady,' said Reggie. 'The death of Dr Fox is such a loss to the medical profession.'

Miss Hockstetter wiped her eyes. 'That's so kind of you. I need to go into the office tomorrow. Perhaps I could have a look for that name if you would like to come in?'

'Thank you so much, Miss Hockstetter. I do appreciate it, but on second thoughts, I shouldn't bother you. I'll come back in a week.'

Reggie glanced at Fox's house and noted that the constable was leaving.

The secretary stood up and put her handbag on her arm. 'I think that I'll go home. This has been extremely upsetting.'

'Can I show you to your automobile?'

'I take the tram. It stops near my house. Tomorrow, I'll need to talk to the other doctors and find out what I'm to do. I hope that I'll still have a job.'

'You seem very capable, Miss Hockstetter. They will not want to lose you.'

The secretary smiled through her tears. 'Poor Dr Fox. Such a good man. It's such a shame.'

She went out through the gate, then walked slowly down the road towards the tram stop.

The doctor's house was deserted. It wouldn't be long before solicitors were involved, and family too, if Fox had one. He had to move fast. It was the perfect opportunity to check the house for his diaries. Perhaps they might reveal whether Miss Webb and he had been acquainted, and, hopefully, provide a motivation for his murder.

He opened the gate and took the path down the side of the house, which was hidden from view by a line of trees. Halfway down was an open window. He peered through it and realised that it must be the bathroom where the body had been found.

Reggie pushed the window up to its full extent and, using the window frame for leverage, squeezed through the gap, his foot reaching for the floor on the other side. He groaned as one of his expensive, two-toned shoes filled with water. The bath was right below the window, the same bath in which the body of Dr Fox had lain submerged. After extracting his foot, Reggie grimaced at the dark stain that was spreading across the leather.

Showing the single-mindedness and determination that marked him as Melbourne's premier crime reporter, Reggie tried to block out the sound of his squelching shoe as he considered if there were another way in. But a quick reconnoitre around the house revealed that the back door was locked, as were the other windows. This was the only entrance available.

Reggie had read somewhere that necessity was the mother of invention, a handy phrase that could be applied to his present situation. In the shed at the back of the house, he found a tool with a hook on the end. Just the thing, he thought, to empty the bathtub. He returned to the window and angled the implement so that it slipped through the ring of the bath plug. He lifted it, then watched with satisfaction as the water drained away.

Once inside, Reggie removed his wet shoe and dried it as best he could with a towel, wrung out his sock, and hung it over the edge of the bath. Hobbling down the hallway, he found the sitting room, which doubled as a study. Above the desk was a glass-panelled bookcase with medical dictionaries, journals, and psychiatric tomes arranged neatly. On the top shelf was a collection of black, leather-bound diaries, their dates in gold lettering on the spine.

Reggie took down the first one and thumbed through it, noting the references to Fox's life in the country, his schooling, and his family, and, revealingly, his employment as a butcher in an abattoir. The Poison Pen's allegation was accurate. Fox's handwriting was neat and regular, although the entries were relatively childish and immature. He put the first diary back on the shelf and took down the ones covering the war years.

Reggie skimmed through the 1915-1916 diary. There were comments about being a medical orderly, his pride in his work, and how he wanted to better himself and be regarded as an equal by the medical staff.

The 1917 volume was devoted wholly to his time on the Western Front. A couple of comments caught his eye. He was referred to as 'Dr Fox' by the patients. Many of the entries detailed the nature of the operations he performed, meticulous and precise in their descriptions, and, ultimately, gruesome in nature. It was clear that he was no longer regarded as a medical orderly, but as a skilled and experienced surgeon. How Fox had ever managed to trick the medical staff into accepting him as one of their own was beyond Reggie's comprehension. A butcher and now, a surgeon. Only the chaos of war could explain it. Yet, Reggie had to question the wisdom of chronicling his journey from slaughterman to respected medico by committing it to print. It was obvious that Fox had been brazen in his deception and overconfident, believing that his duplicity would never be exposed. How wrong he had been.

Reggie had no desire to abscond with the complete set, so he chose the 1917 and 1918 diaries and three of the post-war volumes. Surely, he would find enough in them to satisfy his curiosity.

He pushed the remaining diaries along the shelf so that there were no gaps, and closed the glass door of the bookcase, then hobbled back down the hall to the bathroom, put on his sock and shoe, and exited through the window.

Sitting in the Minerva minutes later, the diaries lying on the seat next to him, Reggie's mind was firmly fixed on one question. It wasn't whether the diaries would reveal Fox's connection to the other victims of the Poison Pen, but rather whether his shoe could be restored to its original state or become the ultimate sacrifice in the cause of crime detection? He feared that it would be the latter.

Chapter Thirty-Four

It had been a particularly busy Thursday for Dusty Rhodes. Around ten o'clock, he had arrived unannounced at the door of Mr and Mrs Longfellow, parents of one of the patients who had been under the care of Nurse Webb at The Melbourne Hospital. He had found it to be a gruelling experience, the grief of the parents still raw, despite the time that had passed. Surprisingly, they had invited him in. He gained the impression that talking about their daughter was better than trying to forget the circumstances of her death.

'Charlotte was such a sweet girl. She'd do anything for you,' said the mother, touching the tip of a handkerchief to a teary eye. 'Only twenty when she died.' She picked up a photograph in a silver frame and showed it to Dusty. The young woman was petite and fair-haired, fragile-looking. 'She fell from a horse when she was young. Suffered terribly from back pain.'

'How awful for her.'

'She bore her suffering with grace and dignity, but you could see the signs on her face.'

'The doctors were planning to operate?'

'They were trying to get her pain under control by trying different drugs.'

The father broke in angrily. 'That woman stole her painkillers. She let our daughter suffer. How a human being could do that to another is beyond me.'

'You found out?'

'Only by chance. One of the nurses was suspicious. When I went to the hospital administrator about it, he refused to confirm it. It came out later that she'd been stealing the drugs from other patients too. The hospital hushed it up. They refused to give us any information until we threatened to go to the newspapers. By that stage, Webb had been dismissed.'

'Your daughter died?'

Mrs Longfellow let out a sigh. 'We brought her home. She was in agony.'

'She took her own life,' added her husband.

There was silence for a time.

'When was your daughter a patient there?'

Mr Longfellow frowned. 'Why are you asking us these questions? We've been through all this before with your reporter. Why don't you talk to him?'

Dusty was perplexed. 'A reporter from *The Argus*?'

'That's right.'

'What was his name?'

The couple looked at each other, then the wife spoke. 'Reggie da Costa. That's it.'

Dusty was at first dumbstruck but recovered quickly. Reggie would never have sent him on a wild goose chase if he had interviewed the Longfellows already. The only possibility was that the 'reporter from *The Argus*' had impersonated Reggie to get information on Nurse Webb. Dusty ran his fingers through his hair, thinking how he should get to the bottom of the matter.

'What did he look like?'

'Average-looking. Thin. Dark suit. Why do you ask?'

'No reason. I'm sorry to make you go through all this again. When did Reggie meet with you?'

'It would have been early September,' said the husband.

'This was before the attempt on Miss Webb's life?'

'I suppose it was,' said the woman. 'I saw the article he wrote in early November. We met him weeks before that.'

'Can you remember what he asked you?'

Mrs Longfellow paused, thinking back. 'How we found out about what Nurse Webb was doing. What effect it had on Charlotte. What the hospital told us. He wanted the details. We told him as much as we could.'

'He said that he knew where Webb lived and told us that he intended to question her personally about our daughter,' added the husband. 'He asked whether there was any message that we'd like to pass on to her. I told him to tell her that she was evil and that I wished she was dead.'

Mrs Longfellow reached out and stroked his arm. 'Enough, darling.' She turned to Dusty. 'I think you should go.'

As he left the house, Dusty's emotions fluctuated between dejection and elation. On the one hand, he felt sympathy for the Longfellows and what they had suffered. On the other hand, he was buoyed by what he had learned from them. The killer had impersonated Reggie to learn more about Beryl Webb's addiction and the damage that she had done, providing him with information that had appeared in the Poison Pen's column. The impostor had also told the bereaved couple that he knew Webb's address and intended to visit her. Given that the Poison Pen's column contained a description of Webb's living conditions, it was clear that either the killer or the columnist had visited the house before the attempt on her life. How else could he have described her as 'wallowing in the filth of a back room, the blinds drawn against the world outside' without having seen it for himself?

Reggie and he were making headway in the White Feather Murders case. For the first time, a shadowy figure had emerged, gathering evidence against one of his targets for publication in the Poison Pen column. Reggie would be pleased.

* * *

Dusty spent the rest of Thursday morning tracking down Jim McTavish, using the address that Ruby had found in the members' file at Temperance Hall. Although McTavish was no longer living with his wife and children, due to the intervention of Mrs Burns, a neighbour told Dusty where he could be found, which was at a worksite two miles away.

'They fought like cats and dogs after he got back from the war. Too much booze,' she added. 'It didn't surprise me when she kicked him out. How do you know him?'

'He's an old family friend, although I haven't seen him in years. What does he look like these days?'

He headed off with a brief description of Jim McTavish in his head. On arriving at the building site, his eyes roamed around the construction workers until they settled on the man he was seeking. McTavish, a thin rake of a man, wearing moleskin trousers, a khaki shirt, and heavy work boots, was sitting on the trunk of a fallen tree. He was in his late thirties, tanned from the sun, and with prematurely white hair and clear blue eyes. Dusty wandered up to him, feigning interest in the frame of the house that was starting to take shape.

'Mind if I ask you about the company you work for?' he asked him. 'I'm in search of a job.'

'What trade are you in?'

'I'm a bit of an odd job man. A bit of carpentry, plumbing, labouring. Have you worked here long?'

'Since I left school, apart from when I served overseas,' McTavish said. 'They're a good company to work for and they pay reasonably well.'

'Enough to support a wife and child?'

McTavish's face darkened. 'Depends on whether you're keeping two households, like I am.'

Dusty pulled a face. 'Sorry to hear that, mate. Women want the world these days, if you ask me.'

'You're right there.' McTavish spat in the dirt. 'My wife got caught up in that temperance movement. Bloody wowsers. They talked her into leaving me. They said I was a bad influence on my kids. It's true that I've got a bit of a temper when I've drunk a bit, but it's all talk, you know? I never touched a hair on her head.'

'Ridiculous the way they go on about the so-called evils of drinking,' agreed Dusty. 'What's a beer or two with friends?'

'That's what I said.'

'You put a roof over their heads, food on the table. You deserve some sort of reward for your efforts.'

McTavish nodded his head. 'I even promised her that I'd come home straight after work, not go to the pub, but that wasn't good enough for her. That wretched woman told her to go, and she did.'

Dusty looked shocked. 'A woman talked her into it? Who has the right to break up a marriage? Who was she?'

'Mrs Burns, the president of the temperance union.' McTavish spat again.

'If it were me,' said Dusty, 'I would have told her to mind her own business. That's what I would have done.'

'She wouldn't see me, so I wrote to her. Never got an answer.'

'That's shocking. It's a wonder someone didn't wring her neck, interfering like that.'

McTavish nodded slowly, his fists clenching and unclenching. 'She got what she deserved in the end. She's dead.'

'Dead? How come?'

The man snorted. 'She drank herself to death. What a hypocrite.' McTavish got down off the tree trunk and wiped his hands on his overalls. 'You know, my wife won't take me back.'

'That's terrible.' Dusty checked his watch. 'I should be going. I'll let you get back to work. Sorry to hear about your troubles. Best of luck, mate.'

'Thanks.' Jim McTavish rallied. 'Go speak to the boss if you're interested. I'll put in a good word for you, if you want a job here.'

They shook hands, and McTavish walked away.

Dusty slid into the driver's seat of his Australian Six and watched as the man put on his tool belt and went back to work. Dusty considered himself a reasonable judge of character, but he couldn't read Jim McTavish. It was hard to align the different faces of the man: a former soldier with a temper, who drank too much and argued forcibly with his wife, as opposed to the man who missed his family and claimed that he had never been violent towards them. McTavish had been upfront about his hatred of Mrs Burns, not hiding his delight that she was dead. Whether he was capable of murder was another matter.

He started the motorcar and drove back to *The Argus*, with the intention of typing up a record of his conversations with the Longfellows and McTavish while they were still fresh in his memory. That would leave thirty minutes to have a bite to eat and get to the offices of *The Truth* in time to intercept the courier. With another column due out the next day and another life potentially in danger, it was essential that Dusty gain the cooperation of the courier and find out where the Poison Pen lived. He patted his pocket in which lay a £1 banknote. Payment for information.

Dusty parked his automobile outside the *Argus* building and headed up the stairs to the newsroom. It was relatively quiet in the early afternoon, given that some of his colleagues were out and about chasing stories or taking a long lunch. It would be bedlam later in the day, with last minute reports being hammered out on typewriters, telephones ringing, people yelling, the office boy dashing from one reporter to another; in short, a mad scramble to meet the afternoon's deadline.

His task completed and the record of the conversations on Reggie's desk, Dusty checked his watch and realised that he needed to get going. He had twenty minutes to get to *The Truth*, which should be more than enough. He took an apple from his desk drawer and was about to take a bite when he heard the thin, reedy voice of Curtis Flange, head of the crime desk, calling his name.

'William! William!'

No one else called him that, except for his mother when she had been angry with him.

Dusty turned. 'Yes, Mr Flange?'

'I need you to do something for me.'

'I'm busy, sir. Can it wait an hour?'

'Indeed, no. Come into my office.'

Dusty put the apple down and followed him, experiencing a sinking feeling as he looked up at the clock, its hands slowly edging towards two o'clock.

Flange flipped through the loose papers on his desk, muttering to himself in frustration. At last, he waved a wad of papers at him. 'These reports need to be typed up and delivered to the typesetters *post-haste*.'

'Can't your secretary do that, Mr Flange? I'm on an errand for Reggie, and it's very important.'

Flange frowned and fiddled with his bow tie. 'May I remind you, William, that I am your boss, not Reginald. When I ask you to do something, you do it. Understand?'

'But this relates to the White Feather Murders. It's crucial to identifying the killer.'

'White feathers? What on earth are you talking about?'

'Reggie briefed you last week. The White Feather Murders.'

Flange shook his head. 'I thought he was talking about birds, not murders. How can birds have anything to do with crime? Unless someone is shooting them. He should explain things better. I had more important things on my mind, including the Melbourne Debutante Ball. The Lord Mayor was holding a reception that night for the young ladies. The cream of Melbourne society was going to be in attendance.' His eyes shone at the memory. 'Beautiful, young ladies from rich families. Lovely gowns and eye-watering jewellery. Simply divine.' He went silent, his mind miles away.

'Mr Flange, I must go. It's a matter of life or death.'

Flange sighed as he registered Dusty's frustration. 'Oh, very well, but I want you back here at three o'clock sharp. Understood?'

Dusty nodded his head and took off, taking the stairs at double pace. He started his motorcar and pulled away from the curb, merging into the traffic as he headed for the offices of *The Truth*. Ominously, the town hall clock was chiming two.

Minutes later, Dusty pulled up outside the building and stared up at the entrance, despair taking hold of him. He was five minutes late. What if the courier had been and gone? Inside, he joined the line of people queued up in front of the reception desk. As each person reached the front, he tried to see if any of them was holding an envelope, but hope faded as he reached second spot in the queue. He tapped his foot in frustration as the woman ahead of him addressed the receptionist.

'The chap next door plays his violin at all hours of the day and night,' she whined. 'He claims to be the reincarnation of Niccolo Paganini, but his playing sounds so squeaky and scratchy that he puts my teeth on edge. It's a disgrace. The council and the police won't do anything about him. I want to speak to a reporter.'

The receptionist sighed. She handed the woman a form and asked her to fill in her name and address.

'A reporter will be in touch, I promise you.'

The receptionist's demeanour changed when she saw Dusty. A smile lit up her face. 'Dusty Rhodes. Fancy seeing you back here. How are you, sweetheart?'

'Fine, thanks, Tilly. It's good to see you again.'

'You too, love. What can I do for you?'

'There's a courier who comes here every second Thursday at two o'clock. He drops off an envelope addressed to the editor. Have I missed him?'

'You're in luck. Ordinarily, you'd have been too late, but we had a telephone call earlier advising that he'd be here at four o'clock sharp.'

Dusty breathed a sigh of relief. 'That's good. You don't know which company he works for, do you?'

'Sorry, love. I reckon it's a private arrangement between him and the bloke he delivers for. If you like, I'll point him out to you when he arrives. That's the best I can do.'

'Thanks Tilly. I'd appreciate that.'

He headed out into the street, relieved that he didn't have to tell Reggie that he'd messed up completely. He'd been lucky, that was for sure. He should have driven directly to *The Truth* instead of going back to work, taking the risk of being delayed by the likes of Curtis Flange. But at least he had a second chance. And he'd make sure that he was back at *The Truth* long before the courier came, hopefully accompanied by Reggie.

A lot hinged on getting the courier's cooperation. If they were unsuccessful in tracking down the Poison Pen, one more life might be at risk. Tomorrow, his column would be published. Another person, unnamed but with clues as to their identity, would be vilified and possibly murdered. And the timing of the column and subsequent murders meant that it was becoming increasingly hard for anyone, including the police, to carry out a proper investigation into each of these murders when there was so little time between them. Making headway in their enquiries was almost impossible, given the differing backgrounds of the victims and the *modus operandi* used by the perpetrator. There was nothing to connect them, not even a weapon. The only common threads were the Poison Pen column and the existence of a white feather at each crime scene.

Dusty shrugged his shoulders as he asked himself the inevitable question: Why?

If only he knew the answers.

Chapter Thirty-Five

Clary Blain was watching the entrance door to the Duke of Wellington Hotel, waiting for Reggie to arrive. He'd left a message at *The Argus* asking for Reggie to join him as soon as possible, but there was no sign of him. The death of Dr Fox had rattled the detective, coming so soon after Dr Dwight's murder. What if Reggie were right? What if Fox were the target, rather than Dwight? Aligned with Clary's desire to discuss the case with Reggie was his need to confide in someone he trusted, who could advise him on what he should do, now that his career appeared to be going up in smoke. Earlier that morning, he had met with Homer Glass and demanded an update on the deaths that seemed to be happening with monotonous regularity in Melbourne.

'I'm working on them, sir,' sniffed Glass. 'I remind you that I have a lot to deal with, what with my focus being on counterfeit currency.'

'We have four deaths, detective sergeant: Mrs Burns, Captain Badger, Dr Dwight, and Dr Fox, as well as the attempted murder of Miss Webb.'

Glass was unperturbed. 'I don't understand why you're concerned. I've read the case notes. Three of them were accidents. Burns drank too much. Webb left the gas on. Fox drowned. Only Dr Dwight's and Badger's deaths look suspicious. Dwight was the victim of a robbery gone wrong and Badger was shot by persons unknown at this stage.'

Blain shook his head. 'My source says there's a link between four of them. A white feather at the scene of each crime. Have you investigated that?'

Glass pulled a face. 'That's not true. It was two white feathers, not four. And it doesn't mean that the crimes are connected. You'd take the word of a crime reporter over mine?'

'That's not what I'm saying. It's not only the feather; it's more than that. Each of these people—Burns, Webb, Badger, and Fox—were mentioned in *The Truth*. Within days, three of them were dead. I've read the report on Fox, and it's ridiculous to suggest that he drowned in the bath.'

'I have explained how it happened. I should think that my report would be good enough for you. Besides, the Poison Pen doesn't mention names, so it's debatable whether these are the people he's talking about in his column.'

Clary went red in the face. 'I don't like your tone, detective sergeant. I'm unhappy with your investigations into these deaths. If it hadn't been for me hounding you, Badger would be listed as a suicide, and we wouldn't be looking for the culprit. And, while I'm asking difficult questions, what were you doing at The Stockade on the night of Horace Striker's Hallowe'en party?'

His question came from out of the blue, unsettling the detective sergeant. Glass took a moment to recover, then he snarled, 'Your mate, da Costa. I should have known.'

'This has nothing to do with Reggie. Why were you there?'

'I can't tell you, sir. It's confidential.'

Blain was at first rendered speechless at this blatant breach of respect, but he quickly recovered. 'You're a brazen, bent copper, Glass. You have the top brass fooled, but you don't fool me. I'll hound you out of the Force if it's the last thing I do.'

Glass looked him up and down. 'No one will listen to you, *sir*. You're the past. I'm the future.'

'We'll see about that. You'll get what's coming to you.'

* * *

Hours later, with Reggie nowhere to be seen, it looked like Clary was destined to stew over his deteriorating relationship with Glass alone.

Blain sighed as he shifted in his chair and eyed the entrance to the pub. Where was Reggie? The switchboard operator had said that he was due back

170

soon, but that was an hour ago. He went up to the bar. 'If Reggie comes, tell him I've been and gone.'

'Certainly, Mr Blain,' replied the bartender. 'Are you sure that I can't get you a drink, sir?'

'Nah. I've lost my taste for it. Maybe next time.'

He walked out, his shoulders slumped, his back stooped, as if he were carrying a heavy burden. How was he going to prove that Glass was not worthy to wear the badge? With no immediate solution in sight and the relationship between the two of them deteriorating fast, Clary clung to the hope that the detective sergeant would make a mistake, but doubts assailed him.

As he entered the main office of the Criminal Investigation Branch, the room went silent. He was aware of ten pairs of eyes watching him. Whatever was going on, it was bad news. One of the constables nodded his head at him and shifted his eyes in the direction of the Chief Commissioner's office. The message was clear that he was in trouble.

Homer Glass had his head down over his desk, but the smirk on his face did not escape Blain's attention.

One of the detectives beckoned to him. 'The Chief wants to see you, Clary. Good luck.'

'Thanks.'

He hitched up his trousers and straightened his tie, then strode purposefully towards Blamey's office. He knocked on the door and heard a muffled reply indicating that he should enter.

'Take a seat, Blain.' Blamey shuffled some papers on his desk before finding the document that he was seeking.

'I have received an official complaint about you, detective inspector,' he said. 'It has come to my attention that, earlier today, you deliberately provoked and harassed one of your fellow officers, Detective Sergeant Glass. He has accused you of interfering in his investigation into several murder cases, and that you questioned his judgment. He asserts that you have been sharing police information with a member of the press. What's even worse is that you have been seen drinking on duty. I believe that you recently attended a local hotel before you returned to this office, is that correct?'

'Indeed, I did, sir. I had arranged to meet one of my sources, who has information on the Squizzy Taylor murder.'

'And did he arrive?'

'He did not, sir.'

'Have you been drinking? Look me in the eyes, Blain, and answer me honestly.'

'I state plainly that no drink has passed my lips today. If you doubt me, you may smell my breath.' He sent out an unspoken thank you to Reggie for not turning up.

'That will not be necessary, Blain. I'll return to the complaints against you shortly. What is your progress on the Squizzy Taylor and John Cutmore case?'

'Three men have been arrested for vagrancy; two of them answered the descriptions of the men who accompanied Squizzy to Cutmore's house. One was the driver, the other went inside with Taylor. They were found on Seymour railway station in the refreshment rooms, waiting for the Sydney Express train. The obvious explanation was that they were trying to avoid apprehension by heading for New South Wales. They have been returned to Melbourne for questioning.

'My final report will conclude that the shootings of Leslie Taylor and John Cutmore were the outcome of happenings originating in Sydney, when Norman Bruhn was murdered. In short, Taylor and Cutmore had history. Eleven shots were fired inside Cutmore's house, resulting in their deaths. The coronial inquest concluded that the bullets were fired by the two deceased men, with others present being interested spectators, nothing more.'

Blamey grunted. 'I'll expect that report on my desk tomorrow. What do you have to say to the other assertions brought against you?'

'They are baseless, sir. As Glass's superior officer, it is my duty to know how police investigations are progressing, and to check if there is a need for advice or support in bringing those investigations to a satisfactory conclusion. As for my contacts in the press and otherwise, they provide me with useful information. I couldn't do my job without them.'

'Glass claims that you defamed him by suggesting that he was associating with the criminal classes when he attended an event at The Stockade.'

'My source said that Glass was waiting for someone.'

'Does that not tally with his comments to me that he wanted information from a snitch?'

'In plain view of Melbourne's gang leaders? That's hard to believe.' He took a breath. 'I believe that Detective Sergeant Glass is not making genuine efforts to uncover the truth around the deaths that followed the publication of *The Truth*'s Poison Pen column. Information has come my way that a white feather has been found at three of the five crime scenes, but Glass does not wish to pursue it.'

Blamey sat back in his chair, studying Clary Blain. 'I have no wish to examine the intricacies of these five cases with you. I trust my men, including Detective Sergeant Glass, and I suggest that you should too. However, in the light of the complaint made against you, I suggest that you take three days' leave from your duties to reflect upon your place in the Victoria Police. Glass has done outstanding work, absolutely outstanding work, on the counterfeiting rackets in Melbourne. I will not have his reputation tarnished. Do you understand?'

Blain was astounded by this development. He squared his shoulders and rose from the seat. 'You are standing me down?'

'I am, detective inspector.'

'That's your prerogative, sir, but I believe that you're making a mistake. You should be looking at Glass, not me.'

'That will be all, Blain. Your leave commences on Monday.'

As he walked from the room, Clary held his head high, full of resolve that no inexperienced or dodgy upstart from New South Wales would throw his career into jeopardy. If Glass wanted a fight to the death, he'd get one. But, despite his show of bravado, Clary feared the worst.

Chapter Thirty-Six

As he settled onto the couch after dinner at Ruby's house, Reggie was totally unaware of the ructions going on in the Criminal Investigation Branch, and the slippery slope that Clary Blain's career was on. If he had to give his opinion on the trustworthiness of either of the two adversaries, he would have chosen the detective inspector any day. It was clear to him that The Undertaker was a shifty character, whose reputation was based on outcomes rather than methods. He had heard enough from his Sydney colleagues to know that Glass was inclined to shoot first and ask questions later, as well as falsify evidence to prove that he was justified in taking the action that he did.

'The Undertaker was doing nicely until he went too far,' Warren T Warren, alias 'Rabbit,' a reporter with *The Sydney Morning Herald*, told him. 'He forced members of the public to act as undercover police agents, and one of them died. Before the truth came out about his strong-arm tactics, Glass moved to Victoria and joined your police force. The New South Wales coppers buried the story because it didn't make them look good. Glass was able to start afresh without a blot on his reputation.'

'Do you reckon he's crooked?' Reggie asked the reporter.

'No doubt about it,' confirmed Rabbit.

That opinion had been enough for Reggie. He trusted his interstate colleague implicitly. And, as he turned his mind to the diaries that he had brought back from Dr Fox's house, he put aside the machinations of the former detective from Sydney who was trying to oust his good friend and contact, Clary Blain.

Ruby finished her cup of tea. 'Can I ask you something before we start reading these diaries?'

'Of course. What is it?'

'Have you heard how things are going with your mother?'

'I spoke to her before I came here.'

'Did she speak to Mrs Bardsley Smith about the ladies making fun of her? That business with Damien and the garage?'

'She did. Apparently, Mildred had words with them today. They apologised.'

'And were they nice to her after that?'

'Mother says that they wouldn't dare go against Mildred, but she caught one of them sniggering behind her back. She is taking your advice to call their bluff, but I know how much that hurts her.'

'Poor Mavis. People are cruel.'

Reggie nodded his head. 'You gave her good advice. Let's hope that it works.'

'When's the next Poison Pen column coming out?'

'Tomorrow.'

'Why don't the police put a stop to it, Reggie? Why don't they order *The Truth* not to publish it?'

'You'd need a court order to do that. I doubt if *The Truth* would take any notice of it anyway.'

'You still don't have an address for the Poison Pen?'

'Unfortunately, no. We did manage to intercept the courier, but he wouldn't divulge the identity or address of the Poison Pen. Even £1 failed to persuade him. He's paid well to keep a secret.'

'What did he say when you interviewed him?'

'Virtually nothing. He wouldn't cooperate at all. I sensed that he might be afraid of his employer.'

'Was he young?'

Reggie shook his head. 'In his late thirties. His cheek was badly scarred, probably from the war. I noticed that he was wearing military identification discs around his neck.'

'Why didn't you follow him after he left *The Truth*?'

'There was no point. He wasn't going back to the Poison Pen's house. He'd already been there.'

'Poor Dusty. He was upset that he didn't get to *The Truth* on time. I hope you weren't too hard on him.'

'I don't blame him for that. Dusty couldn't afford to disobey Flange. At least we got back there in time to speak to the courier at four o'clock. But it was a waste of time in the end.'

Ruby touched his hand. 'Don't dwell on it. You couldn't have done any more.'

'It's frustrating,' admitted Reggie. 'It was the only way to find the Poison Pen. And now, that's gone.'

'Something else will turn up, I'm sure. Are you going to name Dr Fox as the fourth victim, instead of Dr Dwight?'

'There's not enough evidence yet to prove the target was Fox. That's why we need these diaries. Hopefully, they show that Fox and Webb knew each other. Once I have that, I can publish my report.'

He looked at her, a smile on his face, his eyes taking in her flame-red hair and her lovely, green eyes. 'Let's forget about murder for a while. I was lucky to find you, Ruby. I can't imagine any other fiancée showing an interest in my work. If Dusty hadn't invited me to his twenty-first birthday party, I might never have met you. And now, it's only a month to our wedding.'

Ruby smiled. 'Horace says everything is in readiness. He says that the decorations are in storage at The Stockade, and the food and drinks are on order. He's been so kind, even if he is on the wrong side of the Law. Sometimes, I forget that he's a gangster as well as a friend. I wonder what people will think if he agrees to walk me down the aisle.' She studied Reggie's stylish navy jacket, with its wide lapels and red pocket handkerchief. 'I can't wait to see your wedding suit. No doubt, you'll put me in the shade.'

Reggie took her hand. 'Never, my love.'

Ruby laughed. 'I know what you're thinking. You want to be admired as much as the bride.'

He stroked his moustache, a smile on his lips. 'That reminds me. I need to make an appointment with the barber. Can't have my Ronald Colman moustache growing wild.'

'Indeed, no, that would be a catastrophe. Let's get to work, Reggie, and stop thinking about how handsome you will look.'

'Quite right,' he said, handing her the 1917 diary. 'You start with this one. I'll check 1918.'

'Remind me what we're looking for?' asked Ruby.

'Any mention of Beryl Webb. Any link to Badger or Burns, too. Any change to his status amongst the soldiers. Being called "Dr Fox," for example.'

After five minutes, Ruby broke the silence. 'You might want to mark the 4th of February. He's at a Regimental Aid Post located in one of the trenches at the rear of the battlefield. A patient called him "doctor."'

'Interesting. What's his role there?'

'He says that he assesses the wounded, changes bandages, and administers morphine. The conditions sound dreadful. He talks about a gas attack. They covered the regimental aid post with blankets to stop the gas seeping in.'

She turned a few pages. 'He's moved to a casualty clearing station. He's operating on soldiers. This is awful, Reggie. So much blood and yet he seems to almost enjoy it. Perhaps not "enjoy," but it's not healthy the way he describes amputations and surgery. He's so detached. Like it doesn't bother him at all. I'd be totally squeamish if it were me.'

She read on. 'This is interesting. It's September 1917. He's been moved to a field hospital not far from Ypres. He says that some new nurses have joined them. I wonder if Beryl Webb is amongst them?' She skimmed a few pages. 'He mentions them by name, but she's not there.'

She put the diary down. 'I'll get us a bottle of wine. This might take a while.'

While she was out in the kitchen, Reggie read about the influx of wounded soldiers into the field hospitals after the Battle of Amiens in August 1918. Despite his misgivings about Fox, Reggie found his account riveting. Around 2000 Australians were among the casualties. Fox described the pressure of setting bones, cleaning wounds, and performing amputations. He had been accepted as one of the medical staff and was working hard in trying conditions. His journal entries conflicted with the accusations made against him in the Poison Pen column. Fox appeared to be dedicated and diligent, not a butcher let loose in a slaughterhouse.

Ruby reappeared with a bottle and poured two glasses of wine. 'What have you found out, Reggie?'

'Herman Fox is not as bad as you think. He seems to have saved a few lives. He takes his job seriously.'

After ten minutes, Reggie let out a whoop. 'Got her. Beryl Webb. She's been assigned to the London hospital where Fox is working.' He took a sip of wine and read on. 'There appears to be an instant attraction between them. He likes talking to her and she admires him. Let's see where this goes.'

Reggie moved closer to Ruby. 'Listen to this. "Beryl and I are stepping out tonight. She is very useful."' Reggie raised an eyebrow. 'That's a strange expression to use for a lover.' He continued. '"She encourages me to try different treatments with my patients. The use of electrical therapies seems to excite her. I haven't confessed to her about my lack of qualifications, but I think that she knows. She said something the other night about how certificates and academic degrees mean little in real life, then she looked at me in a meaningful way. I must have given something away in what I said. However, she seems besotted with me, and I'll take advantage of that. I've found her weakness too, which I will exploit."'

'What does that mean?' asked Ruby.

'I have no idea, but it may be her predilection to morphine. This is looking like a most unhealthy relationship.'

'I wonder what Miss Webb would think if she read this,' said Ruby, taking up her glass. 'Do you know if she's still in the rehabilitation hospital?'

Reggie looked at her thoughtfully. 'I don't know, but I'll put Dusty on her tail. We've got Dr Fox's side of the story in these diaries. It would be interesting to hear Beryl Webb's version.'

Reggie flipped over a few pages and began to read. '"Beryl has given me a list of patients who would benefit from electrical therapy. She says they're cowards, and I agree with her." Fox goes on to describe how he uses electrodes to cure soldiers who won't or can't speak. It's sickening.'

CHAPTER THIRTY-SIX

'That's terrible. Who could do that?' cried Ruby.

Reggie frowned. 'It's a form of torture, carried out by a sadist. Fox forced one poor patient to walk by threatening him with more electrical therapy. *Therapy?*' He shook his head, disgusted. 'Listen to what he says: "I have to say that working in this hospital has its advantages. No interfering friends or family. Colleagues either collude with you or look the other way. This is a whole new world of psychiatric medicine. Why use a laboratory animal when you can experiment on a human being?"' Reggie scowled. 'I take back what I said about Fox before. He's a monster.'

'I don't think I want to hear anymore, Reggie. It's horrible. Beryl Webb and Herman Fox were treating these poor soldiers as guinea pigs. Those men were traumatised by what they saw on the battlefield. They weren't cowards.' She shook her head in disgust. 'Fox deserved to be punished after what he did. Forgive me for saying it, but it's true. God knows how many people he hurt.'

Reggie placed his hand over hers. 'Enough. No more. I'll take these home and read through the rest of them by myself.' He finished his wine and put the glass back on the tray. 'I think that we've learned what we needed to know about Dr Fox and Nurse Webb. If there's anything more, I'll find it, not you.'

Ruby looked up at him. 'I thought that the Poison Pen was just another rumourmonger, a spreader of lies and gossip. But there's something serious in his intention. He's after revenge, I think. If it's not the Poison Pen, it's the person giving him this information. These people did real harm and should be punished for it.'

'You think they deserve to be murdered?'

'Of course not. In my opinion, it should be up to a judge and jury to deliver a verdict of guilty, not the White Feather Murderer.'

'You're right.' He gathered up the diaries and put them in his bag. 'These journals have proved that two of the victims knew each other. But it still doesn't explain the white feather. I mean, how were they cowards?'

As Reggie put on his hat and prepared to leave, the telephone rang in the hallway. Ruby answered it. 'It's for you,' she said.

He took the earpiece from her and raised an eyebrow as he recognised the voice on the other end.

'Reggie, it's me, Clary. Sorry to bother you at Ruby's, but I've been trying to get in contact with you. This afternoon Glass arrested someone for the murder of Captain Badger.'

'Who is it, Clary? His former wife?'

'No, mate. It's her brother, Herbert.'

Chapter Thirty-Seven

Reggie sat at his desk on Friday morning, twirling the white feather that he'd found at Beryl Webb's house. It seemed that his theory about the deaths being linked was losing traction, given the information that Clary Blain had imparted the previous evening. A review of Captain Badger's financial transactions had revealed certain amounts were being paid regularly into the bank account of Herbert Hawke, the brother of the former Mrs Badger. It appeared that blackmail was involved.

In a way, it didn't come as a surprise to Reggie after he had met the siblings in Geelong. While the sister was plainly dressed and lived in a cheaply furnished home, the brother could afford the latest in men's fashion and drove a new Summit motorcar which, Reggie knew, was equipped with a radio, cigarette lighter, and electric stop lights. Not the sort of automobile owned by an unemployed man who was looking for 'opportunities.' The money to finance his lifestyle had to have come from somewhere. And it was clear that his sister was not benefitting from her brother's illegal activities.

Clary told him that The Undertaker had interviewed Herbert and, faced with the irrefutable proof that he was blackmailing his brother-in-law, Herbert Hawke had broken down and confessed. The Honourable Member had a lot to lose if his bigamous status were revealed. At risk was his second marriage, his reputation as an advocate for the sanctity of the family, and his career as a member of the Legislative Assembly. Herbert had taken advantage of that and had accepted payment for his silence. And, when one took into consideration that Herbert's Summit motorcar was seen parked in the street near Badger's house on the day he died, the case against Agnes's brother became much stronger. Herbert had motive and opportunity.

'It's clear that he was there,' Clary told Reggie. 'He doesn't deny it, but, unlike his sister, he claims that Badger was alive when he left him. He knew Agnes was catching a train to see her ex-husband, and he wanted to meet with Badger before she made it to Melbourne. He drove up the Geelong Road while she was on the train and arrived at the house about an hour before she did.'

'What was his motivation?'

'That I don't know, and he's not saying. Perhaps he saw it as his last chance to extort money from the man. Or maybe he wanted to try to keep the blackmail quiet. Imagine if Agnes found out that her own brother had made money from her suffering? She'd never forgive him.

'What's certain is that he could see that Badger's telegram was going to bring on a confrontation with his sister. Badger threatened her. He was going to sue Agnes if she spoke to the newspapers again, and Herbert knew that she wouldn't be silenced. In Agnes's view, she had little to lose. But inadvertently, she was implicated when Badger turned up dead. Both Herbert and Agnes became suspects when their respective visits to Badger's house became public knowledge.'

'Do the police still suspect Agnes?'

'Glass isn't ruling her out yet, but Herbert Hawke will be charged with murder tomorrow.'

'What about the white feather, Clary? How does that fit?'

'I can't afford to think about that anymore.' Reggie could hear the frustration in his friend's voice. 'I have enough to deal with already. Glass is making life difficult for me. The fact is, Reggie, that I've been suspended for three days, starting on Monday. Three days to consider my options. Three days to decide if my career is over. But I'll be blowed if I'll give in to that underhanded, dirty-dealing, little crook. I'll see Glass off before he does it to me.'

* * *

With that day's edition of *The Truth* about to hit the newsstands and, with it, the latest hypocrite to feel the wrath of the Poison Pen, Reggie waited anxiously for the arrival of his assistant, Dusty Rhodes. The prospect was that the arrest of Herbert Hawke would dismantle his theory that one killer was responsible for three of the deaths as well as an attempt on the life of a fourth.

A dishevelled Dusty arrived, his face flushed and his tie askew. 'I've got it, boss. *The Truth.*'

'Well, let's hear what the Poison Pen has to say today.'

Dusty shook his head. 'Before I do, there's something that I forgot to tell you. You know that I interviewed the Longfellows, the parents of one of Nurse Webb's patients. They claimed that someone from *The Argus* had already spoken to them about their daughter.'

Reggie raised an eyebrow. 'Who?'

'You.'

'What?'

Dusty leaned forward. 'It wasn't you. It was a man who claimed to be you. He wanted to know all the details about Nurse Webb.'

Reggie frowned, his thick black eyebrows knitting together. 'Go on.'

'He told them that he knew Miss Webb's address and that he was going to visit her. This was *before* the Poison Pen's column appeared in *The Truth.*'

Reggie let out a breath. 'Which means that he was gathering information about Webb. It also means that he knew what the interior of her house looked like *before* it was described in *The Truth.*' He tapped the newspaper. 'You know what this means, Dusty? It means that we have the first evidence that someone, either the killer or the Poison Pen, was collecting evidence that these people were corrupt and unscrupulous. He was going to use this information to destroy their reputations.'

'But we still don't know if the Poison Pen and the killer are one and the same person.'

'That's true,' admitted Reggie. 'Or if they're working in tandem. The methods used for gaining information match Crabby's suggestion that the Poison Pen may be a former policeman. What description did they give of this man who claimed to be me?'

'Average-looking. Thin. Dark suit.'

'Average-looking. Unimaginative dresser. Certainly not me.' He tapped the newspaper again. 'Now, let's hear today's column.'

Dusty found the page.

THE IMPIOUS PREACHER IMPLICATED

After a middle-aged, deeply religious, and gullible spinster took a lethal dose of poison in the confessional box of a Melbourne Roman Catholic church recently, tongues were wagging and fingers were pointing.

This Man of the (Tainted) Cloth, this fawning, grovelling, sycophantic, mealy-mouthed priest with the forked tongue, broke his vows of celibacy. Confide in me, he cried, and she did, and more.

A snake in the grass?

She is not the only victim of this viper in the nest. He destroyed others in his early days as a priest when trusting souls, traumatised and troubled, confided in him. They were punished after he revealed their confessions to his superiors. Restraints, medication, and a life in purgatory were their rewards for believing in him. The Viper broke the Spirit of Trust and the Confidence of the Confessional.

And now, he has betrayed a parishioner when he took advantage of her devotion. He destroyed her as he did others, without a pang of conscience. And, when he next sprinkles holy water from the font, he will have blood on his hands. His own.

[*The Truth*, November 18, 1927]

Dusty put the newspaper aside. 'Hopefully, our last hypocrite, Reggie.'

'I hope so too. The suspects are piling up and there's nothing to connect them, except for the link between Nurse Webb and Dr Fox. We need time to investigate, not rush from one case to the next.'

'I agree. We need time to put the pieces of the puzzle together, but first, we need to find the priest. Who do you think he is?'

Reggie shook his head and sighed. 'I don't know. There's nothing here to identify him, except for his religious denomination. However—'

'What?'

He tapped the newspaper article. 'The congregation from the early part of his priesthood is described as traumatised and troubled. Not your usual flock in the suburbs, like Toorak or Brighton.' Reggie re-read the article. 'What are they troubled about? What have they experienced that has bothered them so deeply that they turned to the preacher for advice and comfort? It sounds as if the priest was working in an institution or for an organisation. But what sort?'

'A hospital?' suggested Dusty. 'A seminary? He could be a chaplain in the army.'

'It's possible.' Reggie lit a cigarette and inhaled deeply. 'My thoughts turn more towards a hospital for the insane. Troubled. Traumatised. Restraints. Medication. This "congregation" is supervised, controlled, and under the direction of someone in authority. These people lack the freedom to complain. They are powerless. As in an insane asylum.' He blew a smoke ring and watched it dissipate. 'How does that link with our victims?'

'Dr Fox fits three of those possibilities: army, hospital, and asylum. Webb worked in a hospital. Badger was in the army. He was also in parliament,' suggested Dusty, a smile lingering on his face.

Reggie chuckled. 'They'd have need of a chaplain there.'

'What about Mrs Burns? She doesn't fit with any of them.'

'She's the problem. What do we know about her? Most recently, Mrs Burns was involved with the temperance movement.' Reggie opened the drawer of his desk and flipped back through the pages of his notepad. 'Remember when I spoke to the reporter who wrote the profile of Mrs Burns before he retired? He said that she supported women's suffrage.' He tapped a page. 'She was also in favour of deporting "enemy aliens" at the start of the Great War.'

Dusty ran a hand through his hair. 'I can't see a connection there.'

'Neither can I. I think that we should concentrate on the other victims. Maybe they had contact with this priest. In the meantime, I want you to track down Miss Webb. See if she's been released from the rehabilitation hospital yet. When I get a chance I'll visit her, but I need to pay another visit to Mrs Badger first.'

'Alright, boss, I'll get onto that today.' He sighed. 'We can only hope that victim number five reads it, recognises himself, and heads for the hills.'

Reggie stubbed out his cigarette. 'Let's put some pressure on the Poison Pen. I don't ordinarily do this to a fellow reporter, but I reckon he's gone too far.'

He pulled the typewriter towards him and put a fresh sheet of paper in the roller, then started typing.

THE WHITE FEATHER MURDERS
WHO'S NEXT? LET'S ASK THE POISON PEN
By REGGIE DA COSTA, Senior Crime Reporter

A series of murders has rocked Melbourne in the last few weeks, following the publication of *The Truth*'s Poison Pen column. In his fortnightly denunciation of those he regards as hypocrites, the writer has poured scorn and ridicule on certain 'Pillars of Society,' accusing them of double standards and unethical behaviour.

Although the columnist has not identified his 'hypocrites' by name, there have been clues within the posts as to their identity, which align with each of the victims, namely: temperance advocate Mrs Ida Burns, nurse Miss Beryl Webb, parliamentarian the Honourable Cuthbert Badger, and surgeon Dr Herman Fox. Dr Everett Dwight was originally identified as one of the targets, but fresh evidence has shown this to be incorrect. The latest to be pilloried by the Poison Pen is a priest, not yet identified.

Attempts have been made to interview *The Truth*'s Poison

Pen, but these approaches have been rebuffed by *The Truth*'s editor-in-chief, who insists on the columnist's right to anonymity.

The Poison Pen cannot dodge his responsibilities in explaining his role in the deaths of Mrs Burns, Captain Badger, and Dr Fox, and the attempt on the life of Miss Webb. He has questions to answer: Why has he selected these people in particular as objects of scorn and derision? What is his opinion of the punishment meted out by an unknown assailant? What is his relationship to the killer, if any? And, finally, does he know the significance of the white feather that has been left at each crime scene?

If the Poison Pen is afraid of public scrutiny, then he is complicit in these crimes and guilty of cowardice in not coming forward. He should face the public or resign from his position with *The Truth*.

He re-read his opinion piece and smiled grimly at Dusty. 'What do you think?'

'It's certainly hard-hitting. I don't doubt that it will provoke a reaction from *The Truth*. But honestly? I'd be worried that you're putting yourself in danger.'

Reggie leaned forward, his eyes glistening. 'If it's the only way to find a killer, I'll take that chance.'

Chapter Thirty-Eight

It was a typical day in Spring, the weather changeable, shafts of sunlight cutting through the gloomy clouds that hung low in the south, as Reggie motored down the Geelong Road, leaving Melbourne behind. Faced with an impasse over the latest Poison Pen column, and with no name for the next victim in sight, Reggie had decided to revisit Mrs Agnes Badger in Geelong that afternoon to see what he could learn about her brother. Hopefully, she would agree to speak to him.

The Minerva purred along at sixty miles per hour, its silver bonnet glinting in the weak November sunshine, its six-cylinder engine unleashed as Reggie settled back in the driver's seat with his foot keeping a steady weight on the accelerator. Times like these were uncommon for *The Argus*'s senior crime reporter, whose life in the city was a hectic round of attending crime scenes, pumping out stories for his loyal readers, meeting with his snitches and sources, and ensuring that his wardrobe was frequently replenished with the most fashionable suits available. As he drove, he allowed his thoughts to flow freely, weighing up the pros and cons of the suspects, while trying to untangle a most baffling mystery.

As Mrs Badger's house came into view, he parked the motorcar on the side of the dirt road and sat for a couple of minutes, contemplating how best to conduct his interrogation. With Herbert Hawke a prime suspect in the Badger murder, he wondered how Agnes would react to the arrival of a reporter. Would she be defensive? Would she cooperate? Or, horror of horrors, would he have wasted four hours of his precious time driving up and down the Geelong Road, if she turned him away at the door?

Reggie took a pen and notebook from his bag and slipped them into his pocket, then stepped out of the motorcar. He smoothed the trousers of his new maroon and pink check travelling suit, adjusted his tie, and removed his 'newsboy' cap, which had kept his hair from blowing in the breeze, replacing it with a Panama hat. Glancing up at the sky, he noted that the weather was deteriorating, with a low band of leaden clouds on the horizon. He put the Minerva's top up and secured it into place. With one last look at the sky, he walked through the gap in the hedge, stepped up onto the verandah, and knocked.

Mrs Badger looked at him through the gap in the doorway. 'Mr da Costa,' she said, 'this is a surprise. I thought you might be one of those pests from the local newspaper.'

Reggie breathed a sigh of relief. 'Good morning, Mrs Badger. I was wondering if you would have time to talk to me.'

The door swung wide and she stepped aside to let him pass. He glanced at her as he moved into the sitting room. She was better dressed than last time, but still looked tired, the dark rings around her eyes more prominent.

'I'll get some tea and cake. Please sit down.'

He waited, casting a critical eye over the furnishings. Some attempt had been made to update the furniture. The faded, floral couch had been replaced with a good quality lounge suite, while a reproduction Turkish rug now covered the bare boards. Above the fireplace hung an attractive landscape painting.

Agnes returned, setting a tea tray on the table. She caught him inspecting the furniture.

'I see that you notice the improvement in my situation.'

'How is this possible, Mrs Badger? Might I suggest that you are coming into some money?'

'It's true, but if you expect me to feel guilty about it, you're wrong. I paid a heavy price for being married to Cuthbert. I'll take whatever I can get.'

'The will's been read?'

'It has, and I'm the sole beneficiary. I've had word from his wife that they want nothing to do with Cuthbert: neither his money, his house, nor any of his possessions. Daphne and her family have wiped any association with him from their lives.'

'Will you move into his house in East Melbourne?'

She shook her head. 'Definitely not. But I will sell it and use the money to buy a nicer home for myself.'

'Where will your brother live? Will he move in with you?'

She poured the tea and offered him a slice of cake. 'If he's found not guilty, you mean?' She took a sip of tea, then put her cup down. 'He was never living with me permanently. Herbert has a couple of rooms in a boarding house in Fitzroy. He can stay where he is.'

'The last I heard, he's been released on bail.' He took out his notebook and pen. 'Would you be prepared to answer some questions?'

'I'll talk to you because you and Mr Montgomery treated me with respect when you came here last, and his report in your newspaper was a fair one. He didn't exaggerate or make some melodrama out of my situation, unlike others I could name. I appreciate that. But before I answer your questions, I want to know whether you think that Herbert killed my husband.'

Reggie finished his cake and pushed the plate away. 'I'm of the opinion that Captain Badger's death has nothing to do with either you or Herbert. Your brother's arrest has muddied the waters.'

Agnes nodded. 'What do you want to know?'

'Could you clarify some things for me, information that you may not have shared with the police?'

'Such as?'

'Did you and your brother travel separately to Melbourne on the day of Badger's death?'

'Herbert drove me to the railway station. I took the nine o'clock train to Melbourne, then the tram to East Melbourne. Unbeknownst to me, Herbert left shortly after in his motorcar with the same destination in mind.'

'You had no inkling that he intended to come too?'

'If I had, I would have been asking him why, and he wouldn't have liked that.'

'What did you hope to gain from visiting Captain Badger?'

She paused, taking time to consider her words. 'In hindsight, it was a stupid thing to do. I should have let it alone, but he made my blood boil. He threatened me. He sent me a telegram after Mr Montgomery wrote about me in *The Argus*, ordering me not to speak to the press again. You can imagine that he was afraid of more publicity; what it would do to his career, his marriage. He thought that he would lose everything unless he could stop the flow of accusations against his character. He thought that I would buckle under and do what I was told. He was wrong. I had nothing to lose. I decided to have it out with him. Tell him to his face that I wasn't afraid of him anymore. It's been eight years that I've been hiding away, keeping to myself, with only my brother and my parents visiting me. To tell you the truth, I was sick of it and ashamed that my life had come to this.'

'You were going to tell Badger that you wouldn't be silent anymore?'

'That's right.'

'Was he expecting you that day?'

'I didn't tell him. I wanted to catch him off guard.'

'Weren't you afraid that he might react violently?'

'As I said, I was past caring. But he'd have trouble explaining *my* dead body in his drawing room. Funny, it turned out to be him, not me.' She laughed, mirthlessly.

'What about Herbert?'

'I didn't know he was in Melbourne until I saw his automobile parked at Jolimont railway station. He was waiting for me, ready to drive me back to Geelong. He told me that he'd seen Badger and that they argued. He said that he pushed Badger and he fell backwards, hitting his head on the edge of the hearth.'

'An accident?'

'He says so. In the heat of an argument. He said that there was blood, but that Badger was conscious when he left him.'

'No gun? No shots fired?'

She shook her head and sighed. 'My brother couldn't kill a fly. He was a shaking mess when I saw him at the railway station. He can't cope with stressful situations. The war, you know.'

'What happened to him?'

'He was at Messines. Ironically, my husband was his senior officer. The bastard didn't give Herbert an inch; he drove him hard. When Herbert came home, he spent some time in an asylum.'

'Which one?'

'Mont Park. I'd go to see him when I could. He'd babble about this thing or that.'

'What, in particular?'

'It didn't make a lot of sense at the time. Something about one of his mates being betrayed by a fellow soldier. I don't know if it really happened or whether it was just in his mind. It took a while for him to get better, but he never made it up with my husband. He hated him.'

'How would you describe Herbert?'

She thought for a moment. 'Moody. Hot-headed. Impulsive. Likes money too much, as you know. What he's done is wrong, blackmailing Cuthbert. But he's still my brother and I love him.' She shook her head and stared into space, lost for words.

Reggie waited until she had recovered. 'There are some who say that your former husband was a coward. I've heard that he sent soldiers into battle while he stayed safe in the trenches.'

Agnes sniggered. 'That doesn't surprise me. I told you that he had nightmares. He'd wake up sweating and shaking. Probably afraid that the truth would come out.'

'It was also rumoured that your husband hushed up any criticism by silencing those who were witnesses to his failures. Some were court-martialled or accused of cowardice, according to my source. Did your brother ever say anything about that?'

'Not to me, but I could believe it. Cuthbert would bully people into submission, like he did me. I'm not sorry that he's dead.'

'Did Herbert explain why he went to see your husband that day?'

'After the Poison Pen wrote his column and Cuthbert was identified, Herbert knew that the payments would stop. I can only guess that he saw this as an opportunity to extract one last sum of money, in return for buying my silence. I can't tell you how that affects me. To think that my brother would do that.'

'That doesn't make sense.'

She frowned. 'Who knows what goes on in Herbert's head?'

'Are you talking to your brother?'

'Despite my anger with him, he's still my brother, and I don't want to see him hang for something he didn't do. He's in a terrible way. That policeman, Detective Sergeant Glass, is a most unpleasant person. I don't think he cares who killed Cuthbert. He wants to convict someone, anyone, and move on to the next case.'

Reggie nodded his head. 'An accurate description, Mrs Badger.'

She studied him. 'Please, call me Agnes. Agnes Hawke, not Badger. I don't want to be known by my married name again.' She looked down at his cup. 'Your tea's gone cold. Can I make you another?'

Reggie checked his watch. 'No, thank you, Agnes. I better get going. Here's my card. If you think of anything else, telephone me.'

She followed him out onto the verandah. 'Please, save my brother. I know that he's done the wrong thing, but he's no killer.'

'I'll try. One more thing. Did anyone contact you before the Poison Pen wrote about your husband? Someone wanting to know about your relationship?'

Agnes shook her head. 'No one contacted me, but Herbert told me recently that a man telephoned him, asking questions.'

'Was this before or after *The Truth* article came out?'

'It was before. Why do you ask?'

'The timing is important. Did this man identify himself?'

'It was one of your reporters: Dusty Rhodes from *The Argus*.'

Reggie stared at her in disbelief. Another example of someone using a false identity to gather information. First, the Longfellows being interviewed about Nurse Webb by 'Reggie da Costa,' and now, Herbert Hawke being questioned about Captain Badger by 'Dusty Rhodes.' This person was audacious and determined when it came to gathering information.

'Did Herbert say what this reporter asked about?'

'He knew that I was still alive. He said that he'd checked the registry of births, deaths, and marriages, and that my death wasn't listed. Herbert told him the truth about why I'd left. My brother has always been too impulsive. He doesn't consider the consequences of anything, including revealing my secrets to a man he's never met. Next thing, it's in the Poison Pen column. Herbert didn't have the guts to tell me that he'd let the cat out of the bag. My own brother put me in danger. That's why I contacted *The Argus* because I needed to protect myself in case my husband came after me.'

Reggie sighed. 'I wish I'd known this from the start.'

'Well, I only found out last week; otherwise, I would have told you.'

'Thank you, Agnes. I appreciate your candour.'

Reggie tipped his hat to her, then looked up in dismay at the sky. The sun had disappeared, a shroud of mist descending. He set off down the path, the collar of his jacket turned up, as the drizzle began to fall.

Chapter Thirty-Nine

With her fiancé not due back until late, Ruby decided to visit Horace Striker after work on Saturday. She caught the tram down Swan Street from the Richmond railway station, dismounted at Church Street, then walked the two blocks to Shamrock Street, where Striker lived and worked.

As she approached the unobtrusive brick terrace, Ruby saw the curtains move and the face of Hare, with his cropped, red hair, disappear. It was uncanny, she thought, that he knew when someone was outside, even though she had made the decision to visit Striker on the spur of the moment.

The door opened. Hare stood aside as he greeted her. 'Miss Ruby, so nice to see you again,' he said in his broad, Scottish accent. 'Is Mr Striker expecting you?'

'I'm afraid not. Is it possible to see him?'

Hare's cool, green eyes appraised her. 'If it were anyone else, I'd say no, but I'm sure that Mr Striker has some time to spare before he leaves for his club. However, I'll ask him while you wait inside.'

After checking that the street outside was empty, he ushered her in and closed the door behind her. Shortly after, she followed him along the hallway to Horace Striker's office.

'Ruby,' Horace said as he rose from his chair and came around the desk to greet her.

'Thank you for seeing me,' she replied. 'I should have contacted you first, but I acted on impulse.'

'Please, have a seat. I have a spare hour before I leave.'

'Thank you, Horace.' Ruby looked around her, remembering the first time she had visited him. It was the décor of his office that had impressed on her that she was dealing with someone who didn't fit the mould of the typical gangster. The French imported furniture of maple and burl walnut, with their intricate mother-of-pearl, ivory, and brass inlay, was in the style of Art Deco, while the walls were decorated with posters that were very much in vogue. The only concession to the past was the imposing mahogany desk behind which he sat.

It was also his appearance and demeanour that signalled to Ruby that Horace Striker was not a stereotypical, underworld figure. He was sharply dressed, although not as stylishly as her future husband. As she smiled up at him, Ruby felt the intelligence behind those wary, brown eyes which were directed her way. He was handsome, if in a rather daunting way, and he could be intimidating to those who were not in his inner circle.

'What brings you here, my dear? There's no need to be concerned about your wedding. All is in hand.'

'I can't thank you enough for your generosity. I hope that it's not too much trouble having our reception at The Stockade?'

'Indeed, no. My sister is taking care of the arrangements. She has impeccable taste. The decorations and food will be of the highest standard.'

'It will be expensive. Please let us—'

Striker interrupted her. 'We've discussed this before. I owe you so much for finding my nephew's killer. Without you, that mystery would remain so.'

Ruby sighed. 'That seems so long ago.'

'I agree. Only two years have passed and yet you've changed since I first met you. Once you would never have come here on a whim. And now, you do.' He sat back in his chair, studying her. 'You've gained a lot in confidence, although you were never afraid to speak your mind. You're a sensible woman and that hasn't changed. But you're more like your sister these days, except perhaps not so wild.' He smiled.

'That's true. My sister's murder sparked a change in me. Impersonating her released something in me. I've learned to enjoy life and I found love.'

She blushed. 'But I'm still that secretary from Smith and Sons, despite what's happened.'

'And a good one, I'm sure.'

'And I want to stay that way,' she blurted out.

'Aah, a difference of opinion I take it?'

'My future mother-in-law seems set on me resigning when I get married.'

'And you don't want to.'

'Exactly.' She stared at him defiantly. 'And I suppose that you're going to tell me that I should.'

Horace chuckled. 'I wouldn't dare. I know you, Ruby, and I know how strong you are. Set out your reasons and argue your case. If you could talk me into helping you find your sister's killer, convincing others that you want to continue working should be easy.'

Ruby laughed.

'Now, what's this fiancé of yours working on? I hope that it has nothing to do with me.'

'The White Feather Murders. He believes that there's a killer out there. He's established a link between two of the victims, Nurse Webb and Dr Fox. But when it comes to Mrs Burns, Reggie can't find a connection.'

'That's the Prohibitionist woman?'

'That's right. She died of alcoholic poisoning. She's been succeeded by Mrs Skinner as president.' She looked at him. 'You knew Mrs Skinner, I believe? You spoke to her on the telephone.'

The smile left Horace's face. 'I wouldn't pursue this, if I were you.'

Ruby was embarrassed. 'That was wrong of me. It's none of my business.'

Horace leaned back in his chair. 'Next, you'll be asking me what The Undertaker was doing at The Stockade the night of my Hallowe'en party.'

'I wouldn't dare, although Reggie would want me to ask you.'

Horace nodded his head. 'He would. I saw you talking to Glass. He's a shifty bloke. Talked himself into The Stockade, but, fortunately, he left before he was kicked out. As if I'd want to deal with him. There's nothing like a copper who can't be trusted.'

'Clary Blain thinks he's corrupt.'

'Clary Blain has a good head on his shoulders, despite the amount of whisky he drinks.' Striker's face relaxed again. 'Now, tell me a bit more about these White Feather Murders. It's intriguing, if we believe Reggie's theory.'

'The bodies of Mrs Burns, Nurse Webb, and Captain Badger were found with feathers in their hands.'

'What about Dr Dwight? I read that he did too.'

'Reggie doesn't think that his death is connected. He says that Dr Dwight's death was a robbery gone wrong. The thief left a feather behind to put the police off his trail. The safe was robbed of cash and cocaine, and the doctor's Rolex watch was stolen.'

'That's interesting. Just a minute.' Striker went over to the door and opened it. 'Hare, I need you.'

Horace's bodyguard had been stationed outside the office. 'Yes, boss?'

'Miss Ruby was talking about a Dr Dwight. Don't we have a customer with that surname?'

'That's right. Charles Dwight. A regular customer. Dr Dwight's son. The one who was murdered.'

'What does he buy, Horace?' asked Ruby.

Horace shook his head at her. 'You don't need to know the answer to that one. Suffice it to say, it wouldn't be on your shopping list.' He turned back to Hare. 'How's Mr Dwight's financial circumstances these days?'

'Much improved, boss. Much improved. It seems that Mr Dwight is doing well.'

'But he would have inherited his father's property, wouldn't he?' asked Ruby.

'It's too soon for that to happen. It takes months.'

'Excuse me for interrupting, boss,' said Hare, 'but when we take on a customer, we do a thorough examination of their circumstances. Mr Dwight works as a clerk, so his available cash has been limited until recently. I also know that his father had disinherited him due to his…personal problems. There's no apparent explanation for the improvement in his financial situation that we know of.'

CHAPTER THIRTY-NINE

'Thank you, Hare. That will be all.'

Hare withdrew, leaving the two of them alone again.

Horace rubbed his chin. 'If I were a betting man, I'd put my money on Mr Dwight being his father's killer. I have to say that putting the feather on the body was a masterstroke of distraction.'

'You'll allow me to tell Reggie about this?'

'Certainly. I wouldn't have spoken in front of you, otherwise. Family is so important to me. The thought of a son taking his father's life for a watch and cash is disgraceful.'

'I'm glad that you have ethics, Horace.'

The gangster threw back his head with an uncharacteristic roar of laughter, causing Hare to pop his head around the door, then close it quickly again.

'Now, if that's all?' Horace asked, recovering his equilibrium.

'There is one thing.' She took a deep breath as she fiddled with her engagement ring. 'You've become like a father-figure to me.'

Striker raised an eyebrow. 'Me, a father-figure? I think not.'

'Well, you are, despite what you say. I would like you to give me away at my wedding.'

The gangster was dumbstruck. He took a moment to recover. 'You never cease to amaze me. I've said before that there are very few people in this world that I either like or find remotely interesting. You are one of the few. I would be honoured to walk you down the aisle.'

Ruby glowed. 'That makes me so happy.'

Horace tapped his desk. 'However, if you change your mind, I won't be offended. You should realise that choosing someone in my profession for that role will invite controversy.'

Ruby nodded her head and grinned. 'I have to admit that Squizzy Taylor was my first choice but he's dead, so I've chosen you.'

Horace laughed out loud. 'You're good for Reggie. He's lucky to have found you. Now, if you're ready, we'll take you home on the way to The Stockade.'

Chapter Forty

An eerie twilight settled over the outskirts of Geelong as Reggie began his journey home through the mist and drizzle. He passed through the city itself, with its old graceful buildings, and noticed that the footpaths outside the Union Club and the Orient Hotel were deserted, given the deteriorating weather.

By the time he reached the Geelong Road, Reggie had replayed his conversation with Mrs Badger in his head, committing to memory those points that had relevance to his investigation, and those which raised questions about the involvement of Herbert and Agnes Hawke in the murder of Cuthbert Badger and the other victims.

Originally, Reggie had assumed that Herbert lived with his sister in Geelong, but that was incorrect. Agnes's brother had rooms in a Fitzroy boarding house, so there was no two-hour journey to any of the crime scenes. It put him more in the frame for the White Feather Murders.

It was also apparent that Agnes Badger had benefitted from her husband's death, which meant that she could not be disregarded as a suspect. Judging by the new furnishings in her house and the improvements to her appearance, she was no longer in dire straits financially. However, how could she have known that Badger's will would name her as the beneficiary of his estate when they never corresponded?

In Herbert's case, the death of his brother-in-law had cut off a source of income, but perhaps he hoped that he would share in his sister's good fortune. But again, how would he predict this?

There was also Agnes's revelation that Herbert had pushed Badger, causing him to fall and hit his head. Cuthbert had still been conscious when Herbert left the house, or so he said. But was that the end of it? Badger had been shot with his own gun and, by the time Agnes arrived, he was dead, according to her. There was the possibility that she was lying. No one saw Herbert leave. He might still have been present in the house when she arrived. Reggie had only her word for it that her brother was waiting for her at Jolimont station. This begged the question: Were sister and brother in collusion? Had both participated in killing the former soldier?

Finally, he was interested in the fact that Herbert had served in the war under his brother-in-law, and had suffered from war trauma, necessitating an enforced stay in an asylum to recuperate. It seemed that his relationship with Badger had been fraught, but was that enough to drive him to murder eight years later?

Despite the evidence pointing to the siblings' guilt, Reggie's instincts told him that Hawke and his sister were an unwanted distraction. There was a real culprit out there, responsible for Badger's murder. He knew that someone had been gathering information for the Poison Pen, information that could provide a motive for murder. But surely, the perpetrator had to be experiencing an emotion greater than contempt for his victims? There had to be a significant, underlying reason why they were being targeted with such ferocity.

The mist had thickened and the windows were fogging up as the rain settled in. He opened the split windscreen to get a better view, and was dismayed to see that visibility was reducing, the road seeming to be swallowed up by a dense cloud which was descending rapidly over the countryside. Reluctantly, he slowed down, aware that to do otherwise would be risky in the conditions.

It crossed his mind that his journey home held parallels to his investigation into the White Feather Murders. Although the shapes and shadows of trees and houses might loom up out of the mist on each side and distract him, and potholes might threaten his progress, he needed to keep his eyes on the road in front of him and ignore anything that might divert him from reaching his destination. Like the golden hood ornament of the Roman goddess, Minerva, on the bonnet of his car, pointing the way home, the white feather would be his guiding light in this investigation, showing him the way.

* * *

As he reached the outskirts of Melbourne, Reggie sighed with relief at the thought that the drive would soon be over. It had been a long and tiring journey, with nothing to relieve the monotony of concentrating on the road ahead of him. No signs of life to be seen. Not a bicycle, or a truck, or a horse-drawn buggy. Houses were cloaked in mist. Animals in the fields were no more than ghostly shapes.

His attention was drawn by the reflection of headlights in the rear vision mirror. An automobile was moving up behind him. He smiled to himself. At last, there was someone else motoring on, keen to return to the city, keen to be home. He moved over to the left to allow the driver to pass. But surprisingly, the vehicle kept on coming, drawing closer and closer.

The motorcar was big, black, and powerful, most probably a Dodge judging by its twin chrome bumper bars. He looked again and realised that he couldn't see them anymore, an indication of how close the Dodge was to the Minerva's rear. Its engine roared ominously, as if Reggie's presence on the road was a source of indignation to the driver. Reggie shook his head in disgust and increased his speed, painfully aware that the slimy road and hazardous weather conditions were powerful reasons to keep a good-sized gap between the two automobiles.

Suddenly, the burst of a klaxon horn split the air. Reggie swore loudly. He looked in the rear vision mirror, but all he could see was the shadowy shape of the driver. He put his hand outside the window and signalled for him to go past, his eyes still on the road ahead of him, his foot steady on the accelerator pedal.

Unexpectedly, the Dodge gave ground, leaving a length or two between itself and the Minerva.

'Thank goodness,' Reggie muttered, relaxing slightly.

They travelled on for another five minutes, the Dodge matching the Minerva's speed, not showing any inclination to pass, not showing any inclination to back off further.

Suddenly, the Dodge surged forward, the driver's hand on the klaxon. Again and again, he sounded the horn, while the engine of his automobile roared loudly in the stillness of the late afternoon, reverberating off the pall of cloud which hung in the air. Reggie put his foot down on the accelerator and the Minerva responded, but, to his horror, he saw that the Dodge was not only matching his speed but was drawing ever closer. Reggie glanced briefly at the speedometer as the needle edged upwards. Thirty-five, forty miles per hour, on wet and slippery roads. This was madness. Beads of sweat popped out on his brow.

The automobiles made contact. The Dodge's front bumper bars grazed the back of the Minerva, pushing it forward. Forty-five. Fifty.

Up ahead, the road curved gently to the left. Reggie braked in preparation, the Minerva holding traction on the road's surface, but the big Dodge had locked in behind him, pushing him along faster and faster. The Dodge slowed, then accelerated suddenly, ramming the Minerva and jolting Reggie so unexpectedly that he almost let go of the steering wheel.

Reggie's motorcar hurtled along, drawing ever closer to the bend. Ahead, a row of gum trees loomed up out of the gloom directly in his path, promising a hard reckoning if he failed to make the turn. The Minerva's tyres gripped the road surface as the automobile began to negotiate the curve, but, to his dismay, Reggie saw the bend was tightening. Experience told him that his beloved motorcar would struggle to hold the road at this speed.

His thoughts turned briefly to the motivation of the maniac who was putting him in mortal danger, as the Dodge's engine roared behind him. How could the driver be oblivious to the risk? Was he doing this for a thrill? Or was he acting with deadly intent?

Reggie was certain that he would lose control of the Minerva if he attempted to take the corner at speed. The time for evasive action had arrived. At the last moment, coming into the turn, Reggie noticed a dirt track leading off to the right. Behind him, the Dodge had slowed marginally approaching the bend. Reggie gritted his teeth and swerved across to the wrong side of the road. He jammed his foot on the brake and turned the steering wheel hard towards the track. The Minerva's tail flipped out as it left the sealed road. The tyres gained traction momentarily as they hit the dirt, before raising a flurry of stones as the motorcar skidded sideways across the potholes and puddles. They came to a grinding halt. Thump! Simultaneously, Reggie hit his head against the steering wheel while the front wheels of the vehicle embedded themselves in a roadside ditch.

Blood drizzled down Reggie's cheek. He touched the gash that had opened above one of his eyebrows and stifled a groan. The Minerva had come to a stop in the drain dug next to the dirt road. He waited for the dizziness to pass, then edged across the bench seat and managed to push open the driver's door.

Outside at last, he leaned up against the side of the motorcar and took a few deep breaths. When he raised his head, he realised that he was not alone. An adult, grey kangaroo was not ten yards away from him, grazing close by, its large expressive eyes gazing at him curiously.

He walked slowly back towards the main road and stopped dead. Through the mist, he could see the silhouette of the Dodge parked on the side of the Geelong Road. He ran towards it, stumbling at first, determined to have it out with the driver who had forced him off the road, putting his life in jeopardy. A door slammed and the engine roared. The taillights shone through the drizzle as the Dodge left the grassy verge and regained the road. It rounded the curve and disappeared from view. Reggie swore, then slowly retraced his steps to the Minerva.

Chapter Forty-One

Melbourne was a city of contradictions. Only streets away from the mansions of East Melbourne, where the moneyed classes resided, and the magnificent buildings and churches that had been financed by the unprecedented wealth of the gold rushes, were dark alleyways, brothels, illegal grog shops, and gambling dens. They were frequented by the homeless, the lonely, and the disadvantaged, and were overseen by a shadowy criminal underclass. The latter was the face of Melbourne that police, such as Detective Inspector Clary Blain, encountered most days of their working lives.

It was during a distressing period in his life, when he had been demoted for drinking on duty, that Clary had confided in Reggie that he sought relief from the sordid realities of the city's underworld by spending time in the Edinburgh Gardens, a short walk from his Fitzroy home. Here, he could find some peace and quiet, a chance to regain a sense of perspective when he found life overwhelming. Given that Blain was suspended from the Victoria Police, if only for three days, Reggie was not surprised to find him there.

The detective was in the rotunda, leaning against the low wall that linked the columns. He seemed to be gazing out at nothing in particular. Reggie climbed the steps and stood next to Clary, who seemed oblivious to his presence. The large expanse of lawn below them was broken up by a network of interconnected paths, shady trees, and well-tended garden beds. The park offered a reprieve from the restless city that surrounded them, the sound of traffic a distant murmur.

'How are you?' Reggie asked.

'Been better,' Clary replied, turning towards him. 'I heard that you had an accident yesterday.'

'Word travels fast, even if you are suspended. It wasn't an accident. Someone tried to run me off the road. If that side track hadn't been there, I'd be dead.'

'You're alright?'

'A bit of a gash, that's all.' He touched the bandage on his forehead. 'When I got to work this morning, there was an envelope waiting for me.' He took it from his pocket and handed it to the detective.

Clary unfolded the letter and whistled softly as he read the message. '"You've been warned." What's this?' He reached into the envelope and took out a white feather. 'Well, well.'

'I'm getting close by the look of it.'

'Too close, Reggie. Did you get a look at the driver?'

'Unfortunately, no. By the time the farmer towed the Minerva out of the ditch, the Dodge was long gone.'

'How's your motorcar?'

'A broken headlight, a couple of scratches on the back bumper bar, and a lot of mud. I must say that she's in a better state than my travelling suit. It's ruined.'

'That's not the only thing that's ruined, mate. My career is on its last legs.' He gazed out at the gardens again, his expression mournful. 'Maybe they're right. Maybe I should give it away.'

Reggie shook his head. 'I think that would be unwise. You're a good copper, Clary. Even if you drink too much.' He patted him on the shoulder. 'Come on. Don't let them force you out. Certainly not The Undertaker.' Blain didn't reply so Reggie tried again. 'I've contacted my old friend, Rabbit, up in Sydney. He told me a bit about Glass the last time I spoke to him, so I thought he might have more to add.'

Clary's face registered interest for the first time. 'And did he?'

'It seems that Glass was coming under scrutiny before he moved to Victoria last year. Two years ago, the New South Wales police broke a cocaine importing network. They launched a series of raids and arrested several offenders, one of whom was an undercover agent, a member of the public. According to Rabbit, this man was "persuaded" to cooperate; otherwise, he'd be charged with an unrelated crime. The coppers seized over 250 tins of opium and thirty bottles of cocaine. The opium was being imported from China at £1 a tin and would be re-sold in Sydney for £10, so the projected profits were considerable. When the case went to trial, the offenders were fined, not jailed, so it's likely that they are back on the streets doing it again.'

'What does this have to do with Glass?'

'He was one of the police involved in the raids. He was the one who'd forced the member of the public to go undercover. That agent was killed while on remand. Interestingly, the seized drugs went missing shortly afterwards. Rumours were rife that The Undertaker was involved, and there was a move to take a closer look at him, but he resigned and moved to Victoria before anything could be proved.'

'How does this help me?'

'It confirms what you believe: that Glass is corrupt. And it's a good reason why you should resist pressure to leave the police. Someone needs to hold him to account. It has to be you.'

'Tell me the truth, Reggie. Why are you trying to talk me out of resigning?'

'Because I like spending money on Scotch whisky. Your Scotch whisky.'

Clary shook his head. 'More likely, it's the information I give you.'

Reggie chuckled. 'Why else would I be here?'

Blain hitched up his trousers. 'What do you want to know?'

'Herbert Hawke, Agnes Badger's brother. What can you tell me?'

'He was psychologically damaged when he went to Mont Park, diagnosed with shell shock. They put him in the Military Mental Hospital annexe. Only those soldiers with chronic psychiatric illnesses were sent there. He was released before the military block closed in 1924.'

'When was he admitted?'

'In 1918. He was under the care of Dr John Springthorpe. A compassionate man from all accounts. Apparently, he worked wonders with his patients, including Hawke. Others were not so lucky.'

'Did Herbert start blackmailing Cuthbert after he was released from Mont Park?'

'We've checked Badger's bank account. The payments started six months after Herbert left the asylum.'

'You know that Badger was his senior officer? There was no love lost between them.'

'I heard about that connection. It gives Herbert Hawke a motive to kill him. He must have been doing very nicely until the Poison Pen's column stopped the flow of money. But I don't think Hawke did it,' added Blain.

'Why is that?'

'I can't explain it. Gut instinct perhaps. And the fact that I despise The Undertaker. He messed up the investigation with his suicide theory. Now, he's focused on the easy option of Hawke as Badger's killer, because I forced him to treat it as a murder.'

'Have you spoken to Hawke?'

'I have. He's in a fragile state so it's hard to get at the truth.'

'Has Herbert told you why he blackmailed Badger?'

'Isn't it obvious? No politician wants to be known as a wife-beater or a bigamist.'

'Which brings us to Badger's murder.' Reggie stroked his moustache. 'How does Glass explain Hawke's involvement in the killing?'

'It's straightforward, according to him. With the truth out about his bigamy, Badger stops the blackmail payments to his brother-in-law. Herbert goes to Badger's place and offers to secure Agnes's silence in return for one last payment. Badger is not persuaded. They argue and Hawke shoots Badger.'

'Agnes says that Herbert is incapable of that.' Reggie lit a cigarette and inhaled, then blew a smoke ring. 'Have you had any luck finding out who the Poison Pen is?'

'The editor-in-chief refuses to reveal his identity.' Clary frowned. 'Calls it protection of journalistic sources. The courts won't budge on that one unless we can give them a good reason.'

Reggie shifted position and turned his back on the view over the gardens, his eyes focused on Blain. He tapped the ash off his cigarette and took another drag. 'I wish that you would consider the white feather connection, Clary. Look what happened to me yesterday. It's clear that my article on the Poison Pen ruffled a few feathers.'

Clary chuckled. 'A few white feathers, from the look of it.'

Reggie was not to be distracted. 'It's clear to me that Glass found a white feather at Dr Fox's crime scene but won't admit it. It complicates matters for him if he acknowledges that it was there. We know that Glass is a lazy bugger. He wants a simple resolution.'

Reggie paused, choosing his next words carefully. 'A white feather at the scene of each crime changes everything. It connects them. Burns, Webb, Badger, and Fox. With one exception,' he added. 'The case of Dr Dwight.'

'Really, Reggie? I want to believe you, but it was found at the scene. Don't tell me that some white feathers are legitimate, while others have been planted as a diversion.'

'Listen to me, Clary. That feather was a hoax. I had a telephone call from Dr Lynas Farrington. He's known Everett Dwight for years. He trained with him and worked at the same clinic. He says the claims made by the Poison Pen are false.'

Blain sighed heavily. 'This Poison Pen business is tedious.'

'But the white feather is significant. It's the reason behind them all. Can't you see that?'

'Does it matter? I've been suspended.'

'Consider this. Dr Dwight's son has a drug problem and he's recently come into money. You might want to investigate that.'

'If I don't resign first.'

'Where's your fighting spirit, Clary? We don't want the likes of Homer Glass in the police force. We need good coppers like you to put criminals behind bars.'

Blain brightened visibly. 'You mean that? Thanks, mate.' He paused, nodding his head slowly. 'Dr Dwight's son, eh? That might be worth following up.'

Reggie patted him on the back. 'That's the spirit. Time for a quick one?

Any pubs around here?'

'If you're heading back to the city, the Rainbow Hotel is on the way.'

'That sounds good. You never know: We could find that pot of gold,' said Reggie, chuckling. 'Or perhaps that pot of beer?'

'Make it a pot of whisky, and a large one at that.'

Chapter Forty-Two

<u>THE WHITE FEATHER MURDERS</u>
WHO'S NEXT: A VIPER IN THE NEST?
By REGGIE DA COSTA, Senior Crime Reporter

In the last two months, there have been several unexplained deaths linked to the Poison Pen columns in *The Truth*. The murder of Mrs Ida Burns, president of Melbourne's Woman's Christian Temperance Union, was followed by an attempt on the life of Miss Beryl Webb, a former nurse who suffered from drug addiction. Thereafter, came the shooting of the Honourable Cuthbert Badger, member of the Legislative Assembly, as well as the fatal attack on Dr Herman Fox, who was found drowned in his bath. A white feather was found at each crime scene.

Originally, it was reported that Dr Everett Dwight was a victim of the White Feather Murderer. However, information has been received that disproves this theory. A feather was placed next to the body to mislead the police.

Each one of these victims had been accused of deceitful and immoral behaviour by the person who writes under the nom de plume 'The Poison Pen.' Hiding behind the expedient justification that his claims would open him to reprisals from those he libels, the columnist remains anonymous, making defamatory statements without providing evidence for his sources. He also protects himself by not naming the person, preferring to identify them obliquely by using a play on words. For example, Mrs Burns was referred to as 'The Fiery One,' Nurse Webb was a 'Dope Spider' with a 'Deadly Web,' Captain Badger 'lived up to his name' by bullying and tormenting, or badgering, his wife, and Dr Fox 'outfoxed' the authorities.

Another 'hypocrite' was revealed in Friday's *Truth*. He is referred to as a 'viper in the nest' with a 'forked tongue.' It is impossible to identify this person as he is not named, but the allusions to him being reptilian in nature suggest that his name will align with that description. We can assume, however, that this priest worked for a large organisation or institution, such as the military, a hospital, or a mental asylum, before he was assigned to a parish. It is to be hoped that this person will recognise himself from the description and seek protection from this killer.

The perpetrator of each of these murders is still at large. The latest development in the Badger case is that Herbert Hawke, brother-in-law of the deceased, was arrested and initially charged with his murder, but has been released on the advice of the Crown Prosecutor.

In defiance of evidence to the contrary, Detective Sergeant Glass, of the Victoria Police, has issued a statement:

"There is no White Feather Murderer, as asserted by one of Melbourne's crime reporters. This person is a fabrication created by the press to sell newspapers. The Criminal Investigation Branch has investigated the circumstances pertaining to the deaths of Dr Herman Fox and Mrs Ida Burns and has found them to be unfortunate accidents. In the cases of Dr Dwight and Captain Badger, we are pursuing

lines of enquiry to uncover the perpetrators of those crimes. We stress that these two cases are unrelated. Linking these deaths to the wild accusations aired in a newspaper column is not helpful in the fight against crime in Victoria."

[*The Argus*, November 21, 1927]

Reggie re-read his report, hopeful that it would alert the unknown fifth 'hypocrite' to the danger he was in, before the killer went into action again. Even now, after all that had happened, he couldn't make a guess as to whether the Poison Pen and the killer were one and the same person. The columnist had been writing under his *nom de plume* for about six years, according to Dusty's friend, Crabby Crabtree, and there hadn't been a whiff of murder prior to these latest 'Hypocrite' columns. It was a mystery.

As was his habit when he was cogitating over the facts of the case, Reggie took the white feather from his pocket and twirled it, perhaps hoping that it would divulge its secrets. A white feather: a symbol of cowardice closely associated with the Great War.

The image of the ornament on the Minerva's bonnet rose up before him. What had he promised himself as he drove home from Geelong? That he should not be distracted in his quest to find the connections between the victims. He mulled that over. What of the suspects? Forget Herbert Hawke and Agnes Badger? They had motive and opportunity to kill Captain Badger, but no apparent link with the Poison Pen or with the other victims. The same applied to Mrs Skinner, who coveted Mrs Burns' job as president, and Jim McTavish, the drunken husband, who sent threatening letters to Mrs Burns.

Skinner, McTavish, Hawke, and Agnes were as shadows looming up on the side of the road, threatening to divert his attention from reaching his destination: the identification and subsequent apprehension of the White Feather Murderer.

If the common thread between Fox, Badger, and Webb was the war, what of Mrs Burns? Where did she fit into this scenario?

It was a month since Reggie had spoken on the telephone to his former colleague, the retired journalist who had interviewed Mrs Burns. He took out his notepad and found the page recounting the conversation. According to the reporter, Mrs Burns had been influenced by her next-door neighbour, a supporter of local causes. But Burns' interests were wider than local issues and she had involved herself in all sorts of causes, from women's suffrage to the deportation of enemy aliens.

He sat up in his chair. 'I'll bet that she supported the conscription referenda,' he said out loud. 'That's the missing link.'

Reggie remembered it well. Volunteers had enthusiastically enlisted when the Great War broke out, spurred on by patriotism and the belief that the war would be short-lived. However, heavy losses had been inflicted on the Australian contingent at Pozières and Fromelles in 1916, and enthusiasm had waned. With few recruits, the Australian Government announced a referendum to introduce conscription in 1916 and a second one in 1917, both of which were soundly defeated. Casualties mounted. An air of pessimism hung over the Australian people, that peace and victory were proving elusive.

Back then, Reggie had refused to enlist and had voted against the referenda. From the start, he had held the view that it was an economic war, with British capitalistic interests defending their markets against the growth of Germany as a world power. But he had experienced the pressure exerted by those who believed wholeheartedly in the cause of supporting the British in the war. A white feather had been left on the doorstep of his mother's house when he lived with her, and derogatory comments were thrown at him when he walked down the streets of Melbourne, a healthy, fit man, not in uniform.

He reached for the telephone and gave the operator the number of the former *Argus* reporter who had written the article on Mrs Burns.

'It's Reggie here again. I'm pursuing some lines of enquiry concerning the death of Mrs Burns. Could I ask you a few more questions?'

'Of course, mate. What do you want to know?'

'When I spoke to you last, you mentioned that Mrs Burns was involved in a variety of causes.'

'That's right. She was nothing, if not committed. Fearless, she was. If she believed in something, she carried it through.'

'Was she involved in the conscription referenda?'

'Not only advocating for conscription. It went deeper than that. She said that when she lived in Bendigo, she would stand out in the street and hand out feathers to men who weren't wearing military uniforms. She said they disgusted her, because they weren't real men and were letting down their sex. She was very outspoken about it. Apparently, she was prepared to stand up to any man who questioned her. I'm sure that she cowed many a reluctant young man into joining up. As I said to you last time, everything was either black or white, good or evil, no shades of grey. Her own husband joined up, even though he was in his late forties. He probably couldn't bear being labelled as a coward.'

Reggie breathed a sigh of relief. 'This has really helped me.'

'That's all you need?'

'Without a doubt. This makes my theory plausible. Next time I see you, I'll buy you a beer.'

Reggie hung up and smiled to himself. The Great War. The war to end all wars. That was the connection between the victims. Mrs Burns had handed out white feathers to shame men into enlisting. Captain Badger had forced his men to fight while he cowered in the trenches. Miss Webb and Dr Fox had mistreated soldiers suffering from shell shock. Presumably, the latest rant from the Poison Pen was about a priest who had betrayed military men who confided in him. It was tenuous, but it worked.

Finally, the pieces of the puzzle were coming together, but there were three pieces that were missing. Who was the Poison Pen? Why had he chosen this time to destroy the reputations of these people? And was he connected to the subsequent attempts on their lives?

Chapter Forty-Three

Clary Blain strolled back to the office, damaged, but not broken. Reggie's pep talk had given him the strength to go on, rather than buckle under the weight of the accusations thrown at him by Detective Sergeant Glass. The Undertaker was using every means at his disposal to force him to resign, but Clary intended to resist to the end.

Eyebrows were raised as he walked back in and, to his surprise, he was met with a round of applause. He noted the absence of The Undertaker and wondered if that show of support would have happened if Glass were in attendance. Perhaps not, given that he had the ear of the Chief Commissioner. However, despite that, Clary was cheered that he still had the respect of his colleagues, the ones who mattered.

He raised a hand in response and smiled, then went into his office. His files had been cleared away; the desktop bare. Glass had expected that Clary would hand in his resignation. If that were the case, Clary would show him. He took the folders from his drawer and opened them, spending the next forty minutes re-acquainting himself with the cases that had been assigned to him.

He reached for the telephone. 'Put me through to Dr Lynas Farrington, please.'

Such was his concentration that he failed to notice one of the constables enter the room, until a slip of paper dropped onto his desk. He picked it up and read it.

'I need your advice, sir,' it read. 'It's a confidential matter of some sensitivity. Could you meet me at the café in Franklin Street in ten minutes?'

He looked up. Constable Blanch nodded at him and walked out of the office into the street.

The telephone rang. 'I have Dr Farrington on the line for you, sir.'

'Put him through.'

'Farrington, here.' The man's voice was deep and confident.

'Dr Farrington. It's Detective Inspector Blain from the Criminal Investigation Branch. I'm looking into the circumstances of Dr Everett Dwight's death. Could you answer a couple of questions for me?'

'If this is going to add to the rubbish that was published in *The Truth* and *The Argus*, that Everett was a butcher, I want nothing to do with it,' Farrington declared. 'It's totally ridiculous the lies that are being spread about him. He was a man of integrity.'

'That's not my purpose, sir. I'm more interested in his personal life. I believe that he had a son.'

Farrington's tone changed, becoming calmer. 'Charles. A no-hoper, if ever there were one. Everett did his best for the lad, but his efforts failed. He didn't have anything to do with the boy after he was thrown out of university.'

'Why was Charles expelled?'

'He was studying to become a doctor, like his father, but he got in with a bad crowd. He failed to attend lectures and tutorials and, when he did, he was drunk or worse. Everett told me that he was out of control.'

'Had Dr Dwight seen him lately?'

'I believe that he invited him around for dinner to talk to him; make him see sense. It was a shambles, apparently.'

'When was this?'

'About a month ago. Although we weren't working together, Everett and I met up regularly at my club. We were close friends.' He sighed. 'I miss him.'

'Do you know where Charles lives?'

'A rooming house in Fitzroy. In Gore Street. Why do you want to know?'

'Just making enquiries. Is there a Mrs Dwight?'

'She died of consumption fifteen years ago. Very sad.'

'Thank you so much. I'm sorry to take up so much of your time.'

Blain hung up the telephone and contemplated his notes. Interesting, he thought. They tallied with Reggie's snippet of information. He reached for his hat.

'I'll be back soon, sergeant,' he said to the policeman at the front desk.

* * *

Constable Blanch was waiting for him at a table down the back of the café. He stood up as Blain sat down opposite him.

'Can I get you a cup of tea, sir?'

'No, thank you, constable. Have a seat. What's this all about?'

'It's a delicate matter, sir. It concerns the investigation into counterfeiting.'

'Presided over by Detective Sergeant Glass?'

'That's correct, sir.' The policeman was nervous, fiddling with the salt and pepper shakers.

Blain leaned forward. 'What you tell me remains confidential, Blanch. Unless it's illegal, of course.'

'Thank you, sir.' He took a deep breath and began. 'You're the only one I can talk to. The others agree that there's something wrong, but they're afraid to go against Mr Glass. He makes it clear that he's in charge and that he makes the decisions.'

'Which is the correct procedure, as you well know, Constable Blanch,' said Blain.

'That's true, but we've stumbled over something that deserves to be investigated. Last week, me and a couple of the lads were patrolling Swan Street when one of the shopkeepers came out of his grocery store. He showed us a £5 banknote that a customer had given him as payment. It was counterfeit, but a good one. He only noticed it because it had a waxy feel. When he held it up to the light, he saw that there was no basketweave watermark around the borders. It was also missing the denomination, which appears in watermarks in the centre of the note. We asked if he could identify the customer. He said that it was a woman who comes in every Friday morning. He wasn't too pleased when we confiscated the note, but we told him that we'd be back.'

'I assume that you reported this to Detective Sergeant Glass?'

'We did, sir.' He shook his head. 'We couldn't understand his lack of interest. He said that there were bigger fish in the sea and that we shouldn't concern ourselves with minnows. Those were his words, Mr Blain, not mine. I thought it strange.'

'I agree.' Clary was silent, then leaned in towards him. 'I have a plan, Constable Blanch, if you're prepared to carry it out.'

'I'll do whatever you suggest, sir. But I do have a wife and child.'

'No one's asking you to put your job in jeopardy. It's on my head if anything goes wrong. God knows, my career is almost over anyway.'

'You have my full attention, sir.'

'Very well. Here's what I want you to do.'

Chapter Forty-Four

The terrace house in Brunswick was much neater on the outside compared to the first time Reggie had visited it. The garden had been tended, the path swept, and on the front porch sat former nurse, Beryl Webb, in her rocking chair. No longer thin and drawn, she had put on weight and was wearing a floral dress which looked fresh and new.

'Can I help you?' she asked as she observed the crime reporter standing on the footpath.

'I'm Reggie da Costa from *The Argus*. I was here when you were taken off to hospital a few weeks ago. Would you be prepared to answer some questions?'

She nodded her head. 'Come inside, Mr da Costa. I'll make us a cup of tea.'

He followed her down the hallway to the kitchen at the back of the house, glancing in the sitting room and bedroom as he passed them. It was like a different place, with the floors swept, the rooms tidy, and the bed made, despite the need for a lick of paint on the walls. Nothing like the filthy place that she had lived in when she had been overcome by gas, weeks before.

Beryl put the kettle on the hob and spooned tea leaves into the teapot, then set two cups on the table. While they waited for the kettle to boil, Reggie studied the woman who, only recently, had been at death's door. Her eyes were clear and bright, her hair clean and brushed, but the effects of a life addicted to morphine could not so easily be banished: the lines from years of neglect were etched on her face; her arms scarred from the needle.

She poured the tea and seated herself at the table opposite Reggie.

'How can I help you, Mr da Costa?' she asked.

'Reggie, call me Reggie.'

She nodded and took a sip of tea, waiting for him to begin.

'You're looking so much better, Miss Webb. You've recovered well.'

'To tell you the truth, Reggie, I have no memory of that day. I was in the grip of addiction.'

'You've overcome your problem?'

'I'm not sure that's possible. It's a battle every day, but I have support to see me through it.'

'Family, friends?'

'Unfortunately, I've burned those bridges. The hospital could have released me onto the street but they didn't; otherwise, I would have reverted to my old ways. I was lucky. I timed the lowest point in my life to coincide with a vacancy at the Salvation Army's new sanatorium in East Caulfield. The nurses are specially trained. They are kind but firm, and they cared for me while I withdrew from morphine. Before I came home, the Salvos cleaned up my place and left food for me. They visit me once a week and talk to me, to see how I'm going. They've turned my life around, and, for that, I'm grateful.'

'You are lucky,' agreed Reggie. 'Addicts are usually arrested and sent to prison. They withdraw from drugs in their cells. No help. Nothing. They're released after a month or so. Most relapse, few recover.'

Miss Webb nodded her head, her expression, solemn. 'If the hospital had sent me home, I'd be dead now. Although the doctors cured the effects of asphyxiation, they didn't cure my addiction. I was still wanting to feed my habit when they sent me to the Salvos. Like I said, I was lucky.'

'I'm pleased for you, Miss Webb.'

'I'm not sure that I deserved this. I've hurt a lot of people in my time.'

'Do you remember anything about the day you were gassed?'

She shook her head. 'Nothing at all. I spent a lot of time not being aware of what I was doing or where I was. I've wasted so much of my life.'

'No memory of turning the gas on, or if someone visited you that day?'

She shook her head.

'How did your addiction start?' asked Reggie.

Beryl frowned. 'At the field hospital on the Western Front. It was easy to get drugs. Early on, the British military even provided cocaine to soldiers so that they weren't afraid to go into battle. My problem grew as time went on.'

'Were you familiar with a surgeon called Dr Fox?'

Miss Webb went pale. 'I was.'

'Could you tell me about your relationship with him?'

She passed her hand over her eyes. 'His reputation preceded him. In the operating theatre he was said to be like God. Amputating damaged limbs. Making decisions about treatment without ever doubting himself. Before the end of the war, he moved to a hospital in London. That's where I fell under his spell. There's no other word to explain it. Another addiction. I was in thrall to the man. I thought he was a miracle maker.'

'Do you still feel the same way?'

'I had time to think in rehabilitation. I've revised my opinion.'

'Did you know that he wasn't a qualified doctor?'

'I did wonder at the time.'

'Do you remember any particular cases that didn't go as well as planned?'

She paused, took a sip of tea, and pushed her cup away. 'There were two. A young soldier who was suffering from shell shock. Traumatised, he was. Curled up in a ball babbling away to himself. Wouldn't speak properly and couldn't walk. By that stage, Herman was experimenting with electro-convulsive therapy. He believed that it could make men walk; make men talk.

'This young man was in a bad way. Twitching, shaking, holding his hands over his ears. Herman had him tied face down to a bed. Two orderlies held the soldier steady as he placed electrodes on his back. I'll never forget it. It was horrible. The screams. He thrashed around, but they held him firm. He wasn't the only one. There were more like him. I look back on it and I know it was torture.' She paused, tears forming in her eyes.

'What happened to the soldier?'

'He was transferred out.' She shrugged her shoulders. 'I don't know where.'

CHAPTER FORTY-FOUR

'His name?'

'I can't remember.'

'And the other case?'

'Similar to that one, but it ended badly. He hanged himself with a sheet.' She stifled a sob.

Reggie waited until she regained her composure. 'Did you work with Dr Fox at Mont Park Lunatic Asylum?'

'I never saw him again after London.'

'You regret working with him?'

'Of course I do. But back then, I did what he wanted me to do.'

'You're sure that you never saw Dr Fox again?'

She shook her head. 'But if I do meet him again, he'll find me much changed.'

Reggie took up his hat. 'Indeed, he would.'

The crime reporter studied her. She had turned her life around, although it would be a constant struggle, if he knew anything about morphine addiction. He decided to keep his theory about the White Feather Murderer to himself. He doubted whether she even knew about the Poison Pen column and how it related to her. Back in October, Beryl had been in the grip of addiction, unaware of what was going on around her, except for the need to inject morphine into her veins. And now, the former nurse was emerging from years of addiction and was getting stronger in resisting the urge to submit to what had been her *raison d'être*. Informing her that the gassing was intentional would not be helpful in her rehabilitation. Nothing would be gained from telling her about Dr Fox's death either, only igniting the fear that the murderer, who harboured a grudge against her, might make a second attempt on her life. Let it go, Reggie told himself. Ignorance in this case was bliss.

'Thank you, Miss Webb,' he said. 'I wish you all the best for the future.'

'Thank you, Reggie. I intend to make amends if I can. I've been given a second chance and I mean to make good use of it.'

Chapter Forty-Five

It was bedlam when Detective Inspector Clary Blain entered police headquarters on Friday morning. Not only were there sounds of loud wailing, low moans, and heavy sobs coming from the interview room, but the officers clustered around the woman in question didn't seem to know how to subdue her.

'What on earth is going on, Sergeant?' asked Clary. 'Who is she?'

'She's the ringleader of a counterfeiting gang, sir. Constable Blanch brought her in fifteen minutes ago. The others are locked up in the cells. He's been trying to question her, but she's incapable of explaining anything. We're at our wits' end what to do with her.'

When he saw Clary enter, Constable Blanch broke away from the group surrounding the woman. 'Detective Inspector Blain. I'm glad that you're here. I did as you said and put two of my colleagues on surveillance this morning. They were out of sight in the back room of the grocery store so as not to scare off the person passing the counterfeit banknotes. Sure enough, the woman entered the shop and bought some bread and milk, then gave the shopkeeper a £5 note. He checked it and gave a pre-arranged signal. She was promptly arrested.'

'And then?'

'We escorted her to her house. We put out a call to another wireless patrol car to provide support. Two men were arrested in a large garage at the back of the residence. We took possession of a marble slab which had etchings of the front and back of a £5 banknote, as well as sheets of paper cut to size, similar in texture to that used in the making of genuine notes. We also confiscated tins, bottles, and jars of dyes and inks, and a second marble slab, smeared with green and blue ink.'

'Good work, Blanch. Where are the others?' asked Clary.

'We have the men in custody, sir, if you wish to interview them. They're not talking, as you'd expect.'

'Let me have a chat with this woman,' said Blain.

He took a step towards the interview room and caught sight of her face. Moments later, he was on the telephone.

'Reggie, get down here!'

Clary entered the interview room. 'Right, men, leave us. I'll deal with this.' The policemen looked relieved and made a hasty exit as the wailing continued, the blood-curdling sounds emanating from a plump little woman of advanced years, with a froth of white curls and a rosy-cheeked face. Tears were pouring from her large blue eyes, dripping onto the bodice of her lacy blouse.

'Mrs da Costa, please stop. I'm Clary Blain, Reggie's friend. I've rung him and he's on his way.'

She looked up at the detective and let out a loud sob. 'You know Reggie? He's coming?'

'Indeed, he is. Please stop crying.' He took a handkerchief from his pocket and handed it to her.

'I don't understand, I don't,' she stammered, wiping her eyes. 'Why am I here?'

'You had a counterfeit note in your possession,' Clary explained patiently. 'The grocer says that you've been paying him with fake, £5 notes.'

'Mr Blain, I'd never do anything illegal. You must believe me.'

'I do, Mrs da Costa. Can you remember where you got that note from?'

'I'm renting out my garage to a business. They design and print posters and catalogues for well-known companies. I've seen them. They're very good. The nice, young man who owns it pays me £10 a week. But it couldn't be him. He's very respectable.'

'What's this nice, young man's name?' Blain asked her.

'Damien.'

'Does he have a last name?'

Mavis shook her head. 'I'm in big trouble, aren't I?'

'We need to track Damien down, Mrs da Costa, so we need your help. Where did you meet him?'

'In the park near my house. It must have been around the middle of October. We began talking. He told me that he needed new premises for his business. He explained what he was after, and it fitted the description of the garage at the back of my house.'

'And he offered you a good sum of money to rent it?'

'Oh, yes. Cash in advance and a lump sum up front.' She looked at the detective, sadly. 'I needed the money, Mr Blain. It was like my guardian angel was watching over me, bringing Damien to the park that day. I never would have guessed—'

She started to cry again, the mortification showing on her face. 'What will Reggie think? He'll be so disappointed in me.'

Clary sighed. 'You've been hoodwinked by an expert. He's probably been making discreet enquiries around your neighbourhood. I suspect that he knew that you had a garage just right for his operation. He made it look like a chance meeting, and he won your trust. Did you tell him your surname?'

'I chose not to. I called myself Mavis. That's all.'

She looked up and saw Reggie standing outside the interview room, staring at her in disbelief.

'Oh dear. How can I explain this?'

'Let me do it, Mrs da Costa.'

Blain went outside and closed the door behind him, took Reggie by the arm, and led him to his office.

Using a few, well-chosen sentences, Blain explained Mavis's situation, emphasising the fact that his mother was the innocent victim of an enterprising criminal, who had taken advantage of an elderly, naïve woman.

'Talk to her, Reggie,' he concluded. 'Be gentle. Assure her that she's done nothing wrong, and that everything will be fine. I'll need to take a statement from her first before I can release her. We still have the two counterfeiters to interview and, hopefully, they will identify the boss of this operation. I can offer them a reduction in their jail time in return for information. Don't worry, we will get this fellow.'

'Thanks, Clary. I appreciate this.'

Reggie entered the interview room. Blain watched him consoling his mother as she sobbed on his shoulder.

Constable Blanch approached Clary. 'What's going on, sir? Isn't that Reggie da Costa in there with her?'

'I'll explain it all to you after they've left. I need you to witness her statement and we can let her go.'

'Let her go?' Blanch looked downcast. 'I've arrested an innocent woman?'

Blain patted him on the back. 'Don't worry. You've done well. Let's go in.'

Blanch followed him in, then turned at the sound of raised voices. He went white. 'Oh dear, it's Detective Sergeant Glass, sir. When he finds out about this, I'll be in big trouble. I do have your support, don't I?'

The Undertaker was talking to the sergeant on duty, looking angrily over at Blain and Blanch. He stormed across the room and opened the door to the interview room.

'What's going on here? I demand an explanation!'

And then he saw Mavis.

'Damien,' she cried, a look of relief on her face. 'Thank goodness you've come. Tell them I'm innocent.'

* * *

The next afternoon, in the cosy surroundings of The Duke, Clary paid for the drinks and, together with Reggie, toasted the demise of The Undertaker.

'Your mother will be alright, won't she?'

'It was a terrible shock for her.'

'Not only for her,' said Blain gleefully. 'Glass's face went as white as a sheet when he saw your mother. He never expected to see his landlady in the offices of the Criminal Investigation Branch.'

Reggie chuckled. 'It was fortunate that Mother didn't reveal her surname to Glass, because he would have queried her relationship with the one and

227

only Reggie da Costa.'

'Agreed. I felt vindicated when the Chief Commissioner came out from his office in time to witness the demise of his favourite within the ranks. It was like savouring that first sip of a fine malt whisky.'

'Or the froth on a beer.'

Blain nodded his head. 'With Blamey there, Glass had no choice but to comply when I asked him to empty his pockets. That wad of fake, £5 banknotes.' He smiled, savouring the moment. 'And now he's facing charges of counterfeiting and perverting the course of justice.'

'Good work, Clary.' Reggie raised his glass and clinked it against Clary's. 'To The Undertaker. May he enjoy his stint in prison.'

'And a toast to your mother. She's brought me great happiness.'

Reggie frowned. 'To tell you the truth, I'm concerned about her. I went back to see her last night. She told me that she's worried about testifying in court.

'Not only that,' he added, 'but she's afraid of the repercussions. If Mrs Bardsley Smith and her friends hear that she's been caught up in a counterfeiting ring, her reputation will be ruined. Or worse still, she'll be a laughing stock.'

Clary put down his Scotch, his expression thoughtful. 'Poor Mavis. We can't have that. Do you have your notebook with you?'

'Of course. Why?'

'Take down this statement and attribute it to me. I want this to appear in tomorrow's edition of *The Argus*.' He grinned at the crime reporter and nodded. 'Let's begin.'

By the time Blain had finished dictating, Reggie, too, had a smile on his face.

Chapter Forty-Six

A BRAVE WOMAN
COUNTERFEITING RING SMASHED
By REGGIE DA COSTA, Senior Crime Reporter

The counterfeiting ring led by disgraced detective Homer Glass has been smashed, with those engaged in the illegal operations facing trial. Four premises have been raided, resulting in the confiscation of machinery used to print the fake £5 banknotes that have flooded Melbourne.

The police have revealed the identity of the brave woman who helped bring these criminals to the attention of the Criminal Investigation Branch.

In a statement issued last Friday, Detective Inspector Clary Blain said:

"Acting on information supplied to the police by Mrs Mavis da Costa, regarding suspected illegal activities being carried out in the garage behind her Richmond home, the Victoria Police requested that she go undercover to expose the alleged counterfeiters.

"Over a period of weeks, Mrs da Costa provided police with valuable information about the workings and composition of the gang. Today, the garage was raided. Plant, paper, and ink used in the production of fake banknotes were

impounded and will be used as evidence during the trial. Mrs da Costa was escorted back to the headquarters of the Criminal Investigation Branch where she identified Detective Sergeant Homer Glass as the ringleader of the gang.

"Firebell Lane, Richmond, was one of four locations in Melbourne producing counterfeit banknotes. It appears that Glass had manoeuvred himself into the position of heading the taskforce entrusted with uncovering the gangs involved in the counterfeiting industry. This would facilitate his own illegal activities and allow him to gain a monopoly over the production and trade in fake banknotes. He has been taken into custody. Bail will be opposed.

"The Criminal Investigation Branch commends Mrs da Costa for her bravery in assisting with the arrest of these criminals."

Detective Inspector Clary Blain, CIB.

[*The Argus*, November 28, 1927]

R uby put down the newspaper. 'That's wonderful. Have you heard from your mother?'

Reggie turned back from the window overlooking Swan Street and smiled. 'She's delighted. She'll see her friends on Thursday and they will be impressed. No jokes at her expense now!'

'There's something I want to discuss with you,' said Ruby, her face serious.

'You're not still worried about what happened on the Geelong Road?'

'Of course, I am. You could have been killed.'

'Trust me, Ruby, I can look after myself.'

'Be careful, that's all.' She got up from the chair and stood beside him. 'The fact is that I've been thinking about our arrangements after the wedding.'

'Go on, my love.'

'Originally, we decided that you would move into my house in Tanner Street. But I've changed my mind. I think that we should buy a house that can accommodate your mother too.'

'You think that we should protect her from herself? She's like a babe in the woods. Trouble finds her.'

'No, that's not the reason. I think she's lonely. She only sees her friends once a week. She leads a quiet life. That's why she gets taken in by the wrong people.'

'You'd want Mavis to live with us?'

'My relationship with her is so much better now. We could choose a house that offers some privacy for her and us, such as a place with a bungalow. She could rent out her home in Firebell Lane. It would give her some ready cash, so that she wouldn't be dependent on us financially.'

'Where did you have in mind?'

'I know that you're attached to Richmond. It's a haven for crime, your bread and butter. But I was thinking of Brighton. It's a lovely place to live, close to the beach. It's where Mildred Bardsley Smith lives. Mavis would love that.'

'Move back to Brighton?' Reggie said excitedly. 'Brighton is where I grew up. Can we afford it?'

'I've been checking the classified columns. There's a lovely, six-room, brick house, a short walk from Middle Brighton station, and with sewerage, a made road, all for £1600. It also has an art studio in the backyard which could be converted into separate accommodation. I've talked to the agent. He says that we could do a tour of the house this weekend, if we want to. The truth is, Reggie, that I have enough money left over from my sister's inheritance, without selling Tanner Street.'

Reggie stroked his moustache. 'Brighton. Is there a garage at this house too?'

'A brick one, just right for the Minerva. With a lock on the doors. What do you think?'

'I think that we should take a look. Should I mention it to Mother?'

'Let's find the right house first before we ask her, but the choice to come with us has to be hers.'

'Agreed.'

'I'm so pleased that you like the idea. Now, tell me whether there's been any developments in the White Feather Murders, apart from the threat against you.'

'There have been a few developments. In fact, today, I received a telephone call from Father Adder.'

'Who's he?'

'It took me a moment to register at first, but I realised that he's the priest mentioned in the latest Poison Pen column.'

'A viper in the nest,' said Ruby, nodding her head. 'A snake in the grass. The play on words. A viper is a snake, as is an adder.'

'Clever girl,' said Reggie. 'I'd almost forgotten about the Poison Pen, what with the drama surrounding Mother and The Undertaker. Father Adder told me that he was horrified when he realised that my story was about him, and that he could be a target of the White Feather Murderer. He read *The Truth*'s article and compared it with my suggestion that he worked in an asylum. That's exactly where he worked after the war: Kew Hospital for the Insane, in 1919.'

'Did he explain what he did that was so wrong?'

'He used to visit ex-soldiers who were experiencing shell shock. They were damaged men who couldn't cope with life and needed to be hospitalised. The patients confided in him, telling him their fears and their troubles, of which there were many. It seems that some of these men were regarded as troublemakers, resisting attempts to control them. Some were medicated; some underwent electrotherapy; some were isolated; some were put in straitjackets for long periods. Their treatment was inhumane, Adder admits. But, at that stage in his life, he felt that his duty was to the doctors, rather than to the patients.

'Adder recalls the case of a patient who admitted himself to the asylum. A voluntary inmate. He was troubled, but harmless, according to Adder. A sensitive soul who had seen too much. After a few weeks, he confided in the cleric that he was revolted by the treatment that his fellow soldiers were forced to undergo, which he thought amounted to torture. He told him, in confidence, that he intended to quit the asylum and expose what was really going on there. Rather than keeping a confidence as a priest should do, Adder passed the name of this man on to the authorities who administered the asylum.'

'What did they do to him?'

'Punishment was quick and brutal. The former soldier, who had admitted himself voluntarily, was reclassified as a lunatic and was detained. His property and estate were put under the control of the administrators of the asylum.'

'That's horrible. What happened to him?'

'Adder doesn't know.'

'Did he tell you the man's name?'

'He didn't want to, but I told him that if I knew the identity of this patient, I could track him down and see if he's involved in these murders. Finally, he relented. The patient's name was Leo Kane. He came from Kangaroo Flat. I remembered that someone else had lived there too.'

'And who was that?'

'Mrs Burns. That's a coincidence that can't be ignored. It's a small town outside Bendigo. Population 900.'

'Have you been able to locate Leo Kane?'

'Not yet, but I'll get onto it tomorrow.'

'Do you think that he's the White Feather Murderer?'

Reggie shrugged his shoulders. 'We can't be sure. It depends if he knew Nurse Webb, Captain Badger, and Dr Fox.'

'Is this the only time that Father Adder breached a confidence?'

'He wouldn't answer that question, but I suggest that it wasn't. However, word got out about what he'd done. The patients were scathing, according to him. They drove him out, he said, after he'd been there for three months. He was bitter about that. Said that he was just doing his job. He went back into a regular parish and that's where he got into trouble again. *The Truth*'s Poison Pen asserted that he became involved with one of his parishioners and drove her to suicide.'

'A man of few ethics. How could a Man of the Cloth do that? Betray a confidence and break his vows?'

'I don't know.'

'Where is Father Adder now?'

'He wouldn't say. Somewhere in Victoria, I'd think. But he says that he has no intention of returning to Melbourne until the White Feather Murderer is under lock and key. He's scared that he'll be tracked down and killed, like the others.'

'So why did he telephone you?'

'He says that he wanted me to know that my theory about the White Feather Murderer is true. He also despairs of the police catching the killer, given the statement from Detective Sergeant Glass. I was able to tell him that Glass has been removed from his position, and that there is a good chance that the deaths will be taken seriously.'

'At least you're investigating them.'

Reggie chuckled. 'I worry about you sometimes, Ruby. You show an unhealthy interest in crime.'

'It's so much more interesting than typing up invoices for Smith and Sons' clients. Tell me more.'

'I've also found out that someone pretending to be your brother contacted Herbert Hawke requesting information about Agnes. He asked why she left Badger. This man knew that Agnes wasn't dead, and that Badger was a bigamist.'

'Was this *before* Badger was featured in the Poison Pen column?'

'It was. The same thing happened with Nurse Webb. A person, claiming to be me, questioned the parents of one of Beryl's patients and found out that she was an addict, and that the hospital had fired her.'

Ruby frowned. 'That's risky on his part. I guess he did the same thing with Mrs Burns, trying to gather information for the Poison Pen's column, although her drinking seems to have been an open secret. Did Dr Fox have friends or family that you could speak to?'

'I did make enquiries, but there was no one close to him, so it's hard to know where you'd start.'

'It sounds like the killer is determined and methodical. He built a case in advance against each of the victims.'

'Which makes it even more pressing that we find this killer before he disappears from view, his job done.'

Chapter Forty-Seven

Clary Blain was back in his element, unfettered by the need to defend himself against the allegations made by The Undertaker. Even the Chief Commissioner had mumbled an apology of sorts and had praised Blain for his work in exposing Glass's duplicity. The arrest of those involved in the counterfeiting racket had brought good newspaper coverage for the Force. It had enhanced the reputation of the Victoria Police in being transparent in its investigations, given that many government institutions would have covered up corruption in the ranks.

As for Mavis da Costa, she was feted by her friends for her bravery. Although they encouraged her to reveal the sordid details of her undercover work, modesty prevented her from doing so, as well as her inability to make up convincing lies.

The fact that Glass's criminal associates agreed to give evidence against him, in return for reduced sentences, ensured that Reggie's mother would not be called on to testify in court. Blain assured her that there was more than enough evidence to convict him, and that, once he had completed his jail term, an extradition order would be issued by the New South Wales authorities asking for his return to face separate charges, related to the disappearance of cocaine seized during a raid that he had overseen.

With The Undertaker consigned to the graveyard of corrupt coppers, Clary Blain had been restored to his rightful place as an honest and capable policeman, except for those times when he imbibed a little too much Scotch whisky.

As he sat at his desk, Clary opened the file on what Reggie had dubbed the 'White Feather Murders' and re-read his notes, going through the facts of each case methodically.

Herbert Hawke would be charged with blackmail, based on threatening letters he had written to Captain Badger and the evidence of the transactions paid to him from the dead man's bank account. For this crime, he would face several months in prison.

It was true that Hawke could be placed at the scene of the crime, as could his sister, Agnes, but there was no real proof that either was responsible for Badger's murder. The coroner had confirmed that the bump on Badger's head had not been the cause of death, but rather that a single shot through the heart had killed him. There were no fingerprints on the gun which matched either of the siblings, and Herbert had admitted to nothing more than pushing his brother-in-law. The evidence, at present, was circumstantial, and would not result in Herbert's conviction on a murder charge, according to the Crown Prosecutor. There was also the little matter of the white feather in his hand, tying Badger's death to the cases of Mrs Burns, Nurse Webb, and Dr Fox.

Blain hated to admit it, but the feather gave credence to Reggie's theory that one killer was involved, linked to the Poison Pen columns, but it was far from being proven.

However, Mrs Burns' death was difficult to classify as murder. She had died of alcoholic poisoning, choking on her vomit. There were, surprisingly, no bottles in her dressing room, although there was the chance that the caretaker had removed them and put them in the rubbish before discovering the body. Her bag, too, was missing, which might have contained them. But attempts to clarify this had been fruitless, because the caretaker had left the employ of the Temperance Union and could not be located.

As for Miss Webb, her statement contained nothing noteworthy. She had been under the influence of drugs when she was gassed and could not clarify what had happened on that day. However, the white feather in her hand could not be ignored, nor the ill will felt towards her by her patients' families.

Dr Dwight had originally been linked to the Poison Pen column, but the testimony of his former colleague, Dr Lynas Farrington, disputed that connection. The discovery of Dwight's Rolex watch in the possession of Charles, his son, confirmed that his death was not the work of the White Feather Murderer. Charles had also been found with a quantity of cocaine and a large sum of money, both presumed stolen from Dr Dwight's safe. The Crown Prosecutor was drawing up charges of robbery and manslaughter against Dwight's son, who was being held on remand. It seemed that Reggie had been right all along that Dwight was not the subject of the Poison Pen's column. Clary had communicated his findings to Reggie in a telephone call.

'We've got him, Charles Dwight. Thanks for the tip-off, Reggie. We confirmed with Dr Dwight's secretary and Dr Farrington that father and son had been estranged. The son fell in with a bad lot, drank, and took drugs, and wanted money from his father to pay for his addictions. Dr Dwight refused and cut off contact with him. Charles visited his father again a month before the murder. They argued, according to his secretary.'

'Charles had a key?'

'It's doubtful. On the night of his father's death, Charles came in through a window, leaving footprints in the garden bed, which we've since matched with his. When we visited Charles in the rooming house, he was wearing his father's Rolex. Everett Dwight's initials were engraved on the watch case.'

'He confessed?'

'He did. He said that his father disturbed him while he was rummaging through the house looking for money and jewellery. He threatened Dr Dwight with a knife and told him to open the safe. He did, but the father tried to wrest the knife from Charles' hand. In the scuffle, Dr Dwight was stabbed. Charles took the cocaine, watch, and money and was about to leave when he remembered the stuffed bird on the side table near the front door. He lifted the glass case and plucked out a feather, went back upstairs, and left it on the body. He thought it would point to the White Feather Murderer, and direct police enquiries away from him. We found traces of blood on the glass covering the bird.'

'Is he remorseful?'

'I don't think so, but maybe in time he'll realise what he's done.'

Which brought Clary to the case of Dr Fox. Clary's investigations into Fox's background had uncovered the unsavoury truth that Herman Fox was a slaughterman who had taken advantage of the confusion and chaos of war to put himself forward as a qualified doctor. He had pursued his new profession without being exposed as a charlatan. It was a horrifying scenario, in Clary's view, that a man, whose job was to slaughter animals for the meat market, was able to perform operations on injured soldiers brought in from the battlefield and had been able to continue the charade when the war was over. However, despite the case files stating that no white feather had been found in the bath, Blain guessed that Glass was responsible for its removal. The fact was that Reggie's theory appeared credible, but, as a detective, Clary needed more than a hypothesis.

In order to identify the man who called himself the Poison Pen, and to bring the investigation to a close, Clary had visited the offices of *The Truth*. He had been angry when the editor-in-chief had refused to co-operate.

'I have never met the Poison Pen,' he claimed. 'I don't even know where he lives.'

'That is ridiculous. How do you pay him if you don't know anything at all about him?' Clary argued.

The editor looked at him defiantly. 'It's confidential. It's against our principles to expose our journalists to police examination.'

'Even if you're harbouring a murderer?'

The editor had pooh-poohed the suggestion. 'According to that hack, Reggie da Costa, there's some crazed killer on the loose. That's no reason for me to throw *my* reporter to the wolves. The Poison Pen has been doing his column for six years. Until this point in time, there's been no one calling him into question, either as a murderer or someone inciting a person to violence. The fact is that the identity of the people in question is kept deliberately vague. There are no names mentioned. The details in his column could fit any number of people.'

'Such as the Honourable Cuthbert Badger?'

The editor winced. 'But the others remain anonymous.'

As he turned to go, Clary said, 'Talk to a lawyer if you won't listen to me.

There's blood on your hands, mate. Co-operate; otherwise, you might be an accessory to murder.'

Chapter Forty-Eight

Reggie contended that a crime reporter's most important asset was not his ability to sniff out incriminating evidence or have a sixth sense as to whom was responsible for a crime, but the strength of his circle of contacts. Information, particularly insider information, was vital. Over the years, he had acquired informants and contacts from a wide variety of sources, including Melbourne's underworld, the coroner's office, the mortuary, and, of course, the Victoria Police, in the form of Clary Blain. As a result, he was able to access information that was not publicly available, and which kept him ahead of the competition.

After his telephone call with Father Adder, Reggie had sent a letter to Theo Georgiou, his contact in the Registry for Births, Deaths, and Marriages. He requested information on Leo Kane, who, according to the priest, had been victimised while he was a patient in the Kew Hospital for the Insane. Kane's status—dead or alive, resident of or released from the asylum—would have a huge bearing on the direction of the investigation. He was taking shape as the White Feather Murderer. Kane, an ex-soldier, was one of few suspects who could fit the bill of being associated with Adder, Burns, Fox, and Webb, as well as Captain Badger.

* * *

On Wednesday morning, Theo and Reggie met at The Rose Hotel in Fitzroy, Theo's favourite pub.

'My father used to bring me here when I was young,' he said. 'The conversation was always about football. Look at the photographs on the wall.'

'The ghosts of football teams past,' observed Reggie, glancing at the black and white pictures of Australian Rules Football Premiership teams, the players sitting in rows with their arms folded, staring into the camera.

Theo had added a few pounds to his frame in recent years, being short and solidly built. His untidy, thick moustache was still intact, despite the hair on his head consisting of only a few white strands. Conservatively dressed in a grey, double-breasted suit, which had been his staple at work for years, Theo's appearance contrasted with Reggie's fastidiously good grooming and stylish navy pinstripe three-piece suit, paired with a gold tie.

They ordered beers and found a table close to the horseshoe-shaped bar.

'Any luck, Theo?' asked Reggie.

'I have a friend who located Kane's Army service record.' Theo removed a notebook from his jacket pocket and referred to it. 'Leo Warwick Kane. Born in Kangaroo Flat in the county of Bendigo. Enlisted 23rd December 1916, aged 18 years.'

'Go on.'

'Joined the 37th Australian Infantry Battalion.'

Reggie whistled. 'Messines. He fought at Messines. I wonder—'

'What, mate?'

'If he served under Captain Cuthbert Badger.'

Theo shook his head. 'I can't answer that.'

'But I know someone who can,' said Reggie, his eyes shining with anticipation. 'Herbert Hawke. He was Badger's brother-in-law. We're making headway. Have you got any information on his medical history?'

Georgiou referred to his notes. 'Not much, unfortunately. There's an official letter from Base Records advising that Corporal L.W. Kane of the 37th Battalion was returned to Australia, departing England on April 10, 1919. He was due to arrive in Melbourne in late May of that year.'

'That's great news, Theo. This means that Leo Kane could have been sent to the London hospital where Webb and Fox were working before he came home. Any mention of him being released from the Kew Hospital for the

Insane?'

'That's beyond my scope. My sources don't go that far. What's this all about?'

'What it means, Theo, is that Leo Kane is in the frame for murder. He's the White Feather Murderer.'

Theo shook his head. 'There's one problem with that theory, Reggie. I found his death certificate. Leo Kane died three months ago on the 31st of August.'

Chapter Forty-Nine

I t was an uncharacteristically subdued Reggie da Costa who returned to the offices of *The Argus* that afternoon. Kane was dead. And he was back to square one in his search for a killer.

He sat at his desk and stared at the fresh piece of paper on the roller of his typewriter. The blank sheet signified the dead end that he'd reached in his investigation. After all this time and intensive research, he had nothing to show for it. Three deaths and one attempted murder had led to this moment—one which was a crime reporter's worst nightmare—of having no obvious suspect.

He was being forced to review the suspects whom he'd discarded. It was an underwhelming selection, most with no links to the others defamed by the Poison Pen. The one and only viable suspect—Leo Kane—had been wiped from the list.

With nothing else to do, Reggie picked up the telephone and rang Mrs Badger, asking her if it were possible to contact her brother. At the least, he could confirm whether Badger and Kane had known each other.

Shortly after, Herbert Hawke was on the other end of the telephone.

'What do you want, Mr da Costa? Nothing good, I'd suspect.'

'A quick question for you, Mr Hawke. Was Corporal Kane in your company at Messines?'

There was silence at the other end of the telephone. 'Leo? Yes, I knew him.'

'Was Captain Badger his senior officer?'

'Indeed, he was.'

'Do you know what happened to Kane?'

'From memory, he was evacuated to a field hospital suffering from war trauma. An extreme case. The last I heard of him was that they'd shipped him to London for further treatment. After that, I don't know.'

'You were at Mont Park asylum after the war. He wasn't sent there?'

'Not in my time. As I said, I don't know where he was sent.' There was silence for a moment or two. 'Why do you want to know about him?'

'I'm following up a line of enquiry. Thanks for your assistance.'

'Mr da Costa. Have you heard if I'm going to be charged with Badger's murder?'

'As far as I know, the police don't have a case.'

'Thank you. I didn't kill him, you know.'

Reggie hung up the telephone and sighed. He started to type, methodically expounding on the connections between each of the Poison Pen's hypocrites and Leo Kane.

Mrs Burns had been a resident of Kangaroo Flat, as had Leo Kane, but what her part had been in this saga was unknown. It was highly likely that they had crossed paths while living in the same town, and her aggressive and opinionated stance on many issues might have been a source of conflict.

Corporal Kane and Captain Badger had both been at Messines in 1917. After one million pounds of explosives were blown up behind enemy lines, thousands of German soldiers were obliterated. As smoke, dust, and debris shrouded the landscape, Leo Kane was one of many Australian, British, and New Zealand soldiers ordered to advance across No Man's Land to storm the ridge, while his senior officer, Captain Badger, cowered in the trenches. It was fair to assume that Kane held Badger in contempt, even hated him.

According to Herbert Hawke, Kane had been sent to a field hospital and went on to London for treatment for war trauma. Was it possible that he had suffered at the hands of Nurse Webb and Dr Fox, who had practised electro-convulsive 'therapy' to cure their patients? In hindsight, Webb had called it 'torture.'

There was also the confession of the priest, Father Adder, who had betrayed Leo Kane's confidence and alerted the authorities of the Kew asylum to his intention to publicise the inhumane treatment of the patients.

Reggie tore the piece of paper from the typewriter and screwed it up. It was a useless exercise bringing a case against Kane because he was dead.

Dusty strode into the office and threw himself into a chair, his long legs stuck out in front of him. 'You look like your best friend died, Reggie.'

'In a sense, he did.'

He frowned. 'Tell me about it.'

Over the next few minutes, Reggie shared with his colleague how his theory had been blown to smithereens.

'In two days,' he added, 'the Poison Pen will feature another of his hypocrites. And I'm back at the beginning in bringing a case against any of the suspects.'

Dusty looked thoughtful. 'Have you checked the death notices for Leo Kane? Perhaps there's something there that might help you.'

Reluctantly, Reggie got up from his desk. 'I suppose it's worth a try. Are you busy?'

'Happy to help, boss.'

Downstairs, they entered the room dedicated to housing back copies of *The Argus*, presided over by the librarian. He looked up from his work.

'Reggie. Dusty. Good to see you. What brings you to the bowels of the building? Is this a social call?'

'Afraid not. Duncan, can you spare us a moment?' asked Reggie.

'Of course. I'm finishing up my card file on Squizzy Taylor's murder. If you need anything on him, it's all there.'

'Thanks for that. Today, we want the newspapers from the 1st to the 14th of September this year. It's the Death notices we're interested in.'

'That's an easy one.'

He walked over to the bookshelves and slid the relevant copies onto a trolley, then pushed it over to the two reporters.

'There's a table over there that you can use. I'll file them back when you've finished.'

Shortly after, they were poring over back copies of *The Argus*, searching for a reference to Leo Kane in the classified section.

'Here it is, Reggie,' said Dusty. 'Friday, the 3rd of September.'

KANE. –On the 31st of August, at Melbourne Hospital, Leo Warwick, dearly loved brother of Kendrick, aged 29 years.

He came back from the Western Front a shadow of a man. He was all but destroyed. While others returned with ruined lungs, scarred faces, missing legs and arms, he was damaged beyond repair: his mind all messed up, like a pot of stew that has boiled down on the hob, just a few lumps left, no broth to hold it together.

They put him away. They eradicated any chance of re-covery. Medicated to the eyeballs, his memory gone, just existing.

They let him out two months ago without telling me.

He stood in front of a train.

The two reporters exchanged looks.

'I've never seen a death notice like that before,' commented Dusty.

'Nor I. But Kendrick Kane? That rings a bell,' said Reggie.

'Bluey Talbot will remember,' said Dusty. 'He's a walking encyclopaedia of crime.'

Back in the newsroom, Bluey was sitting at his desk. He looked up in surprise as Reggie and Dusty sat down in front of him.

'Bluey, we need your help,' said Reggie. 'Have you ever heard of a bloke called Kendrick Kane?'

Talbot pulled a face. 'That's a name I haven't heard in a good while. Kendrick Kane. Sergeant KK, as he was known. A country cop, in Bendigo. Unpopular with bootleggers because of his habit of dressing as an AIF soldier and buying illegal grog from them, then arresting them. He wasn't afraid to root out corruption in the ranks by blowing the whistle on his fellow police. He became obsessed. The shame of it was that he was an honest cop who didn't know when to stop. Ultimately, he upset his masters. They didn't like their dirty linen being aired in public.'

'What happened to him?'

'He was demoted and created a stink about his treatment. He was forced to resign and hasn't been heard from since. Dropped from view.'

'When was this?'

Bluey tapped the desk. 'About six years ago.' He looked from Reggie to Dusty. 'What's this about, laddies?'

'Wish I could be sure,' said Reggie. 'Thanks, Bluey.'

They were silent as they returned to Reggie's office.

'What do you think?' asked Dusty.

'Sergeant KK.' He opened his notebook and checked an entry from the start of November. 'Ruby and I were reading threatening letters sent to Mrs Burns. This one was particularly sinister:

"I know your nasty little secret. You're not only a hypocrite but you've ruined the life of someone special to me. Revenge will be sweet.

KK."'

'You don't think that it's a coincidence?' asked Dusty.

'You only have to look at the language he used. Calls her a hypocrite. Not much doubt, I'd say.'

Dusty nodded in agreement. 'Not much doubt.'

Reggie tapped his pencil on the desk. 'Kendrick Kane holds a grudge because of the way he was treated when he was in the police force. He believed that he was rooting out corruption and was punished because he upset people in power. He leaves Bendigo and heads for Melbourne. Finds himself a job at *The Truth* where he can vent his anger and stay anonymous. Writing the Poison Pen column gives him the perfect opportunity to denounce and ridicule those he despises.'

'You're right, boss. Then Leo kills himself.'

'The little brother that he loves is let out of the asylum, not knowing where Kendrick is. Perhaps Leo goes to Kangaroo Flat and finds him gone. Lost and alone, with no one to turn to, Leo commits suicide. Somehow, Kendrick finds out. Perhaps he tries to visit his brother at Kew and is told that he's been released. He contacts the police, the hospitals, and discovers that his brother has died. He's already angry and Leo's death pushes him over the edge.'

'He takes revenge on those who ruined his brother's life.'

'Somehow Kendrick learned Leo's story and apportioned blame on those people who impacted on his brother's life so callously. Ex-copper. Knows how to gather background information on Burns, Webb, Fox, Badger, and Adder. He impersonates me to find out about Nurse Webb's dirty deeds.'

'And he pretends to be me when he telephones Herbert Hawke, asking questions about Badger,' added Dusty.

'He writes about them in his Poison Pen column in such a way that they will recognise themselves and fear the consequences when the public realises the truth about them: that they are hypocrites. Their legacy, being people in roles that the public trusts and admires—nurse, doctor, priest, and politician—will be tarnished. But the column is not enough. He must make sure that they suffer, like his brother did. They must die.'

Dusty let out a long breath. 'And the white feather?'

'The white feather. That's the clue. That's the symbol behind these murders.' Reggie raised a finger, a smile on his face. 'The first victim. Mrs Burns. Always advocating for a cause. The white feather. She gave Leo Kane a white feather.'

'You're right, Reggie. The symbol of cowardice, handed out to those who hadn't enlisted.'

'Mrs Burns started it: Leo's descent into despair. He joined up, obviously pressured into it. A sensitive young man, not equipped to deal with the horrors of the battlefield. He becomes, as his brother says in his obituary, "a shadow of a man…all but destroyed." As you said, Kendrick took revenge on those who ruined his brother's life.'

Reggie added portentously, 'I think we have our White Feather Murderer.'

Chapter Fifty

'It's perfect,' thought Ruby, as she stood out the front of the red, brick house in Brighton.

The previous weekend, she and Reggie had inspected the pretty Edwardian home in Carpenter Street, convenient to both the beach and the railway station. It consisted of two large bedrooms and a smaller one, a kitchen, a comfortable sitting room, and dining area. A highlight was that the house had been refurbished in the last couple of years, adding an indoor toilet in the bathroom and a hot water service.

In the large backyard was a roomy studio, which could easily be converted to accommodation for Reggie's mother, if she decided to join them. It had been built to cater for their artist son, but since he had moved out, the owners had decided to sell.

Fretwork, painted green, embellished the verandah, and stained-glass windows, featuring brightly coloured parrots and gum leaves, surrounded the magnificent, oak front door.

The icing on the cake, according to Ruby's future husband, was the brick garage at the end of a paved driveway, perfect for storing his Minerva.

'Protected from bad weather and out of sight of car thieves, what a bonus!' he had declared.

'There's a very large closet in the main bedroom,' added Ruby. 'You shouldn't forget that.' She had stifled a giggle as Reggie nodded his head enthusiastically.

Inside, the house had all the features of the Edwardian period: ceiling roses, ornate cornices, timber skirting boards, and solid timber doors, as well as polished floorboards.

After the tour by the estate agent, they had returned to his office to discuss what they were prepared to offer.

'The owners want £1600. It's a bargain,' he said confidently.

Reggie and Ruby exchanged looks, then the crime reporter went into action. 'I read about this area recently. There was some crazed fellow—the Death Mask Murderer—on the loose here a few years ago.'

The agent looked uncomfortable. 'I seem to remember something about him. But he's locked up now.'

'And he was shaving the heads of young women and making death masks from their faces. It happened close to here, I believe.'

Ruby looked suitably uneasy. 'Death masks. Murderers. I'm not sure if we should—'

The agent sat upright. 'The owners are keen to sell. Perhaps we could offer them slightly less. Perhaps £1500?'

'I don't know,' whispered Ruby.

'What about £1400?' suggested Reggie. 'Given the unsavoury reputation of this area, I think that's a reasonable compromise.'

'It's all that we can afford in the end,' added Ruby. 'And it will be cash.'

'Cash? No mortgage?' said the agent. 'In that case, they might be interested. Let me contact you tomorrow evening. I should have an answer by then.'

On the way home, they had stopped at Mavis's house in Firebell Lane. She was surprised to see them, but invited them in.

'Mother, we have a proposition for you,' said Reggie, watching her pour three cups of tea from a floral, porcelain teapot.

'What is it, dear?'

'Ruby and I are looking for a house together, and we've found just the place in Brighton. We'd love you to move in with us. It's not far from Mildred Bardsley Smith's house.'

Mavis put the teapot down in shock. 'Brighton? Close to Mildred? Live with you?'

'If you'd rather not, we won't be offended,' Ruby assured her. 'But it has a lovely studio in the backyard, which could easily be converted into living quarters for you. It even has a bathroom. It's light and airy and overlooks a rose garden.'

'You wouldn't mind, Ruby?' asked Mavis uncertainly. 'I don't want to impose on you when you're starting out on married life together.'

'Not at all. In fact, I suggested it. You could dine with us each night and sit with us until bedtime, if you choose.'

'That sounds very nice.' She smiled. 'Would I have to sell Firebell Lane?'

'Not at all,' Reggie assured her. 'You could rent it out. Have your own source of income to buy clothes, go on outings with your friends, even have a holiday.'

'My own money? A holiday?' Her face lit up. 'I'd be close to Mildred and my friends. That would be lovely.'

'As soon as we sign the contract, we'll take you through the house and you can make the final decision,' said Reggie. 'We'll renovate the bungalow according to your wishes.'

And thus, the purchase of the Brighton house was completed, at the price offered by the future Mr and Mrs da Costa, with settlement occurring after their return from the honeymoon. Mavis was delighted at the prospect of living, albeit independently, with her beloved son and his bride, in a location so convenient to her best friend, Mildred Bardsley Smith.

'It's perfect,' said Ruby as she gazed at the immaculate front garden with its row of roses. 'Absolutely perfect.'

Chapter Fifty-One

The body was slumped forward in the chair, the head resting on the carriage of the typewriter. Adult male, dressed in pyjamas. Detective Inspector Clary Blain approached the corpse tentatively, his eyes searching for those random clues so beloved by the police. He reviewed the items that were arranged on the desk in front of the corpse: a dictionary, a pile of blank, white paper, the typewriter, and a bottle of ink with its cork removed. A pool of black liquid had dried on the wooden floorboards to the right of the man's foot. Clary leaned down and rubbed it, leaving a smudge on his fingertip. Ink.

The victim had been typing. A sheet of paper was in the roller, the first line partially obscured. The detective moved around to the left of the body to get a better look. That's when he noticed it. The shaft of a white feather had been jammed into the back of the dead man's left hand, which was resting on the desk. A thin trail of blood had leaked from the wound. But this was no ordinary feather: It had been crafted into a quill with a metal nib.

Clary turned his attention back to the paper in the typewriter and pulled it out gently. As he read, his eyebrows rose and he grunted. It appeared to be both a confession and a suicide note:

I am the Poison Pen.

I have taken it upon myself to lay bare the hypocrisy of those whom we foolishly admire for their principles and

integrity. Burns: an Intoxicated Temperance Advocate; Webb: a Noxious Nurse; Badger: a Dis-Honourable Humbug; Fox: a Phoney Physician; and Adder: a Prevaricating Priest. All have been exposed to public view and ridicule. All deserved to die.

I can hear the dogs baying for my blood. The end is near.

I am content.

Oliver Short.

Clary inspected the ink bottle. It was half full, but not of Indian ink; rather a clear, colourless liquid. He lowered his head and sniffed the contents. 'Strong odour. Bitter almonds. Cyanide? Certainly not ink,' he muttered to himself.

'Hmm.' His gaze shifted from the ink bottle to the feather protruding from the man's hand. 'I wonder? Help me, constable.'

Together, they took hold of the man's shoulders and shifted him back so that the chest area was visible. No sign of a bullet or knife wound. A few bubbles of foam had congregated around his mouth.

'Looks like cyanide.' They gently lowered him back against the desk and the typewriter.

Blain inspected the room. The bed unmade; no drawers pulled out of the tallboy; the clothing in the closet hanging tidily; everything in its place. A fire had been burning in the grate at some stage. There was no sign of a struggle. No sign that the room had been searched for valuables or cash. No sign that the dead man had met with foul play. It must be suicide.

Clary visualised the scene. The man got out of bed, having made the decision to end it all. He sat at the desk wearing his pyjamas and typed the suicide note. Judging by the fact that there were no lights on in the room, it had to be sometime after sunrise. He emptied the ink bottle, filled it with the colourless liquid that he had purchased in preparation for this moment. He drank some of the poison, took the quill in his right hand, dipped it into the ink bottle, and drove it into the back of his left hand.

Blain addressed the constable. 'Doctor and photographer on the way?'

Blanch nodded. 'Yes, sir.'

'Who found him?'

'A courier. He says that he was employed to collect an envelope every second Thursday at 1:00 p.m. According to the courier, the envelope was sealed with a wax stamp. The client was very specific. Take the letter and leave. The courier rang the doorbell, but no one answered. He looked through the window and could see a man sitting at the desk in the front room. He called out to him but received no reply. He tried the door and found it open, entered, then contacted the police.'

'Did he interfere in any way with the body? Touch anything?'

'No, sir. He had a quick look and got out.'

'Where was he to deliver this envelope?'

'*The Truth* newspaper, sir.'

'Where is he now?'

'Giving a statement to one of the constables. He's out the front, sir.'

'Good work, Blanch. Hold him there, so I can speak to him. I want photographs of the crime scene first, then the doctor can check the body. Take the ink bottle away to be analysed after you put the cork back in. Careful, I suspect it's cyanide. I want the letter placed in a bag as evidence after the medical examiner removes the body. No one is to enter the house without my permission. You know the drill.'

As an afterthought, Blain returned to the desk and pulled out the drawer. Inside was a rental agreement in the name of Oliver Short. He smiled. We have the Poison Pen, he thought.

The telephone was in the hallway.

'Put me through to Reggie da Costa, at *The Argus.*'

Chapter Fifty-Two

The telephone on Reggie da Costa's desk began to ring, interrupting his train of thought. He was putting the finishing touches to his next article on the aftermath of the Squizzy Taylor shooting and its implications for gang activity in Melbourne.

'Call for you, Mr da Costa. Detective Inspector Blain.'

'Put him through, Doris.'

'Reggie, it's me.' The growling tones of Detective Inspector Clary Blain were as music to his ears, heralding another tipoff, which would be repaid with copious amounts of the finest Scotch that the Duke of Wellington Hotel could provide.

'Clary.' Reggie leaned in, pencil and paper handy.

'We've found him.'

'Who?'

'The Poison Pen.'

Reggie dropped his pencil. 'Where?'

'Carlton. Dorrit Street.'

The telephone line went dead. Reggie knew better than to waste time. Grabbing his hat and coat, he pushed back his chair and hurried across the newsroom, his sense of urgency drawing the attention of his colleagues.

'What's the rush, mate?' cried one, while another called, 'Is there a suit sale at Leviathan's Menswear?'

He ignored them both.

Out in the laneway, the Minerva was waiting, her red and silver body glinting in the December sunshine. Reggie started the motorcar, threw it into gear, and slammed his foot on the accelerator, the tyres spinning on the roadway. The engine thundered as Reggie changed gears, the needle on the speedometer swinging sharply, edging upwards.

'The Poison Pen!' cried Reggie, above the roar of the engine. 'The White Feather Murderer in custody.'

Part of him was regretting that he had not been instrumental in arresting the fiend, but he consoled himself with the knowledge that he would be there to record the details of the Poison Pen's capture at the hands of the police. Kendrick Kane—ex-policeman and *Truth* columnist, killer, and avenger of his brother—would no longer terrorise Melbourne. What a story that would make when *The Argus* hit the newsstands!

Reggie guided the Minerva expertly, weaving between trams and trucks, ignoring the cries of foolhardy pedestrians who deigned to cross the road at traffic lights, and the clenched fists of enraged drivers whose inferior vehicles were cut off as they tried to come between Reggie and the story of the century. One shocked bystander described the passage of the Minerva up Elizabeth Street as that of a silver comet with a fiery tail.

Reggie turned into Victoria Street, then chose Cardigan Street, avoiding the clogged roads and foot traffic associated with the University of Melbourne. Past Argyle Square, right into Grattan Street, and left into Dorrit Street. As he drove, Reggie marvelled at his encyclopaedic knowledge of Melbourne's streets, one of the reasons why he never needed to waste time consulting a map on his way to a crime scene.

Up ahead he could see two police cars, part of the wireless unit, but no other signs that his competition had made it there ahead of him. He braked hard, the Minerva coming to a screeching halt just short of a group of bystanders who jumped out of the way in fright.

Standing on the footpath was a policeman in uniform, taking a statement from a man wearing a hat. Reggie rushed past, taking no notice, eager to find Clary and discover the latest on the apprehension of the Poison Pen. As a constable blocked Reggie from entering, Clary appeared in the doorway, a big smile on his flushed face.

'Let him through, Blanch. Come in, Reggie. He's inside. The Poison Pen.

You'll never guess what his name is—'

'Kendrick Kane,' Reggie interrupted, a smirk on his face.

Blain frowned and shook his head. 'Oliver Short. And he's dead.'

'What?' exclaimed Reggie. 'Oliver Short? It can't be.'

He followed Clary inside, the wind blown out of his sails, his excitement dissipating with each step.

They stood, contemplating the body sprawled over the desk, the head propped against the typewriter.

'He wrote a suicide note,' explained Clary. 'He mentioned each of his victims by name. Short is the Poison Pen. He thought that he was on the verge of being arrested, and he was right. According to the rental agreement, he's been living here for four months. There's also a notebook detailing the background information he found on each of his victims. As I said, it's clearcut.'

'Do you mind if I have a look at the body?'

'Don't touch him.'

Reggie approached Oliver Short, noting the quill driven into his left hand and the typewriter with the suicide note next to it. He shook his head as he read the note.

'I have to agree. It looks straightforward. Do you know anything about him?'

'What does it matter? He's dead. The case is closed.'

Reggie leaned in so that he could see the side of the man's face. A scar snaked down the right cheek. Around his neck was a chain from which was hung two identity discs, one round, the other octagonal. It was the type issued to soldiers during the Great War. He let out a breath and stood up.

'I've met him before. He was the courier.'

Clary shook his head. 'The courier is outside. He reported it. This is the Poison Pen.' He walked to the door and pointed at the thin man standing next to a constable on the footpath. 'See, there's the courier, giving his statement.'

'Clary, if you've never trusted me before, I want you to do so now. Listen to me. I want you to send two of your men outside, and station them near to the courier, in case he tries to make a run for it.'

Blain frowned but didn't hesitate. 'Constable, you heard Reggie. Get another of your men and position yourselves out there. Don't let him leave.'

He turned back to the reporter. 'What's this all about, Reggie?'

'The dead man is indeed Oliver Short. But he's the courier. I spoke to him at the offices of *The Truth* when he came to drop off the envelope from the Poison Pen, whose real name is Kendrick Kane. Short is the only person who could identify Kane and now, he's dead. The Poison Pen lured him back here, killed him, and swapped places with him. Kane planted enough evidence to make it appear that Oliver Short was the Poison Pen.'

'Such as the rental agreement and the suicide note?' suggested Clary.

'That's correct. Kane wanted to make sure that you'd find Short and think he was the killer, so he telephoned the police and reported finding the body. He hoped that his statement confirming the identity of the Poison Pen would be sufficient to stymie an investigation. To all appearances, the Poison Pen committed suicide, end of story. If the police decided to make further enquiries, Kendrick Kane would be long gone, with no one any the wiser.'

Clary looked down at Oliver Short's body, his face taking on a determined expression.

'Let's go.'

Three constables had gathered on the footpath, close to where the courier was standing. The man was in his forties, his face partially hidden by his hat.

Clary approached him, a genial expression on his face, his appearance that of an over-indulged but affable, distant relative, rather than a detective inspector in the Victoria Police.

'Thank you, sir, for reporting this to us. Could I have your name for our records?'

'John Tennyson.'

Reggie sidled up next to Blain and smiled at the man. 'I think that we've met twice before, Mr Tennyson. Isn't that so?' He reached forward and knocked off his hat. 'Although your hair was black, not blond.'

The man stared hard at Reggie, and slowly recognition dawned. He went to run but was grabbed by one of the constables. In the mad scramble that followed, he pushed the constable to the ground and shoved another aside. Only Reggie blocked his escape. He lashed out but didn't see Reggie's left hook until it was too late.

'Handcuff him,' ordered Clary.

Sprawled on the ground, Kendrick Kane looked up at Reggie, a wild look in his eyes. 'You. Da Costa. You're the scum of the earth.'

Reggie smiled benevolently. 'The caretaker at Temperance Hall. And, most probably, the driver of the Dodge on the Geelong Road. Kendrick Kane. Former Sergeant KK. You're the scum of the earth, not me. Take him away, Detective Inspector Blain.'

Chapter Fifty-Three

The following evening found Dusty and Reggie at Ruby's house, celebrating the arrest of Kendrick Kane, and a satisfying conclusion to the case known as the White Feather Murders.

'It's Friday,' commented Dusty, 'and *The Truth* has published a *mea culpa* apologising for harbouring a killer and using the newspaper as a forum for the Poison Pen venting his rage. They claim that they were ignorant as to his identity. They thought that they were protecting a columnist from retaliation. It's the first time I've ever heard of them issuing an apology.'

'How was he paid, if they didn't know his name?' asked Ruby.

'According to my mate, Crabby, at *The Truth*, his pay was sent to a post office box at the Melbourne General Post Office,' said Dusty. 'The editor insists that he didn't know Kane's name. The fact was that he was prepared to accept anonymity because Kane's column was immensely popular. The situation changed abruptly towards the end of September when the Poison Pen became, as Crabby put it, more *poisonous*. However, it was getting attention and that was the main thing. The problems arose after Badger was killed. It was murder and couldn't be written off as an accident. Like most people, the editor failed to see the connection between the victims, until the one and only Reggie da Costa drew attention to it.'

Reggie chuckled, enjoying the attention. 'It was the white feather. Such a peculiar thing to find at a crime scene. You had to ask the question when it was found at both the Webb and Badger houses.'

'You saw Detective Inspector Blain today, didn't you, Reggie?' asked Ruby.

'He's delighted now that he has the killer in custody. Kendrick Kane has confessed. He says that he will plead guilty, if he's permitted to make a statement to the court.'

'What else did Clary tell you?'

'Kendrick Kane's sole motivation was revenge. He wasn't carrying out a crusade against hypocrisy at all. It was all about his brother. Apparently, Leo was a gentle soul who, according to Kane, couldn't kill a fly. There was no way that he would have enlisted, but for the coercion applied by Mrs Burns. Kangaroo Flat was a small town. Everyone knew everyone. When Mrs Burns decided to pressure Leo into joining up, she used every means to publicly humiliate him. Every time he left the house to go to work, she'd find some way to intercept him. She wrote letters to him, harangued him in the street, gave him a white feather. It was a concerted campaign.'

'Why didn't Kendrick protect him?'

'He had moved to Bendigo and was working as a policeman. He saw Leo infrequently, so had no idea how bad things had become. Leo bowed to pressure and joined up. Things got worse for him. He was under the command of Captain Badger in the 37th Battalion. Messines happened. He told Kendrick later that he was almost buried alive in the battle. He had to fight his way out of the dirt, push past the remains of his fellow soldiers to breathe. Leo was under immense stress and he cracked. He was diagnosed with war trauma. They sent him to a field hospital, then on to London. You already know what happened to him there. Nurse Webb and her paramour, Dr Fox, almost finished the poor man off.'

'Back to Australia,' said Ruby. 'What happened after that?'

'He was struggling, but sane. He saw Kendrick occasionally. Told him what he'd experienced. Kendrick was angry, but he wasn't in a position to help him. He was still employed in Bendigo, fighting his own battles with authority.

'A couple of months later, Leo admitted himself voluntarily to Kew Hospital for the Insane. According to Kendrick, Leo was unemployed, drinking too much, and having nightmares. He thought that if he could rest, he'd improve. How wrong he was. After a few months, he'd seen and heard enough to be appalled at the treatment meted out to the patients there. He confided in a visiting priest, Father Adder, that he intended to inform the public about what was going on. Leo wanted to be a spokesman for the inmates after he was released. Before he could do anything constructive, he was reclassified as insane. Everything he owned outside of the asylum was confiscated.'

'Did Kendrick see his brother again?'

'Very occasionally. By this stage, Kendrick had taken up a position at *The Truth*. He had a bone to pick with authority and he intended to use it, considering himself unfairly treated.

'In May this year, Kendrick visited Leo for the last time. He was horrified. His brother was medicated and had undergone some form of electrotherapy. Leo didn't recognise him. When Kendrick went back a month later, he found out that Leo had been released. Weeks passed with no word as to his brother's whereabouts. Finally, he found out that Leo had died at The Melbourne Hospital, after standing in front of a train outside of Spencer Street station.'

'Kendrick must have been devastated,' said Ruby.

'He was. And angry. He swore an oath that he would avenge his brother. He methodically tracked down those whom he thought had contributed to Leo's decision to end his life. We know who they were, and what they did, but whether they deserved to die is another question.'

'Certainly, Oliver Short, the courier, didn't deserve to die,' said Ruby. 'Who was he? Did Kane tell Clary?'

'Kane said that he was a homeless man. He'd been wounded in the war. I think Kane thought that he did Short a favour, by giving him six years of payment for services rendered.'

'The house in Short's name?' asked Dusty. 'When did Kane start renting it?'

'Early September, when he conceived of the idea to avenge his brother. It's clear that he was planning to use Short as a scapegoat from that point on, so he put the house in Short's name. With me closing in on him and refusing to be warned off, and Father Adder making his escape, he knew the game was up. Oliver Short was the only man who could identify him, so the poor man had to die. Clary doubts that Kane feels any remorse.'

'What will happen to Kendrick Kane?' asked Ruby.

'He'll plead guilty to murder and beg the court for mercy on the basis that he was justified in killing Burns, Badger and Fox. Webb and Adder can regard themselves as lucky to have escaped his clutches. No doubt he'll hang from the end of a rope in due course.'

'Have they identified how Short died?'

'The quill in the back of his hand was dipped in cyanide. That wasn't enough to kill him, though. Clary thinks Short was forced to drink the poison. We'll have to wait for the coroner's report on that. There were ligature marks on Short's wrists, suggesting that he was restrained.

'Kane went to a lot of trouble setting up the crime scene,' added Reggie. 'The quill made of a white feather, the typed suicide note, the rental agreement in the top drawer, the notebook containing information on each victim. Even dressing Short in his pyjamas was a masterstroke. On the surface, it was designed to convince you that the killing spree of the White Feather Murderer had come to an end.'

'Lucky that you were on the scene, Reggie,' commented Dusty. 'Otherwise, he might have got away with it. Case closed? You're satisfied?'

'Case closed, Dusty.' He paused, a glimmer of a smile on his face. 'There's one thing that I should mention. When I first met Kendrick Kane, as the caretaker at Temperance Hall, the light was bad. But, yesterday, out in the sunlight, it was too obvious to ignore. Kane has the most intense blue eyes. Hypnotic, blue, staring eyes. You couldn't ignore them.'

'You believe in Count Lombroso's blue-eyed killer, after all?' asked Dusty, smirking.

Reggie chuckled. 'Let's just say that I'm prepared to countenance it.'

Ruby smirked. 'You're lucky that mine are green or you'd be in trouble.'

'I think that I'm in trouble anyway with you as my future bride.' He winked at her and smiled.

Dusty turned to his sister. 'That reminds me. What about your job at Smith and Sons? Have you resolved that situation yet?'

'Mr Smith asked me if I was resigning. I told him that I didn't want to.

You know what he said? He told me that I was indispensable, and he wanted me to stay as long as I feel inclined.'

'Good news, sis.'

'Indeed,' added Reggie. 'Now, Dusty, what about your wedding suit? Is it ready?'

'I'm pleased to say that it is.'

'And your shoes?'

'Shoes? I thought that I could wear these.' He pointed at the scruffy pair of brown ones that he was wearing.

One look at Reggie was enough.

'I'll buy some tomorrow.'

Chapter Fifty-Four

<u>SOCIETY WEDDING OF THE YEAR</u>
By CURTIS FLANGE, Social News Reporter

The chimes of St Andrew's Church, Brighton, rang out last evening, heralding the wedding of Reginald Mario, only son of Mr and Mrs Mario Silvio da Costa, of Richmond, to Ruby Amelia, daughter of the late Mr and Mrs Ernest Giles Rhodes. The church was beautifully decorated by the Ladies' Auxiliary, and the service was conducted by the vicar of the parish, The Reverend Doctor Abel Herring. The bride was given away by prominent Melbourne businessman, Mr Horace Striker.

The bride wore a splendid wedding gown created by Madame du Barry of Toorak, inspired by the latest Parisian fashions. The cream silk confection fell to mid-calf, with crystal-encrusted fringes and a plunging back, set off by a long, tulle veil embellished with sequins and a Juliet cap of brilliants, which was extremely becoming to the tall and slender wearer. Her bridesmaid was Miss Lucy Smith, daughter of the owner of Smith and Sons Furniture in Carlton, who was dressed in a frock of chiffon, taffeta, and georgette, in varying shades of green, with clusters of damask red roses at the back.

The groom wore an impeccably cut morning suit, courtesy of Savile Row, London, with a black cutaway jacket, revealing a silver waistcoat and matching bow tie. On closer inspection, the apparently black suit had been intricately woven with threads of silver to catch the light. The bride's brother, Mr William Rhodes, was best man.

The bridegroom's mother, Mrs da Costa, was frocked in pink georgette, with frills around the bodice. She wore an ostrich-trimmed hat of the same shade and carried a bouquet of red roses. The groom's father is vacationing overseas and was unable to return for the celebrations.

After the wedding, the reception was held at The Stockade, a private club owned by Melbourne businessman, Mr Horace Striker. The guests, who numbered 100, were treated to the best French champagne, and danced to a six-piece band, while supping on hors d'oeuvres of the finest Russian caviar, devilled eggs, shrimp cocktails, fresh rock oysters, and canapés.

Subsequently, the happy couple left for the honeymoon, with the bride wearing a travelling frock of Oriental crepe de chine in a deep green shade, and a hat to harmonise. The groom wore a cornflower blue and cream checked travelling suit, with a straw boater.

[*The Argus*, December 12, 1927]

The ceremony and reception were certainly regarded as a great success, according to those who attended. However, there were moments that caused some reflection on the nature of the bridal party itself and on the entry requirements for those who wished to see the happy couple joined as one.

At the church door, the Reverend Dr Herring had his name checked off the guest list and was frisked for weapons when he arrived well before the commencement of the service. He had felt obliged to protest, but was discouraged by the two men who were stationed at the door: a particularly intimidating man with cropped, red hair and cold, green eyes, and another who was smaller, with coal black hair and whose muscles bulged beneath his dinner suit.

As the first strains of Mendelssohn's 'Wedding March' were heard, the congregation stood up. The bride entered the church, on the arm of none other than Horace Striker, a name not unknown to Melbourne's police force. He was wearing a sharply cut tuxedo, with sparkling white waistcoat and white bow tie.

'Who's that?' Gladys Onions had asked Edith McGillicutty, as she glanced at the tall, lean, grey-haired gentleman walking alongside Ruby. 'He's very handsome for his age. Is that her father?'

Edith leaned in. 'He's a gangster. He's a friend of hers.' She raised her eyebrows and pulled a face. 'Illegal booze, gambling, and prostitution.'

'Oooh,' replied Gladys, reacting to the news. 'Really? What does Mavis think?'

'I don't think she knows.'

As he walked past, Striker looked down at Edith, seeming to read her mind. She withdrew into herself, a state which was as alien to her as keeping her opinions to herself.

Despite the complications of Melbourne's most intimidating gangster hosting the reception, the wedding went off without a hitch, although it was said that Clary Blain made a hasty departure immediately after the speeches were made, not wanting to be under the same roof as Horace Striker. However, he managed to consume large quantities of the finest Scotch whisky that Horace's money could provide before he exited The Stockade.

*****

The happy couple, surrounded by love and, in Reggie's case, admiration for his stylish travelling suit, took their seats in the highly polished Minerva, and drove off towards Queenscliff, with a collection of old shoes and hobnail boots trailing behind, attached to the bumper bar.

'Where did they come from?' asked Reggie, as the footwear bumped and bounced on the road behind them.

'Dusty cleared out his closet.'

Reggie chuckled. 'Good man.'

'What lies ahead for us, Reggie?' asked his bride, her gaze resting on her new husband's handsome profile.

'A wonderful life together,' he replied, above the roar of the Minerva.

'And perhaps another murder to solve?' she suggested, a sly smile on her face.

He grinned at her. 'Certainly, but let's wait until the honeymoon's over.

'That reminds me,' he added, reaching into his pocket. He took out the white feather which had accompanied him throughout his investigation, twirled it twice, and tossed it in the air. It hovered above them briefly, then floated away in the breeze.

A Note from the Author

I have retained Australian spelling, punctuation and word usage, where possible.

Acknowledgments

I began this journey to published crime writer ten years ago by joining Writers Victoria, whose short courses and manuscript appraisals contributed to my development as a writer. Dr Kate Ryan's editing skills have helped me polish my manuscript and prepare it for publication.

The historical side of my research relies heavily on the National Library of Australia's portal, *Trove*, which provides access to digitised newspapers from the past.

My thanks must go to the Dames of Detection—Verena Rose and Shawn Reilly Simmons—of Level Best Books, for publishing my books. Thank you for your continued faith in me. I wish to acknowledge Harriette Sackler, my former editor, for her wise counsel over the years and her suggestions regarding this latest book. I also wish to thank my fellow Level Besties for making me feel that I am a part of a writing community.

Family is so important. My two children, Trevor and Angela, and their partners, Lauren and Sam, support and encourage me in my writing. Angela, my talented designer daughter, also created the location map.

My grandchildren, Ellie and Maddie, give added joy to my life. Thanks also to friends, family, and my golfing buddies at the Victoria Golf Club for showing a keen interest in my writing.

Kate Becker, my partner-in-crime from Thesaurus Booksellers, Brighton, has been fabulous, accompanying me to many of my author events. The support of Cheryl and Andrew, of Beaumaris Books, has been appreciated also.

Last, but not least, thanks to my best friend and beloved husband, Bob, for his unstinting support. He must know my novels off by heart, and yet he continues to read them and offer advice and encouragement. Thanks sweetheart.

About the Author

Laraine Stephens lives in Beaumaris, a bayside suburb of Melbourne, Australia. With an Arts degree from the University of Melbourne, a Diploma of Education and a Graduate Diploma in Librarianship, she worked in secondary schools as a Head of Library. On retirement, Laraine turned her hand to the craft of crime writing.

AUTHOR WEBSITE:
  https://larainestephens.com

SOCIAL MEDIA HANDLES:
  Laraine Stephens | Facebook

Also by Laraine Stephens

The Death Mask Murders: A Reggie da Costa Mystery

Deadly Intent: A Reggie da Costa Mystery

A Deadly Game: A Reggie da Costa Mystery

Lies and Deception: A Reggie da Costa Mystery